MURDER IS A MONKEY'S GAME

MADIGAN AMOS ZOO MYSTERIES

RUBY LOREN

Copyright © 2017 by Ruby Loren

All rights reserved.

No part of this book may be reproduced in any form or by any electronic or mechanical means, including information storage and retrieval systems, without written permission from the author, except for the use of brief quotations in a book review.

❦ Created with Vellum

BRITISH AUTHOR

Please note, this book is written in British English and contains British spellings.

BOOKS IN THE SERIES

Penguins and Mortal Peril
The Silence of the Snakes
Murder is a Monkey's Game
Lions and the Living Dead
The Peacock's Poison
A Memory for Murder
Whales and a Watery Grave
Chameleons and a Corpse
Foxes and Fatal Attraction
Monday's Murderer

Prequel: Parrots and Payback

1

IT'S RAINING MEN

I was discussing boredom busting toys for the big cats when the man fell out of the sky.

I'd been at the L'airelle Zoological Park for one week and had already made firm friends with the big cat keepers, Luna and Adele. There were many charming things about the medium-sized French zoo, situated in the Aude commune in the South of France, but there were also many things that made me want to pull my hair out by its roots.

Luna and Adele were more receptive than most to the changes I was suggesting, which was why we were currently discussing various toys to encourage the big cats to exercise. It was lunchtime and the zoo was practically deserted. I was suggesting giant footballs and blood ice lollies. Albeit gory, they were something I'd seen work really well for the cats. It also doubled up as a way for them to cool down. Having said that, we were in September, so it was probably an idea to save for the next summer season.

"Hey, look, a paraglider," Adele said, as I was trying to figure out how to construct a ball that dispensed treats when you batted it along the ground, or perhaps something like a piñata that needed to be broken into…

I looked up at the yellow, banana shaped canopy. "They're flying pretty low," I commented and then returned to my workings out.

Adele's gasp distracted me and I lifted my head in time to see flailing arms and the canopy veering from side to side. Now that they were closer, I could just make out that it was a tandem jump, but the person on the front seemed to be panicking. We all watched as they reached out and appeared to tug on one set of wires that attached to the 'chute. The person behind made no move to stop them. Had something happened to the instructor? I noted that they were now nearly directly above us.

Luna made an exclamation of horror when the front person unstrapped their harness. They fiddled with something to their left. All of a sudden, one side of the 'chute released, sending the tandem jumpers into a downward spiral that could only end in death!

We watched, filled with dread, as the front person jumped clear, falling for a second or two before pulling the string on a backpack I hadn't realised they were wearing. A second 'chute blossomed in the air and I watched the helmeted figure bank sharply to the left, away from the zoo.

The yellow canopy was now a mere streak of colour with a flailing-limbed figure beneath it. We all heard the sickening thump when the body hit the ground.

What followed was much worse.

There was the familiar roar of the zoo's three tiger brothers disagreeing. Then we heard tearing sounds as something was violently ripped apart.

Now over the initial shock, we all ran to the tiger enclosure and looked down from the aerial viewpoint. A squirrel monkey perched on the fence that stopped visitors from falling in. It screeched in my face and I resisted the urge to push it into the enclosure.

"Mon dieu! We've got to get him out!" Adele said, turning to rush down to the keepers' entrance. I grabbed her arm, knowing she would probably do something foolish. More than one keeper had underestimated their charges in the heat of the moment.

"There's nothing you can do. He's already dead," I said.

The man was actually embedded several inches into the ground, despite the tigers' best efforts at pulling him apart. You couldn't get much deader than that. I was just glad we couldn't see his face.

"What do we do?" Luna's hand fluttered to her face.

"We call the police," I said, sorry to be so familiar with the correct procedure.

By my side, the squirrel monkey screeched again and I realised he was a witness. I wondered what he'd seen from his front row seat to murder.

2

FATAL RECALL

"Madame Amos, please tell us what you saw." The lead detective pulled out an ancient, leather bound notebook and a free promotion pen.

I reflected that it was fortunate indeed that the village of L'airelle and its police force were all well used to tourists. This whole situation could have been much more complex if no one spoke English. My French was barely up to conversational standard.

"I was working on some ideas for an enclosure. We were standing by the lions' habitat on the aerial walkway and I was discussing my thoughts with Adele and Luna. We all saw this tandem paraglider come over the zoo and I thought they were flying pretty low. Then the person at the front struggled for a bit and then unstrapped themselves. I guess they must have somehow sabotaged the main 'chute because one set of wires came loose and they just fell from the sky. The person at the front jumped clear and opened a new 'chute. The one behind kept falling and landed in the tigers' enclosure. We ran over to check to see if they were alive and then called the police." I thought back over my words. That definitely covered it.

"Were there any other witnesses?" the detective asked.

I thought about the squirrel monkey but knew he'd hardly be any help. "Not that I know of, although you should ask all of the staff. It was lunchtime, so any visitors were probably in the restaurant. I'm not sure if they'd have seen anything."

The detective wrote it down anyway.

A woman wearing the same gendarme uniform walked over. She had brown hair tied back in a plait and an apologetic look on her face. "Sorry Sir, I didn't realise it was so serious and I had a soufflé in the oven."

"We'll discuss it later, Detective Girard. Please go and interview one of the witnesses." He gestured to Adele and Luna, and rolled his eyes when she had gone. "Soufflé!" he muttered and looked back down at his notes.

"Just a few more questions for you, Madame Amos."

I winced a little at his chosen term of address. The last time I'd visited France I had definitely been a 'Mademoiselle'. I wasn't best thrilled to discover I was now a 'Madame'.

"Do you think this was a deliberate act?" he asked.

I paused to think. "Do you mean the sabotage of the 'chute, or dropping a man into the tiger enclosure?" I asked.

"Both," the detective clarified.

"I don't know anything about paragliding, but it really did look like the person at the front reached round and did something to make the canopy come loose. I'm also going to assume that carrying a second parachute isn't a usual practice in paragliding, so I'd say that what I saw was pretty suspicious." I thought a little more. "As for dropping the victim off in the tiger enclosure, I don't know. I've already told you they flew very low over the zoo, but when the 'chute broke, it twisted around a lot. I don't know if you could aim something like that. However, if the target was just the zoo in general, I could believe it."

The detective nodded, still scribbling.

I took a moment to look down into the tigers' enclosure. Justin, Adele's husband, had been drafted to tempt the tigers indoors with food. It had worked and the detective and other gendarmes had already inspected the body. The coroner had just arrived and would soon move the body. I looked away, still not wanting to see the man's face.

"Did you recognise the victim?" the detective asked.

"No, but I didn't see him very well and I've only been here for a week. I haven't met everyone in the village. He could have been a local." I hesitated. "I'm assuming the victim was a man. He looked like one." He hadn't been wearing a helmet either, I suddenly realised - unlike the person who'd got away. While I was still thinking about that, the detective asked another question. I shook my head, having missed it, and asked him to repeat himself.

"I said, do you think the victim was dead or alive before they hit the ground?"

"I think he was already dead. Or at least unconscious," I said, surprising myself.

I thought back to the way the body beneath the sabotaged 'chute had flailed and fallen in silence and realised that the way their limbs had moved had been almost boneless. They hadn't actually been struggling.

The detective scribbled down a few more notes, his mouth set in a grim line.

"The paraglider who got away is probably a murderer, right?" I asked.

The detective half-nodded. "It's too early at this stage to make any judgements about what really happened, but we would definitely like to speak to this person for questioning. As soon as you called, I sent a team out to scour the local surroundings but so far, they haven't found a thing. The second paraglider must have repacked their 'chute and disappeared."

"Suspicious behaviour," I commented, but the detective wouldn't be drawn.

Detective Girard came over again and apologetically tapped the lead detective on the shoulder.

He turned around with the grim expression still etched on his face and the other detective quailed even further. I mentally raised an eyebrow, speculating over what kind of boss he must be to make her act like such a mouse.

"I interviewed the other witnesses, Detective Prideaux. They didn't recognise the victim, but then, he was falling when they saw him," she said with a little shrug.

"Perhaps it's time we took them all for a closer look," the intimidating Detective Prideaux said.

I felt my stomach clench with worry. I did not want to see what falling from that height did to a person.

Detective Girard must have noticed my face because she smiled. "Don't worry, we won't let the coroners move him until you've had a look. Someone will probably be able to identify him, even if it's not right away."

We all turned at the sound of running footsteps. My boyfriend, Lowell, jogged along the aerial walkway towards us, concern lining his face.

I'd met Lowell when he'd been working undercover as a private detective. He'd been posing as a builder at Avery Zoo - the place where I'd been a zookeeper. We'd initially hit it off, but after he'd concealed the truth of his assignment from me, I'd had a hard time forgiving him. To make up for his misconduct, he'd visited me while I'd been working a case for Snidely Safari and Wildlife Park and had nearly been framed for murder. During our time at Snidely, we'd talked and had discovered that there were more than just a few sparks of attraction between us. We'd started dating and as a sign of good faith, I'd invited him along to this new job at L'airelle, with the intention that it would be a holiday for him.

Things had already gone a bit pear-shaped on that front.

"What's happening? I was walking through the village and I heard that the police had all rushed up to the zoo. Are you okay?" he asked.

I summoned a smile to reassure him. "I'm fine. Luna, Adele, and I just witnessed a…" I hesitated. "…a death," I decided.

"Who are you?" Detective Prideaux asked. I decided to forgive him for his abruptness on the off chance it was due to the language barrier.

Lowell quickly filled him in.

"May I come, too?" Lowell asked, when it was announced that we three witnesses would now be expected to go down to the tiger enclosure at ground level to view the body before it was moved.

The lead detective shrugged, which Lowell took to mean acceptance.

We all traipsed back along the walkway and through the park until we reached the tiger enclosure. My eyes kept focusing on the beautiful, nearly tropical flowers along the way to the enclosure. I wondered if my brain was trying to distract me from the nastiness that awaited us.

I took a deep breath and walked around to the big viewing window, set in the side of the enclosure.

It afforded the perfect view of the body.

I could tell now that it was definitely a man. He had dark, white-streaked hair that curled a bit at the back, and I could also see the silver glint of an ear piercing. His body lay at a horrible angle that made it clear several limbs were broken. I was grateful once again that we couldn't see his face, although that meant there wasn't exactly a lot to identify him by.

"It could be anyone," Luna said, voicing my thoughts aloud.

Next to me, I felt Lowell shift uncomfortably. "It's Pascal Devereux," he announced, much to the surprise of everyone - myself included.

Muttering broke out and I overheard several people suddenly saying that it could well be Pascal.

"What?" I hissed at Lowell, at the same time as the detective.

My boyfriend sighed, keeping his eyes fixed on the body. "I met him when he was over in the UK, many years ago, when I was just starting out as a private detective. He was also in the business and it transpired we were on the same case, so we teamed up. We were trying to uncover the ringleaders of a gang of criminals who were smuggling firearms out of France and into the UK. We both went in undercover but got caught out. The gang tried to kill us and nearly succeeded. A bullet creased the back of Pascal's neck and left him with that scar. One inch deeper and it would have severed his spinal chord and killed him. That's how I recognised him. The scar and the ear piercing."

There was more muttering and I picked up that Pascal's history had not been common knowledge. Perhaps his past had finally caught up with him.

"Monsieur..."

"...Adagio," Lowell finished for the lead detective.

"If you don't mind, we'd like to ask you a few more questions down at the station about your history with Monsieur Devereux."

I frowned at the brusque tone. "You're not treating him as a suspect in all this, are you? He was walking through the village when it happened."

Detective Prideaux shrugged. "We are keeping our minds open at this point in the investigation."

I resisted the urge to throttle him. At least with the village being as small and closely knit as it was, it wouldn't be difficult to find people who could attest to Lowell's whereabouts if the police did decide to escalate their suspicions.

"I need everyone present to recount the last time they saw Monsieur Devereux alive," the detective said, whipping out his notebook again.

He looked at me meaningfully, and I tried to iron out my frown.

"I never met him. I've only been here a week," I reminded him.

He did that infuriating shrug again but thankfully moved on.

To my surprise, it was Luna who first lost her temper with Detective Prideaux.

"Look, the man was practically an outcast! No one in this village particularly liked him, but all the same, he's lived here for years and none of us have killed him for it. Why are we suspects? We watched him fall!" she said and then choked up. Her blue eyes were wide and unseeing and her wispy, done at home highlighted hair fell forwards to hide her features.

"We're just trying to establish some facts," Detective Girard said, offering Luna a smile. She hastily wiped it from her face when Prideaux gave her a sharp look. He was clearly against any show of emotion that might hinder an otherwise robotic job.

"I, uh, spoke to Pascal last week," Adele admitted. "I'd gone into Angoux to do some shopping and parked in the pay and display car park." She shrugged. "Tourist season, you know? Everywhere else was packed. I got back to my car two minutes later than the time on my ticket and Pascal was already writing out a fine. I wasn't too happy about that."

I noticed that Justin looked surprised by Adele's confession. He hadn't known about the altercation.

"Two minutes late does sound unfair," Detective Girard commented and received another quelling look for her trouble.

"You argued?" Detective Prideaux prompted.

"Well, I said he was being unreasonable but he refused to rip up the notice. I wouldn't normally have made such a fuss but he'd seemed surprised to see it was me when I confronted him." Adele threw an apologetic glance at Luna before continuing. "Luna and I drive the same brand and colour car. We even have identical L'airelle Zoological Park stickers. I think he thought it was her car when he wrote out the ticket."

The detective was scribbling frantically now. "And why would he be so keen to give a ticket to Madame Fleur?" he said, referring to Luna.

Luna shot an understanding smile at Adele before responding. "Pascal and I have never really got along. He and my father once went into business together and there was some discrepancy that meant Pascal believed my father had cheated him. He couldn't afford to take the case to court and get a judgement. Instead, he contented himself with being bitter. Since my father passed away, he's transferred my father's punishment to me." A light frown creased her forehead. "But I haven't spoken to him for at least a year. I thought he'd given up, but what Adele said sounds just like something he'd do. He used to try all sorts of things! In the past, he's painted double yellow lines outside our house and sent false parking fine notices in the post." She shook her head. "It was an annoyance, but it was something I weathered. For years," she added, making sure she made eye contact with the lead detective. Her implication was clear - why would she have snapped now and had someone murder

Pascal Devereux when he'd finally let his petty attacks wane?

"I hope Rico, Julian, and Boba, are okay," Adele murmured, looking over at the shut-off sleeping compartment in the tiger enclosure. They would have finished the meat Justin had given them and would no doubt be bored. I tried to give her a reassuring smile. There would probably be some bickering between the brothers, but I was sure it wouldn't be much longer before the coroner would have taken the body and they could be let out again.

Adele was the tiger keeper, so this situation was most stressful for her. Luna looked after the lions and Justin handled the leopards and panthers. The smaller cats were divided between them. They also all helped out with the zoo's guided tours and other duties. One thing I really liked about L'airelle was the way that everyone pitched in. Despite the zoo's larger size, there were only a few more staff than there'd been at Avery Zoo, and I knew it was because everyone had a wider range of responsibilities. The team effort was the upside of having a smaller staff. The downside was that certain health and safety measures were overlooked.

"Mr Adagio, please come with us. We shall be back to ask more questions as needed," Detective Prideaux announced to the rest of us.

I made eye contact with Lowell but he didn't seem nearly as angry about being considered a suspect as I was on his behalf. On the contrary, he seemed mildly amused.

"I'll see you this evening," I said, rather pointedly. If Detective Prideaux thought his small-town jurisdiction meant he could wrongfully detain innocent people, he'd have another thing coming. I may be a foreigner, but I could still kick up a fuss.

"Don't worry, Theo Prideaux likes to talk big, but he's

fair. He just thinks acting tough is how you get people to respect you," Adele reassured me once the police had left.

I looked back towards the body and couldn't help feeling a bit resentful.

An old acquaintance of Lowell's - who had lived in L'airelle village for his whole life - had just happened to show up dead one week after we'd arrived.

I wanted to believe it was down to chance, but I couldn't help wondering if someone else had known about Pascal Devereux's dangerous past... and his convenient connection to Lowell.

I'd just put the tartiflette in the oven when Lowell unlocked the door to our little rental cottage.

"Good timing!" I said, giving him a smile that he returned. I'd worried he'd have to microwave his portion of the cheesy potato dish, and I knew he'd been looking forward to the indulgence for days.

"Don't worry, I'm not nearly as guilty as Detective Prideaux made out," he told me, moving over to wrap his arms around my waist, while I fiddled with the oven timer.

"It wasn't that bad?" I enquired.

I felt him shrug. "I think the detective was hoping I'd come clean and admit to murdering a man I haven't seen for a good ten years, but I disappointed him. He just asked me some more questions about the work we did together and I told him he'd get more answers if he contacted British law enforcement. The gun smuggling case was one we actually did on behalf of the authorities, so it was all above board."

I turned a little and raised my eyebrows at him. "What made you stop doing official assignments?"

He grinned back at me. "Money... obviously."

"You're shameless," I told him, turning back to the cooker to double check it had accepted my instructions. The archaic oven was quirky to say the least.

Lowell bent his head and lightly kissed my neck, sending a shiver right through me.

"I guess I just need someone to realign my moral compass for me. I'm a bad person," he teased.

"Oh, shush," I told him, sorely tempted to give in to the distraction he was offering. Instead, I got free of his arms and walked over to the fridge. I'd bought some exceedingly cheap sparkling white wine, flavoured with peach, that was meant to be served as an aperitif. It was the sort of thing you thought was a great idea on holiday but would never have contemplated back home. I had a feeling it wasn't going to be my last drink of the evening either.

"Don't you think it's weird though? Some guy you haven't seen for a decade suddenly winds up dead, right after we come into town?"

Lowell sat down at the round kitchen table and toyed with the vase of dried flowers. "Except for the law enforcement officials that Pascal and I were contracted by, no one else knew about the case. Well, other than the bad guys who found out who we really were. But they all got caught, or died when the police moved in."

"You're sure about that?" I said, thinking that it was a hell of a coincidence that someone had taken out Pascal immediately after Lowell had visited the village.

"There's just no way it could be connected like that," he said, standing up again. He walked over to the kitchen window that overlooked fields as far as the eye could see. "It can't be about that. I might never have come to this village. Even if someone did know our connection, why would they have waited all this time?"

"Unless they were following you, hoping you'd lead them to Pascal," I offered.

Lowell grunted. "Then they've been stalking me for a hell of a long time without me noticing." He rubbed a hand through his dark hair. "I don't know, Madi. It's a hell of a coincidence, but I don't think this has anything to do with me. You should worry more about your friends."

I took a sip of my frivolous aperitif. "My friends? You heard what they said. Luna has put up with this man being antagonistic towards her family for years. She said it herself - he hadn't done anything mean for a whole year! Until the car parking thing," I added and tilted my head to the side. "But you could say that was justified. Maybe he was just overzealous like that with every car in the car park."

"Not from the way Adele described his surprise at seeing her. What about her and her husband's motive? Perhaps they had a bone to pick with old Pascal, too."

"No more than Luna had!" I said and bit my tongue. That had been exactly what Lowell had wanted me to say.

"Luna is probably going to find herself under a lot of scrutiny," he said. "She could have paid someone to take out Pascal and then deliver the body right where she'd see it - in the tiger enclosure."

"Adele is the one who looks after the tigers," I corrected.

Lowell just shrugged. "Who knows? Maybe their aim was off."

I crossed my arms and gave him a look. "Be that as it may, do you really think a zookeeper could employ an assassin? This is rural France! Assassins don't hang out on street corners waiting for clients. Anyway, she's put up with his behaviour for years. There's nothing to suggest that she'd snap now."

"Then I suppose we are at an impasse. I'm sure the police will figure it out. Unless it was an especially psychopathic tourist who took being given a parking ticket badly, there isn't an endless pool of suspects. It's a small village."

Lowell looked away from the window and caught the end of my thoughtful expression.

"Really? You took that seriously?" he said with a grin, referring to his psychopathic tourist analogy.

I turned back to inspect the interior of the oven, where the tartiflette was bubbling away nicely. "I don't know, it could have been! People get pretty steamed up over parking tickets," I huffed.

"So, what was with the whole paragliding thing? The tourist wanted to kill someone and dispose of the body whilst enjoying a bit of aerial sightseeing? I admire their ability to multi-task," Lowell said with a sideways grin.

I smirked a little in spite of myself. "You'll be sorry if they find out that's what really happened! Hey - where are you going?" Lowell had walked over to the front door and opened it.

"Oh! I was going to visit the police to tell them we'd solved the murder. It was a very angry tourist all along."

I rolled my eyes at him. "Anyone who leaves the house will miss their dinner. I may be small, but if I put my mind to it, I bet I could eat the whole tartiflette."

Lowell shut the door. "Now that's one thing I don't doubt," he said, walking towards me with a twinkle in his dark eyes.

I tried to bat him away with a spatula, but my resistance was half-hearted at best. I only realised how much time had slipped by when the cooker beeped to let me know that dinner was done.

No matter how much chemistry there was between Lowell and me, nothing would distract me from a dish that included cream, cheese, and bacon.

It was all too easy to forget about the events of the day

and dig into one of the greatest savoury comfort foods I knew. Solving the murder could wait until after dinner.

I woke up next morning when my phone beeped to let me know I had a new Facebook message. I wasn't the biggest fan of social media. Fans of the comic I wrote told me it was important to spread the word, but I'd been burying my head in the sand... until now.

My best friend Tiff was looking after my kitten, Lucky. I knew Tiff from Avery Zoo, where I'd worked as a zookeeper, until my success with encouraging animals who didn't usually reproduce in captivity to breed had launched my career as a breeding and habitat consultant.

Lucky was just starting to become more independent, so I didn't feel too terrible about leaving him in Tiff's care for a few weeks. Her house was already full of waifs and strays. I'd also thought it would be a good opportunity for Lucky to do some socialising. When he'd been really young, I'd taken him around the zoo with me in a carrier case, but he hadn't seen much of the world beyond his carrier. I was hoping that if he met other animals, he would be more likely to accept a life on the road. There was a chance it wouldn't work out and I'd have to settle down back at Avery Zoo, but that would be Lucky's choice. I'd taken on a responsibility when I'd rescued him, after he'd been rejected by his mother. If Lucky didn't like travelling or other animals, I would gracefully accept that my career as a consultant was over.

I opened the Facebook message and smiled at the photos Tiff had sent over. This was why I'd been persuaded to actually use the account she'd set up for me years ago. It would have cost her a bomb to text over the slew of snapshots. Tiff had written a note, too.

Lucky is doing great. Everyone here loves him and he's even weaselled his way into One-Eyed-Jack's heart, which I'd never have believed possible! It's given the old fusspot a new lease of life. Here they are sharing a bed:

I looked at the pictures of Lucky, flopped on top of a very disgruntled looking off-white cat. I'd have to take Tiff's word for it that they were best buddies. One-Eyed-Jack was the bane of Tiff's life. He was a stray who'd turned up out of the blue, probably attracted by the mass of animals in Tiff's care. She'd done all she could for him, but he was half feral and didn't like people.

He was also long-haired, which was a disaster. When he'd first arrived, his fur had been so matted, Tiff said he'd looked like a walking dread lock. She'd had to keep her own animals inside so she could trap him and take him to the vet, where they'd sedated him in order to sort his fur out. Despite his new, cushy lifestyle, brushing him was still out of the question. Tiff dragged him, kicking and screaming, to the vet to be sedated and shaved at regular intervals.

I smiled and closed down the images. It was nice to hear that things were going well back at home. While I was still thinking about it, I wrote a text to Auryn Avery - my friend, who was almost singlehandedly running Avery Zoo, now that his grandad was so unwell.

I'd managed to spend a week back at the zoo before I'd left for France. In that time, I thought Auryn and I had figured out a lot of things and made some great changes to the way the zoo operated. Board meetings had once been comprised of a bunch of crotchety middle-aged men, deciding the future of the zoo. Now they were a free for all, with managers expected to find their own solutions to the problems they faced and a chance for any staff member at all to have their voice heard. Turning the zoo into a democracy was something I thought would both take the weight off Auryn and also result in a better zoo for visitors and staff alike.

I sent the text and hoped things were going as well as they had been when I'd left. Mr Avery Senior was largely believed to be in his final furlong. I hoped he'd stay a little longer, if only to see what his grandson accomplished. Hopefully my text would let Auryn know I was thinking of him.

I leant over and kissed Lowell on the forehead. He mumbled something in his sleep.

"I'm off to work. See you later," I told him.

He opened a bleary eye. "Shhh, I'm on holiday."

I threw a pillow at him and he complained. *It's all right for some,* I reflected.

L'airelle Zoo was already busy first thing in the morning. The French liked to rise early. The natives always arrived at opening time in order to get in a full day. It was the international tourists who liked to sleep late.

I nodded to Justin, who was on tour guide duty this morning. Although the keepers weren't always thrilled to have to do this job, I actually thought it was pretty great. Who better to show visitors around the zoo than someone who actually worked with the animals? It also meant that at the end of the tour, the keeper would feed one of the animals they looked after, or find a way to interact with them, depending on the time of day. This was a great way for tourists to learn more about, and appreciate, the animals we were all working hard to conserve.

I walked through the green and leafy park, smelling the heady scent of the many oleander bushes. They were beautiful flowers, but their presence was yet another thing that bothered me about the French zoo. In England, having a deadly poisonous plant all over the place would probably result in some kind of lawsuit.

A squirrel monkey jumped across the path in front of me and landed on a wooden stake that made up the rope barrier between the path and another health-and-safety-defying hillside drop.

"I don't have any popcorn," I told him.

This was yet another issue I would be bringing up with the zoo's manager: the squirrel monkeys and their popcorn addiction. While I thought (on the whole) that popcorn was a pretty healthy snack to hand out to animals like goats and deer, the squirrel monkeys did everything they could to secure the bulk of it. I'd even seen them snatching the cups out of visitors' hands. I worried that it wouldn't be long before they grew even more bold.

"You should be in your enclosure!" I told the monkey who tilted its head at me, probably still looking for any popcorn I might be concealing.

When I'd first arrived at L'airelle, I'd assumed that the squirrel monkeys must have broken out of their enclosure. They were master escape artists, so it hadn't surprised me. But then I'd discovered no one was trying to put them back where they belonged. After further enquiry, I'd found out that the monkeys had escaped only a few weeks after the zoo had officially opened. The first couple of times they'd been rounded up, but eventually they'd stopped trying. The monkeys' enclosure stood empty and unused while the monkeys themselves were free to roam the zoo - much to the delight of the visitors. While I was all for animals having the space they needed to roam around, I quailed at the thought of what might happen if someone caught a monkey on a bad day, or even tried to aggravate the monkeys. Saying it would all end in tears was an understatement.

"Hey, Madi! Come on in, we're having coffee," Luna said, waving to me from the little tiki hut that was one of the staff's bases.

"How is everyone?" I asked Luna, when she turned to go back inside.

She paused for a second. "I think we're all fine. It's just one of those things, you know? I know it's harsh, but I don't think too many people will miss Pascal - not even his wife."

"He had a wife?"

She nodded. "Yeah. Maybe that is too harsh. She's probably still upset. I guess my view is just skewed because of what I put up with over the years. He had so many ways to ruin your day." She sighed. "Then something like this happens. I hope that wherever he is, he's looking back and questioning whether it was worth it - all of that bother he gave me and my father! I know it's certainly made me think twice about how I behave towards others."

"At least you're looking on the bright side," I told her.

She turned her head and looked at something off in the distance. Her lightly tanned skin seemed to glow beneath her blonde and mouse coloured hair. I briefly reflected that Luna, Adele, and I had probably been so quick to click because we were all of a similar age. Luna was still in her late twenties and Adele was in her early thirties. I wondered if the social element of my new career would make me happy or sad. On one hand, I was making friends in all kinds of places, but on the other hand, it wouldn't be long before I'd have to leave them behind.

"Morning," I said to Adele, who wordlessly handed me a strong, black coffee and then walked away to stare out of a window. I noticed her hands were twisting restlessly and I wondered if she was worried that her recent disagreement with the late Pascal Devereux would be taken out of context.

"Hey, are you looking forward to tonight?" Luna asked and I turned to her in surprise.

My brain finally whirred into gear. "The staff outing. That's still happening?"

"Of course!" Luna said. "You've got to live in the present, you know? Anyway, like I said before…" she lowered her voice, "…no one in the village is going to particularly miss Pascal."

"Adele, what are you wearing tonight?" Luna called over to the other keeper.

She jumped a little and turned to look at us with wide eyes. Her mind had clearly been on other things.

"Oh, I don't know. A dress, I suppose," she said.

Luna looked back at me and very obviously shot Adele a suspicious look. "A dress she says… she could wear a bin bag and still look great!"

Adele's mouth quirked up, just enough to show that she appreciated the gesture, but it wasn't long before she looked back out of the window again. Perhaps she'd known Pascal better than she let on, I reasoned to myself, watching the way the attractive thirty-something woman's forehead creased. Her dark eyes were far away and even her usually shining locks looked as though they'd missed a wash that morning. Something was definitely up.

"I'd better get to work. That review needs to be written! Even though I'll probably have to fight tooth and nail to get through to the manager here," I said, throwing my hands up in the air in exaggeration.

"That's it Madi, spoil all of our fun!" Luna joked with a mischievous grin. I noticed that she automatically looked to Adele for a witty remark but none came.

"I'll see you both tonight. You're still okay to pick me up?" I confirmed and Luna nodded. I hoped by the time the evening rolled around whatever was bothering Adele would have faded away.

"Oh, Madi, I hope you don't mind but we've decided to go and visit Madame Devereux before we drive to the restaurant. We were going to be early anyway and Adele…" Luna looked over at the dark-haired woman in the passenger seat who smiled and shrugged.

"She's a family friend. I feel it's only right to check on her, especially as we're in such a small community. It will be good for Luna to go, too," she said with a sly smile.

Luna rolled her eyes back in protest.

"I notice Justin managed to weasel out of this sympathy visit," she grumbled.

"You know he's setting up at the restaurant. Now stop complaining," Adele chided.

I smiled, pleased that Adele had shaken off whatever had been bothering her earlier.

"You look great by the way, Madi," Luna said, as she drove through the village and turned down one of the narrow, cobbled lanes in-between houses. I thanked her for the compliment. Having been caught out at Snidely with only one smart dress in my luggage, I'd been more extravagant this time and brought a few with me. If I were being really honest, I'd also done it in the hopes that Lowell might take me out to dinner one night. *Or perhaps I'll ask him,* I thought, making a mental note to do so.

"You both look wonderful, too," I told them in turn.

Luna was wearing a taupe coloured dress, covered with a print of butterflies. Adele was beautiful as ever, clad in a dress that had a divine print of lemons all over it. I couldn't think of anything more summery! I was pleased that I'd managed to fit in with the dress code. I'd spent a good half an hour questioning whether or not my halter neck, quirky cat print dress had been a good choice.

We pulled up outside a detached village house. My first impression was that the garden wasn't nearly as well cared for as the neighbouring plots, but when we walked up the garden path, I revised my opinion. The owner of this house clearly cared about their garden, as was evident from the neatly gravelled path, but they also loved wild flowers. It was only the overly manicured neighbours who had contrived to make the cottage garden look out of place.

The lilac coloured door opened a second or two after Adele knocked. A middle-aged woman with short, curly brown hair opened the door.

"Adele! It's so good to see you here. How is your husband?" the woman asked and I realised I recognised her from the village's little convenience store, where she worked behind the till.

"He's fine, and yours?" Adele asked, her mouth twitching up at one corner.

"Still dead - thank God!" the woman replied and they both laughed at what must be a joke between them. I threw Luna a look of alarm but she just smiled and shook her head. Apparently a twisted sense of humour was common around here.

"It's good of you to come and visit Louis. She's still in shock, poor thing," the village woman said. "And I see you brought some dishes, too! That's so thoughtful."

Adele had opened the car boot when we'd arrived to reveal a beautiful tarte au citron and a delicious looking chicken salad. She'd passed the salad to Luna without a word and had then explained that I wouldn't be expected to bring anything as I wasn't a local. She'd thrown Luna a pointed look when she'd said that.

"We'll just go in and put them in the kitchen, Madame Myrtle, if that's okay?" Adele said, hinting that we were being kept on the doorstep.

"Of course, of course!" The other woman said but didn't step aside. "Terrible business, isn't it? You know, the one thing I can't figure out is what was he doing paragliding? I never thought I'd see the day that Pascal Prideaux got up in one of those things. We leave all of that to you village youngsters," she said, shaking her head.

"I really don't know, Madame Myrtle," Adele said politely and to our collective relief, the woman moved aside and led the way into the house.

"Louis is just through here with some company," Madame Myrtle told us on the way down the narrow corridor. There was something about the way she said 'company' that piqued my interest. It didn't sound like she was talking about another village well-wisher.

We walked into the main room, Luna and Adele still carrying their dishes. A smart looking woman with a neat grey bob was sat on the sofa, her hands clasped in her lap. Opposite her were a man and a woman dressed in suits. It looked like 'The Men In Black' were filming a spinoff in a tiny French village. I noticed I wasn't the only one frowning at how out of place they looked.

Louis Devereux looked round when the suited man stopped talking and fixed us all with a stare. It wasn't a particularly friendly one.

"Madame Devereux, we just wanted to say we're sorry for what happened. We thought we'd bring you a few bits," Adele said, raising the tart a little higher.

"Thank you girls, that's so kind of you." She turned back to the suited couple but they remained seated.

"Who are you?" Luna abruptly asked the pair and I felt

like patting her on the back for calling them out on their impoliteness.

"I'm Mr Flannigan and this is Ms Borel."

The man's clipped British accent came as something of a surprise. I felt Luna and Adele both look towards me, as if our shared nationality would somehow mean I could explain their presence at the widow of the deceased's house. The man raised his eyebrows and we introduced ourselves in turn, sharing just as little personal information as he had done.

"Madame Devereux, would you be okay to come to the kitchen and make sure that we put all of this in the right place? Perhaps we could dish you up a plate, if you haven't eaten?" Adele offered.

The widow nodded and stood up. "I'll be back in a minute," she told the pair.

I certainly didn't imagine the stab of annoyance that crossed Mr Flannigan's face.

The kitchen was almost unnaturally spotless when we arrived, probably due to a well-wisher's attentions. Louis Devereaux looked around blankly, like she didn't even recognise where she was. Hoping to help, I opened the fridge and found there was already some sort of meat pie in situ. I had no doubt that the fridge would soon be full to the bursting, if bringing food round in times of trouble was the local custom.

I took the pie out and lifted it up, catching Adele's eye. She nodded and gestured towards the plates. I made up a single serving, adding some of Luna's gift-salad on the side. If the mysterious couple in the other room were staying for much longer, they could jolly well help themselves.

"I just can't believe he's gone," Madame Devereux said to Adele, who nodded sympathetically.

"I know. His absence from village life will definitely be noticed," she replied, rather tactfully.

It didn't get past Madame Devereux. "If he'd drunk a little less, perhaps more people would have known his better side." She looked at Luna when she said it.

"I'm sure," Luna finally concurred, after Adele shot daggers at her from behind Madame Devereux's back.

The grieving widow nodded in silence.

"Madame Devereux, who are those people in the other room?" Adele ventured.

"Oh, I don't know really. They say they're some special branch of the police. They hadn't got far with their questions when you all came in but that's what they seem to be here for - asking questions."

I exchanged looks with Adele and Luna, the three of us none the wiser. No doubt time would tell. Nothing stayed secret for long in a village the size of L'airelle.

"You girls... you saw him, didn't you?" the widow said, looking at each of our faces in turn.

"We did, Madame Devereux," I acknowledged, when no one else spoke. Too late, I realised I'd taken on question answering duties.

"Please, just tell me one thing... did he suffer before he died? Would he have felt it?" she asked.

The image of Pascal Devereux's flying limbs and eerily silent fall jumped straight back into my mind.

I swallowed.

"No, Madame, I don't believe he knew he was falling at all," I said, honestly.

She nodded again, looking a little more comforted. I hadn't been able to reassure her that her husband's death had been painless. All I could be sure of was that he hadn't been aware of the fall.

The suited man popped his head around the corner of the kitchen.

"Madame Devereux, I wondered where you'd got to."

His mouth sort of attempted to move up at the corners but he gave up before he achieved a full smile. "We still have questions we need to ask you. When you're ready, please come back into the living room," he said. He folded his arms and leant against the door frame, apparently determined to stay.

I got the funny feeling that he didn't want us to be left alone with Madame Devereux for too long. I wondered what he thought she knew that he didn't want her to share with us.

"Are you sure you'll be okay here? If you'd rather come with us and have some company, that would be fine. You'd be more than welcome to come to the dinner tonight," Adele said, deliberately ignoring Mr Flannigan's looming presence.

The widow gave her a little smile to show she appreciated the offer. "It's fine. I've got family coming over later and I'm sure I'll have many more visitors tomorrow. Thank you for stopping by and for the food you brought with you."

Adele nodded and kissed the widow goodbye, once on each cheek. She walked out of the kitchen, but not without throwing a baleful look in Mr Flannigan's direction.

Mr Flannigan clearly wasn't satisfied with our claim that we were leaving, as he escorted us right to the door.

"Do you know when the funeral is?" Luna asked, before he could shut the door in our faces.

He frowned and then shrugged. "I don't know. It hasn't been decided yet."

"Will you put up a notice about it tomorrow? Where will it be?" she pressed.

Mr Flannigan looked even more annoyed.

"Yes, I'm sure it will be done," he said vaguely and succeeded in shutting the door.

We all looked at the lilac painted wood for a second or two.

"He's definitely nothing to do with anyone around here," Luna concluded, when we walked back to the car. "Anyone with any local knowledge would know that if something important happens, or if there's an event that concerns the whole village, you put a notice up in the boulangerie. He didn't have a clue."

"What do you think those parasites wanted with poor Madame Devereux?" Adele mused, but none of us had the answer for that, or why they clearly hadn't wanted us to talk to her alone for too long.

What had they thought might slip out?

"Ah, bien! We are still on time," Luna said, when we'd found a parking place in the small field behind La Traittoria Restaurant.

I still wasn't quite sure what to make of an Italian inspired restaurant nestled in rural southern France, but I was willing to keep an open mind.

"You're going to love the pizza they do," Adele told me when we walked into the foyer.

A waiter materialised to take the light jackets that we'd all brought with us.

The building the restaurant was in was beautiful. It was made of stone that had been left bare. A large fireplace dominated one side of the room and I noticed that above the already roaring fire was a pizza oven. To my surprise, the kitchen was just another part of the big, open plan room.

"Hey, look, Justin did great, didn't he?" Adele said, pointing to the gold streamers that hung all around. There was also bunting stretched across the room and (I noticed with no little delight) a table full of cheese and charcuterie, as well as one laden with all kinds of desserts.

I'd clearly been wrong to judge La Trattoria as just another pizza place!

"Excuse me," Adele said, giving us both an awkward smile before walking off in the direction of the loos.

I watched her go while Luna waved at a group of people who'd just walked in. I wondered if Adele's strange behaviour had just resurfaced.

The room filled up with zoo employees and I greeted them, just like Luna and Adele, secretly marvelling at how I already felt as though I'd been accepted as a part of the team. Even being invited to the quarterly zoo night out was wonderful.

"Here's the best part… the chefs make the pizzas, but you can go right up and tell them the toppings you'd like as they make it for you. It's great! You can have whatever you want," Luna told me.

"Pinch me, I think I'm dreaming," I murmured, and she giggled, hooking her arm in mine and leading me over to a table filled with bottles. She selected one and poured us each a glass.

"Welcome to the way we do things at L'airelle Zoological Park," she said, raising her glass to meet mine.

"I don't think I ever want to leave," I told her with a smile.

3

IT'S A DOG'S LIFE

"So, what do you think?" I said to Lowell after I'd returned home from dinner and filled him in on the mysterious visitors at Madame Devereux's house. I hoped by now she had some friendlier guests to look after.

Lowell rubbed his dark stubble thoughtfully. I noticed his already tanned skin had darkened even further during the brief time we'd spent away. He certainly seemed to be busy enjoying himself. It was the first time I'd managed to catch him since that morning. At least it was the start of the weekend tomorrow. After working for seven days straight at Snidely, and experiencing a whole lot of stress I hadn't anticipated, I'd made the decision to slow down. I didn't see why my time at L'airelle Zoological Park couldn't be both work and play.

"You said the woman's name was Ms. Borel? What did she look like?" he asked.

I thought about it for a second. "Hair in a bun and a central parting that looked like it was done with a ruler. I guess she was a dark blonde. She had some good cheekbones but I think she's probably in her late thirties," I estimated.

"Try early forties," Lowell said.

I tilted my head enquiringly, and he gave me a rueful smile.

"I know who they are. Or at least, who she used to be. I worked with Adrienne Borel on that gun smuggling case and others like it, back when I was working for the officials. She was just an underling back then, but it looks like she's risen through the ranks. I don't know about this Flannigan guy. He sounds like someone to watch," he commented.

"So, who are they?" I pressed.

He half-shrugged. "Well, it's been years, but I assume they're government agents." He narrowed his eyes. "Why they'd be here though… I could have a guess?"

"Let's hear it," I said, curiosity well and truly piqued.

He took a breath. "Pascal might have known something back from when he worked with them. He had more dealings with the French side of operations, of course, but perhaps there was something international that went down while he was on the job. For example, there might be someone in a witness protection programme who's settled nearby. Pascal might have known their real identity and someone might have killed him in order to find that information out for themselves. That's my best guess anyway. It would explain why the agents are in town. They'll be looking to protect the people who've been hiding and find out if he blabbed to anyone else." He sucked in another breath. "If Pascal didn't crack, that's the person the killer will go after next."

"That could be why Flannigan didn't want Madame Devereux to talk to us. Perhaps he thought she'd say something about the protection programme." I frowned. "But if whoever is looking already knows the person they're hunting is in the area, why would they have needed to question Pascal? Surely they'd just hang around and recognise the person when they popped out to the shops?"

Lowell tipped his head from side to side. "Perhaps, but people do have plastic surgery. It might also have been years since they saw their target. A lot of things could change and if I were after revenge, I know I'd want to make damn sure I got the right person," he finished.

I kept my face blank, hoping he wouldn't see the little flash of worry that had entered my mind. Lowell had sounded awfully passionate when he'd made that statement. He'd also had past dealings with the man who'd died and the agents who were in town right now. What if he was more deeply involved with the case than I realised? Could someone to whom Lowell owed revenge be in the village right now, living their life under a false identity?

I collected Lowell's dirty plates from the table where he'd left them, taking a moment to turn away and start the hot water running to do the washing up. Sure, I didn't know Lowell incredibly well, but he'd never seemed to me to be someone who would hold grudges. But what if I'd misjudged him?

I sprayed some washing up liquid onto the plates and dunked them in the sink. I was jumping to conclusions. Lowell definitely had a shadowy past I didn't know nearly enough about, but he wasn't the second paraglider. I'd thought back and had realised that the paraglider who'd sabotaged the 'chute and jumped free had been slighter than Lowell's large build.

I breathed a sigh of relief and watched the iridescent bubbles float upwards into the air, bursting and spreading their lemony scent. Lowell was not responsible for this man's death.

"Huh!" Lowell said, in-between drying plates.

"You'd better not be trying to get out of drying duty," I warned him, seeing him look at his phone.

"I swear I'm not," he said, flashing me a grin. He picked up his phone anyway. "I shook down some local sources… mostly private detectives who've retired to their place in the sun. One of them has a contact in the local police force who feeds them any info they want to know."

I shut my eyes briefly, wondering at all of the shady deals and corruption I'd been introduced to since Lowell had entered my life.

"This guy says that his informant's been working on the Devereux case. They've found out that the paragliding gear was rented from a local place and they're investigating that," he said.

I frowned, remembering the village woman's surprise that Pascal had been paragliding. "Do you think Pascal himself hired it?"

"They didn't say. After what you said you saw, it doesn't sound like the excursion was voluntary on Pascal's part, but who knows?"

I nodded but the fact that the gear had been hired was interesting. Had someone persuaded Pascal to take a jump with them, for old times' sake? Or had he never known that he would end up airborne?

I was uncomfortably reminded of Lowell's shared past history, both with Pascal and the mysterious Ms. Borel. I wondered if the agents really had only just arrived.

"But why the zoo? Why the tiger enclosure?" I mused out loud.

"Do you think it was picked on purpose? The killer might not have had a clue and could have ended up above the zoo purely by chance. Who knows who they rent gear out to?" Lowell countered.

Yet again, I was forced to scour my memories. I slowly shook my head. "No way. They knew how to sabotage the 'chute and they didn't look like they panicked, even for a second, when they did manage to jump clear. Then they steered themselves away from the crime scene and clearly packed up and disappeared before the police could find them. This person knew what they were doing."

I chewed on my lip for a second as a fresh thought occurred to me. "What if it was a threat? The killer could have aimed for the zoo on purpose, knowing that the person they wanted to reach would see. You know, 'Here's a body, now we're coming after you' type of thing."

"Could be," Lowell admitted. "Then the question is... just how good was their aim?"

"Hmmm," I acknowledged, thinking about Adele's encounter with Pascal just a week ago. What if it had been more than just a parking ticket that been exchanged? Might someone have seen them talking and realised... something? I shook my head and sighed. If there was someone in witness protection, it could be anyone in the village. There simply wasn't enough information to draw any conclusions. I strongly suspected that whoever had dropped Pascal's body had been targeting someone in the zoo, but I didn't have a clue who that target might have been.

Lowell opened the fridge and pulled out a beer, pausing to offer me one. I shook my head but got him to pass me the milk. I upended the carton into a pan and began heating it on the stove. Whilst in France, I'd found a new brand of hot chocolate that I absolutely adored and I was determined to make the most of it. I tried not to think about all of the food I'd already consumed that day. My waistline wasn't going to thank me. *Oh, but it's so worth it!* I thought.

Lowell let out a big sigh from where he'd flaked out on the sofa. "I'm sorry Madi. This is all happening again, isn't it? I know I joked about you being a magnet for murder, but this one's on me." He ran a hand through his dark hair and looked pensively at his beer can. "I can't help thinking that my coming here has somehow triggered this whole thing. I mean, a guy I haven't seen in a decade suddenly winds up dead one week after I come into town? I'm actually surprised the police didn't lock me up when they had the chance."

I sat down next to him and patted his leg. "I know it wasn't you, Lowell," I reassured him.

"I guess that's something," he said. "I'll be sure to let you know if I ever have the urge to go on a murder spree."

"How thoughtful," I said with a smile, resting my head on his shoulder and smelling the scent of holiday sofa. There was always something different about the furniture in rented properties when you stayed abroad. Perhaps it was the cheap materials, but it reminded me of being on holiday.

"Hey, Adele was acting a bit weird today," I said, snuggling into Lowell's neck.

"She's probably in shock. What you witnessed was pretty harrowing," he gently reminded me.

"Luna seems okay," I said, not really thinking. I frowned into my hot chocolate. "I guess we all deal with it in our own ways."

"Exactly," Lowell said, lifting a hand and lightly stroking my wavy, blonde hair. I adjusted my glasses and smiled up at him, feeling tiny sitting next to him.

"Do you wanna go to bed?" I asked.

His own smile turned a little more wolfish. "Take the drinks up there? I don't want to wait," he told me, a familiar spark igniting in his eyes. I felt a shiver run through my body. For once in my life, I was actually anticipating finishing my hot chocolate.

The sun shone through the thin curtains the next morning. I glanced at my phone and realised I'd woken up early, despite not setting an alarm. I clearly hadn't got used to the idea of having the weekend off again.

"Oh well, the best baguettes always go to those who buy them early!" I said, peeling myself away from the still sleeping Lowell.

Despite it being Saturday, the other villagers still rose early. Many of the zoo staff were working today and there was always the daily rush to get first pick of the fresh bread at the boulangerie. Lowell had once paid them a visit close to midday and had reported back that they had nothing more than a few stale sourdough loaves in stock. I'd laughed and explained the truth to him. Since then, I'd been the one to get the bread every day. He was now in charge of making sure we had any essentials we needed to tide us over until market day rolled around again on Monday.

"Bonjour, Madi!" One of the girls who worked in admissions at the park said. I waved to her and she and her friends waved back.

"Bonjour, Madi. There's still some good bread left, don't worry," the friendly baker told me when I reached the front of the queue. "Anything special today?" he asked.

I thought about it for a second, reflecting that it was the weekend. The idea of a picnic lunch sprung into my head. "A baguette, two slices of that quiche and…" I eyed up a couple of severely tempting choux pastry buns. "Two of those please," I said, caving. I knew they wouldn't travel well as part of my picnic lunch but to be honest, I wasn't even sure they'd make it back to the cottage…

On my way back, I happened to glance at the headline printed on the board outside of the convenience store. My French really wasn't brilliant, but even I could figure out it said 'Death at L'airelle Zoological Park'.

"Great," I muttered, knowing what **that** was going to do

for the zoo's attendance. Couldn't they have been a little more specific?

I picked up a paper and glanced at it, but the article was lost on me. I decided to buy it anyway, thinking I'd figure it out with Lowell over breakfast.

When I arrived back at the cottage, Lowell already had a pot of coffee on the go. He'd also got out the jam and butter, ready for breakfast.

"That's presumptuous! I might have just brought back some cereal," I joked, but he pointedly looked at the long loaf I was carrying. "Bit hard to hide," I admitted with a smile.

"You've got that Skype meeting with the agent today, haven't you?" Lowell asked.

I nodded, doing my best to look like I hadn't forgotten about it. How had it come around so soon? I would have to hustle in order to get my notes ready right after breakfast. Perhaps the picnic would have to wait until tomorrow after all, I realised, with a slightly sinking heart.

My webcomic, *Monday's Menagerie*, had attracted a reasonable amount of attention online and my fans had been dedicated enough to set up a crowd funding campaign for me. They'd wanted a paperback copy of the comics and had been willing to pay for it. At first, I'd said yes because I hadn't really believed that people would be interested enough in the comic to fund a project like that. I'd costed it all out, doing my best to account for the hours of time it would take me. The final figure had not been small. However, we were now two weeks into the campaign and the funding was already at 170%. If it reached 200%, I would have to include some stretch rewards, although I had no idea what to offer! I'd definitely have to put my thinking cap on.

The campaign had attracted the attention of more than just the usual fans of the comic. A publishing agent had contacted me, wishing to pitch me to publishers for future work. Despite my misgivings that I might not have the time for it, Lowell had encouraged me to hear the agent out. When I'd got back in touch and explained the nature of my job and how I moved around a lot, they'd said we could talk on Skype and today's meeting had been scheduled.

I still wasn't convinced I was going to accept anything that was offered to me, but that didn't stop me from feeling a few pre-job interview butterflies fluttering around in my stomach. I smiled and poured myself a cup of orange juice. It would be nice if all of my worries were as simple.

"Hey, I bought a copy of the paper. I thought we could look through the article and see what's been said," I told Lowell, unrolling the local rag and placing it on the table. We both looked at the picture of the tiger enclosure, taken after the body had been removed. The man-shaped dent in the ground was still visible.

"Not the kind of publicity the zoo's hoping for, am I right?" Lowell said.

I nodded, bleakly. I may not be in charge of PR, but my job often influenced the success of a zoo. Improvements to habitats tended to result in better breeding and more active, happy animals. Visitors liked to see that. If there was a sudden dive in attendance, I hoped I wouldn't become the scapegoat.

"I'll get the dictionary out," Lowell said, reaching behind him for the little blue book. The rest of breakfast was spent in near silence as Lowell hovered a finger over nearly every word, flicking back and forth through the pages of translations.

By the time we'd both finished our jam and baguette, he'd done.

"From what I can gather, it doesn't say anything we don't know. It names the victim and reports that they died in a tragic paragliding incident and that enquiries are still ongoing. Most of the article is basically an obituary for Pascal Devereux. It lists his job in security and as a parking warden and his local renown for growing pumpkins." He raised a dark eyebrow at me, both of us wondering what it would be like to merely be remembered as a pumpkin grower. I supposed that it really amounted to what you were most passionate about. Perhaps those pumpkins had been Pascal's pride and joy.

"Then it offers condolences to his widow and that's it," Lowell finished.

"Nothing about the agents who've turned up out of the blue," I said, voicing what we were both thinking.

"Nope, but it's not surprising. They have a fair whack of power. I'm sure the local press have been advised exactly what they can and can't print," he said, knowingly.

I shook my head, not wanting to dwell on it. We were already too far into a situation that didn't concern us.

"I wanted to go on a picnic today. I even bought food for it, but I'd forgotten about that Skype thing," I admitted with a sigh.

"It's at lunchtime, right? How about we have dinner at lunch and go for an evening picnic?" Lowell suggested.

"The locals will think we're crazy," I said with a smile.

I'd noticed that several of the villagers had started wearing jumpers, despite it still being warmer than it often was at the height of British summer. There was probably already a lot of talk around the village about the crazy English couple who liked to eat outside most nights.

"Let's do it," I decided. I tilted my head at Lowell. "Hey, wasn't it going to be your turn to cook dinner tonight?"

"Drat, I was hoping that the picnic idea would distract you," he admitted, standing up and gathering our breakfast plates together. "How about you take a nice relaxing walk while I get started on a gourmet feast... the likes of which you'll never have tasted before."

I raised an eyebrow. "I hope it's better than the microwaved pasties you tried to pass off as your own last time."

He winced. "Definitely. It's definitely better than the pasties, which were actually homemade. But, you know - in a factory."

I raised the other eyebrow.

"It said homemade on the packaging!" he argued, the grin growing on his face.

"Are you sure I need to take much time on my walk?" I said.

He pretended to frown. "Have some faith! I swear this time I'm going to cook you a masterpiece. It just er, might take one or two goes. Which is why you need to leave right now," he said, shepherding me to the door.

"Okay, fine! But after all of this build up, it had better be good," I teased.

"I'm sure the result will surprise us both... one way or another," he admitted. "How does lunch at two sound? Your meeting will have finished by then, right?"

"Sure! I guess I'll take my laptop," I said, a little nonplussed. "Lowell, what exactly are you planning to cook?"

"You'll find out," he promised, opening the front door and handing me my laptop case on the way out. "Go and have some fun. It's time you took a holiday!"

I walked through the sunny village, reflecting that the agent would probably think I was showing off when the time came for our meeting. There was wifi at the boulangerie, but if I bought coffee and sat outside at their table, my picturesque surroundings would be all too apparent during the Skype chat.

I adjusted the strap of the laptop bag, so that it sat

comfortably over my shoulder. My eyes scanned the mountains that surrounded the valley village of L'airelle. Although I was supposed to be planning a walk that would while away the rest of the morning, I couldn't help but wonder where Pascal had rented the paragliding gear from. Also, where had the killer jumped from in order to end up at the zoo? I didn't know a thing about paragliding, but from the naked eye, I thought they could have jumped from any number of cliffs and peaks. The village was completely surrounded and I was certain that not every mountain was a tourist trap. Even from where I stood, it was clear that some presented more of a challenge than just a gentle hike.

I'd looked up for so long my head was starting to spin. I blinked and focused on something closer to home, which just so happened to be Adele. She was sat on a bench next to a fountain. I noticed her hands clasping and unclasping - the same way they had the day after the incident.

I decided it was time I got to the bottom of Adele's worries. She was my friend and I knew something was wrong.

"Did you have the day off, too?" I asked, sliding onto the bench beside her.

She jumped when I sat down and I realised she must have been deep in thought.

"No! I mean... yes, I suppose," she fluttered and then frowned.

I waited a beat before I asked. "What's the matter Adele? Whatever it is, you can tell me. I've seen and heard more than you'd imagine," I reassured her. "Is it about what we saw when Pascal fell?" I prompted when she didn't respond.

She looked at me in surprise. "No, it's not that."

"Then what is it?" I asked.

She moved to shrug but then sighed. "It's Justin's dog... I'm really worried about her. I left this pot of prescription medication pills on the counter, and then they vanished. Not just the pills - the whole pot! I didn't really think too much of it, but Jolie, his Labrador, started acting strangely yesterday. She's practically dragging herself around the house whining all the time. I think it's because she might be in pain. I feel terrible! I know I should have done something sooner. I should have taken her to the vet yesterday but I just thought I'd find the pills under a chair, or something. She can't have got the lid off..." Adele put her head in her hands and looked up at me, tears glistening in her eyes. "What if it's already too late? What if I've killed her? Justin is never going to forgive me."

I made myself maintain a sense of calm, knowing that any other reaction would merely make Adele panic further. "I'm sure you're right and it's nothing to do with the pills, but all the same, you should take Jolie to the vet today. Let's not panic too soon, all right? We'll take her in and find out what's wrong. I'm sure it will be fine," I said, crossing my fingers when I said it.

Adele nodded, a tear sliding down her smooth cheek. "Okay, you're right. Jeez, I should have done this earlier. I'm just so scared she's going to die and it's all my fault."

"I'm sure that won't happen," I repeated, praying I was right.

"Come with me, Madi. Please!" she said, grabbing my hand. "If it's really bad, I... I'd just be so grateful if you were there with me. I told Justin I was too sick to work today but really I just wanted to stay home and check on Jolie. I hoped she'd get better, but she seems even more listless today. She's not even walking around anymore. She just sits in her basket whining."

"All right, we'll get her to the vet," I said and then frowned. "Is there a vet around here?"

"Yes, because of the zoo, they have quite a good business,

although they run the practice on their own. The doctor works in the same building," she said.

I noticed that her hands were still clasping and unclasping but less frantically than they had been.

"Let's go pick up Jolie," I said, summoning up what I hoped was a reassuring smile.

I was forced to agree with what Adele had said about the vet running a successful business. When we arrived with Jolie and asked for an appointment, we were told that the wait was around an hour. I'd checked the clock on the wall and had realised I was going to be late for my appointment with the agent. I bit the inside of my cheek and made a decision. There was no telling how long we'd be hanging around for. I pulled out my phone and quickly fired off an apology email, citing an animal emergency and asking if the agent would be kind enough to postpone our appointment.

To be honest, I wasn't convinced I'd hear from them again, but perhaps it was for the best. I hadn't been sure about this whole business from the start. My comic was only ever meant to be a hobby.

We sat down in the waiting room with Jolie, who tried to fit beneath the seats and then gave up. She whined and looked at us piteously.

"Did, uh, the vet tell you to cut down on her food?" I said, surprised that Jolie had managed to get as large as she was in the hands of two trained zookeepers.

Adele sighed and threw up her hands. "We've tried everything! She just has a knack for getting into food. The neighbours once left a pie on their outside table to cool. Not anymore," she said, grimly.

We both looked at the dog.

"You know, she doesn't seem that sick to me, just unhappy. If she did swallow the pills, I think they were probably still in the bottle. That would certainly be enough to make her unhappy," I said, reminded of Mr Limey, the snake, who I'd looked after at Snidely Safari and Wildlife Park. He'd had a solid item stuck in his tail but had fortunately lived to tell the tale... as had I.

I looked around the waiting room and recognised a few of the villagers, who seemed to be sniffling and clutching tissues to their faces. I resisted the urge to immediately disinfect my hands. Adele had already told me that the vet and the doctor shared the same building, but I couldn't help wondering if visitors to the vet returned the next day to see the doctor, after catching whatever bug was currently incubating in the waiting room.

My eyes skated across several fluffy animals, from rabbits to guinea pigs and then - slightly more unusual - a pig wearing a collar and leash. I was still marvelling at that when I saw a familiar suit out of the corner of eye. I turned in time to see Mr Flannigan rise up from where he must have been seated around the corner of the waiting room and walk across to the reception desk.

"How long until I can see the doctor? I'm not a patient. This is a criminal investigation," he hissed. It was clear that he didn't want to be overheard but the room had hushed as soon as he'd started talking, so we all picked up every single word.

The receptionist stopped typing on the computer and fixed him with a glare that would have made most people retreat. The agent just gritted his teeth and stared back.

"I've already told you the waiting time. Saturday morning surgeries are busy. Perhaps you could come back another day?"

"No, I can't! The whole point of this is to resolve the situation quickly. You are being unhelpful, Madame. Have you at least asked the doctor if he could just spare a couple of minutes between appointments?"

I winced at his tone of voice. He was going entirely the wrong way about it if he wanted to hurry things along. You never antagonised the gatekeeper. I wouldn't be surprised if his wait had just doubled.

"I never disturb the doctor while he's working. It is my job to run the waiting room and I am merely abiding by what is fair. You may wait, or you may come back another time," she told him and deliberately looked back at the computer screen.

Mr Flannigan's face was redder than I remembered when he turned round and saw me sitting with Adele. To my annoyance, he walked over and sat in the empty seat next to me.

"You didn't mention that you and your friends witnessed Monsieur Devereux's death," he said, accusingly.

"You didn't ask, so I assumed you already knew. Anyway, we didn't see his death. He was already dead when he fell… unless you know otherwise?" I probed, overstating the facts a little.

Mr Flannigan's face closed down but I took from his grumpiness that I was correct.

"Well, I need to interview you all. There are some questions you must answer. Will this afternoon do?"

I shook my head. "I have the weekend off. You should come by the zoo on Monday. All three of us will be back at work then, although you'll probably have to ask the manager if it's okay," I added, secretly pleased to be making things a bit difficult for the man. I hoped it would teach him to use a little more common courtesy, but I had a feeling that ship had sailed a long time ago.

He sighed, openly and rudely, merely affirming the judgement I'd already made. I opened my mouth to ask him about Lowell and then thought better of it. If Ms Borel hadn't chosen to say anything to him, there was probably a good reason for it.

"I can't believe this is taking so long," he muttered. When I made no comment, he looked at me for several seconds without speaking. I studiously ignored him and instead reached down to pat the miserable Jolie.

"What are you here for?" he asked.

I felt like rolling my eyes at the social faux pas. Was this man really so out of touch, or did he just trade on being impolite?

"I'm helping Adele with her dog, Jolie," I said, as shortly as I could. "Did you get the information you wanted from Madame Devereux?" I asked, equally rudely.

He shrugged. "The old man never told her much of anything."

I nodded and unzipped my bag, pointedly taking out my laptop and opening it in order to do some pretend work. Anything to escape this conversation.

"Still working on your day off?" Flannigan said, looking over my shoulder at the review document for L'airelle Zoological Park, which had been the first thing to come up.

"Just making good use of time spent waiting around," I said, forcing myself to read the document.

Next to me, the government agent slumped back in his seat. "Are you sure you two couldn't get the other one and talk to me after this?"

I shook my head without even looking at him.

Fortunately, Adele's name was called and I didn't have to start the argument all over again.

"I'll see you on Monday," Flannigan called after us.

I waved a hand behind me, which he could take however he wanted to.

Adele shot me a wide-eyed look once we were safely inside the vet's office. I returned it and added a relieved grin.

"Madame Nice, what can I do for you today?" The vet asked with a kindly smile.

I immediately decided I liked Monsieur Lupin, the vet. Everything from his half-moon glasses, to the smile lines around his mouth and eyes, hinted that he was a nice person.

"It's Justin's dog… Jolie. I think she may have eaten some pills of mine. I left the whole bottle on the counter and then they were just gone - bottle and all! Jolie's been acting strangely and you know what she's like around food," Adele blustered and then stopped.

"Okay now, let's not worry ourselves too soon, shall we?" the vet said placatingly. "Let's try to get her up on the counter."

Seeing that Adele was still wringing her hands over the potential fate of her husband's dog, I moved forwards to assist the vet in hefting Jolie onto the examination table. Once there, the dog let out a long and pitiful whine.

"There, there, I'm sure it's nothing to worry about," the vet said to the black dog, patting her on the head. "She never liked coming here at the best of times, even when treats were on offer," he confided with me.

"I can see she's put on weight again, although perhaps there could be bloating if she did eat those pills, but you said they were in the bottle…" He squinted his eyes and started to examine the Labrador, looking into her eyes and mouth. "Hmmm, yes, I see," he said, cryptically.

He got out a stethoscope and began moving it up and down Jolie's body, tapping it every now and then.

"How are your tigers, Adele? I heard they may have had an unexpected dietary supplement the other day." The vet raised a bushy eyebrow.

"Justin got them to come away by bribing them with food, so I don't think they got much," Adele said with a thin smile.

I realised that this vet had a rather dark sense of humour.

He chuckled. "Well, I'm just glad you haven't brought **them** in with indigestion. Every time I go up to the zoo I'm amazed when I come back with all of my limbs still attached. I've no doubt that my luck will run out one day."

He started to hum a little tune as he lifted Jolie's tail and then, to the dog's distaste, popped in a thermometer and took her temperature.

"How is she?" Adele asked, anxiety winning out.

"Oh, she's fine," the vet cheerfully informed her.

"There's nothing wrong?" Adele frowned. "But her behaviour…"

"Yes, it's quite characteristic. I think Jolie here was just trying to get your attention. There's nothing wrong with her - she's just pregnant."

Adele's face turned white. "Pregnant?"

"Yes! I can see from your face that it must have not been intentional. Not to worry, these things happen, although I recommend you get her spayed after she's had this litter. You have another dog, don't you?"

"Yes, but he came to us already neutered," Adele said. "You're sure it's nothing to do with the pills?"

The vet shook his head. "No, I heard several little heartbeats when I listened to her tummy. She and the litter seem healthy to me. I reckon you'll be meeting them yourself in a day or so." He smiled fondly at the forlorn dog. "You must have got loose and met Mr Right, eh?"

"But, she's never got loose!" Adele cut in, visibly distressed. "Since she started stealing the neighbours' food, Justin shored up all of the fences around the garden. This doesn't make any sense."

The vet shot her a rueful smile. "Well, something

happened, or we're looking at a miraculous birth." He looked down at the dog, who to me seemed to look back very guiltily indeed. "You'd better talk to your husband. Perhaps he knows how it happened. Call me if there are any complications or the pups don't appear within the week." He rubbed his bearded chin thoughtfully. "You'd better take her off that strict diet I gave you. It's no wonder she's unhappy. She's probably very hungry indeed. Sorry old girl," he said, rubbing the dog's head. "How about a treat to make it up to you?" He pulled a twisted chew out of a glass jar and Jolie's tail started to wag for the first time since we'd arrived at the vets. "There, I knew that would make it all better. Now, don't forget to bring the puppies in for a checkup and to get their jabs. If you think you'll have trouble finding homes for them, I'd be happy to put the word out once we know how many we have on our hands. And what they look like," he added, throwing Jolie a curious look. "It's rather exciting, isn't it? Only time will tell."

He cheerfully waved us out of the room, leaving Adele and me at reception to pay the vet's bill. My new colleague handed over her bank card without a word.

"It's good that Jolie is all right, isn't it?" I said once we were outside. Adele hadn't said a word since we'd left the vet's office.

"Good? I'm going to kill her! How could she be so irresponsible! Running off and getting pregnant!" she ranted, but I thought I saw the beginnings of a smile there. She sighed. "I don't know how I'm going to tell Justin. I know I said in the vets that she hadn't got out, but there was this one time… She ran out of the front door when I had a day off and Justin was doing extra time at work. I found her with a whole roast turkey in her mouth. Luckily, I never found out who it had belonged to, but perhaps that wasn't the only thing she got up to during her taste of freedom."

"At least she's in good health. Poor dog, I bet you cut her food down even more when you saw her putting on a paunch," I said, shooting Jolie a sympathetic look.

"We did," Adele admitted, patting the dog on the head. "Oh, how irresponsible for two zookeepers to have an accidental dog pregnancy. We're meant to be the guiding lights in animal welfare!"

I gave her a reassuring smile. "Accidents do happen. Don't worry, I'm sure there'll be lots of people in the village and at the zoo who'll want one of her pups. Well, unless the father was something really odd," I amended, thinking of the strange Rottweiler, West Highland Terrier cross I'd once seen on the internet. Despite it being a rather implausible breeding mixup, homes had been found for all of the puppies. "Just get her fixed after she's given birth. I'm sure Justin will forgive you," I added.

"Nothing to be done now. I'm sure it will work out in the end. We'd better get you home then and start making preparations for the new arrivals," she said to Jolie, ruffling her ears.

The dog still had a forlorn air about her, but that was probably just because being this pregnant was no fun. *Still, it'll make a great addition to the storyline for my comic!* I thought.

I reflexively reached down to pat my laptop, only to discover I wasn't carrying the bag any more. I thought back to taking it out in order to dissuade the agent from talking to me and then recalled hastily packing it away again... and not picking it up.

"One sec, Adele. I left my laptop case inside. Are you and Jolie okay to wait?" I asked.

She nodded and waved a hand. "I've got all the time in the world now I know my husband's dog isn't at death's door because of me. I do wonder where my pills went. Perhaps Justin knows." Her cheeks turned a little pink. "I didn't actually ask him. I was so sure Jolie had got into them I didn't dare bring it up, but perhaps he just moved them somewhere else."

"I'm glad this mystery had a happy ending," I told her, before I disappeared back inside the surgery.

The waiting room had emptied a lot since we'd been in there and it was with some relief that I noticed Mr Flannigan must have finally been admitted to see the doctor. My laptop case was right where I'd left it, next to my chair, and I picked it up.

I was about to exit the building for a second time when I overheard a conversation. The doctor's office was on the way out and he'd left his door open a crack. I hadn't intended to eavesdrop, but Mr Flannigan's clipped British accent stood out a mile in the rural French village.

I glanced around, but no one was looking my way. I pretended to notice my shoelace was undone and bent to retie it.

"I'm with the British government. You are authorised to share medical records and opinions with me," I heard Mr Flannigan say, and by the tone of his voice, it wasn't the first time he'd said it. He was evidently having a hard time persuading the local doctor that it was okay to talk about one of his past patients. "His widow's already told me he liked a drink or two. I just want to know what your opinion was."

I heard the sound of papers being shuffled and then the doctor spoke. "Monsieur Devereux certainly had a reputation for drinking to excess. He never came to me about it, but as he was getting older, I did warn him of the dangers for a man of his age. Now, I only feel authorised to share Monsieur Devereux's records - and his alone - with you, but I will say I'm not at all sorry he's gone… if you catch my meaning."

I realised the consultation was coming to an end and

hastily stopped pretending to tie my shoelace. I walked out into the bright sunshine and rejoined Adele. Together, we got Jolie back into the car - admittedly being a little more careful than we had when we'd been rushing her to the vet in what we'd both thought could be a life or death situation.

On the brief drive back to Adele's house, I considered what I'd heard. Pascal Devereux had liked to drink and it sounded like he hadn't been particularly pleasant when he'd been liquored up. The doctor had definitely hinted that he'd got violent on occasion. I wondered if there were other people in the village who'd known that little secret and might have finally decided to put a stop to the behaviour... permanently.

"Madi, would you like to come in for tea? I'd love to say thank you for coming with me to the vet," Adele said when we pulled up outside her house.

I glanced at my phone screen and realised it was already half past one. It wasn't long until Lowell's promised feast would be ready.

"Lowell's cooking dinner at home and I should really be getting back," I said, wondering if I'd regret turning down the opportunity for what would no doubt have been more substantial fare than just a cup of tea.

"I see," Adele said with a curious look. "Is cooking one of his talents?"

"I think I'm about to find out one way or the other," I admitted.

She laughed. "Well, just in case, I'll pack you a bag of madelines. I made them this morning. When I worry, I bake."

"When I worry, I eat," I confessed, which made her laugh some more.

"It sounds like we should have been friends long ago."

She took Jolie inside and I waited in the hallway until she

hurried back with a large bag, filled with madelines and other assorted biscuits.

"I added a few other bits." Adele smiled. "I really was worried this morning."

"Let me know when the puppies come… and what happens when you tell Justin," I added.

She nodded. "If it goes badly, you'll probably hear it from your house."

I left Adele with the very pregnant Jolie, who was no doubt officially in the dog house. In spite of the dark secret I'd learned during my eavesdropping session, my steps were light on the way back to the cottage. An animal had been pronounced well, I had a bag full of treats, and I was even looking forward to discovering what Lowell had cooked up for me.

My nose twitched when I was only a couple of houses away from our little rented cottage. Something smelled fantastic. Could it really be…? I checked the time on my phone and realised it had only taken me five minutes to walk back from Adele's house. Drat! I should have taken a detour so as not to return too early. Lowell had definitely wanted me to give him space and not come back until two. Still… it smelt like it was nearly ready. Surely he wouldn't mind if I was a little less than half an hour early…

The door to the cottage sprung open and a woman walked out.

Without thinking, I dodged into the space between houses, just one building away from our cottage. I stood in shocked silence with my back pressed against the cool stone wall. Why had one of the village women just walked out of our cottage? I'd seen her around the square a few times. She must have been in her late thirties, but her natural red hair and creamy skin made her undeniably attractive and helped her to stand out in a land full of *St Tropez* worthy tans. My heart jumped in my chest.

I was going to have to risk a second look. I poked my head around the corner.

She was waving towards the still open door. It blocked my view, but I had no doubt that it was Lowell who was stood there.

"Au revoir! Merci Monsieur," she said, half laughing. I suddenly realised her waving hand was stuffed full of euro notes!

I whipped my head back around the corner, all kinds of possibilities running through my mind, before I calmed down a bit and realised the truth of what I'd just seen.

It was far worse than I'd imagined.

I gave it five minutes and then walked up to the cottage door and knocked. Lowell answered, wearing the pink gingham apron that had been supplied with the rental property. He used the corner to wipe his dramatically sweating brow. I inwardly raised an eyebrow and wondered how he'd managed to achieve that little touch. Press-ups in the back garden?

"Madi, you're early! No problem, I think it's all about ready. If you sit down, I'll get the starter out of the fridge and plated up."

I tried not to laugh at his sincerity. He'd really gone all out!

"I can't wait to try it all. It smells amazing," I said honestly, still somehow managing to keep a straight face.

"I told you I could cook," he said, proudly placing what looked like a salmon roulade on the table.

"Wow, what is it?" I asked.

He only hesitated for a fraction of a second. "It's salmon and a mousse. I just, you know… whipped it up, using all sorts."

He cut us both a slice and we dug in.

It was brilliant. Somehow that just made me want to laugh even more.

"What's for the main course?" I asked.

"It's uh… duck leg. With like, a cheesy potato."

"Dauphinoise?" I queried.

"Yeah," he said, seizing on what must have been a familiar word. I took a sip of the pink wine he'd poured for us both but I didn't miss the look of relief that crossed his face.

I let him dish up the duck and decided to fill him in on the morning I'd had, including what I'd overheard at the doctors-cum-vets.

"So, Pascal turned into a drunk. I can't say I blame him. When I knew him, he was already old and bitter. It was probably just his way of dealing with things. Although that never excuses any domestic violence," he acknowledged.

I nodded in agreement. "I can see why the doctor all but said it's a blessing he's dead. But it made me wonder how many people noticed what was going on over the years."

"You think it might be a motive?" Lowell asked, taking a bite of the duck and appreciating it.

The whole dinner really was superb.

"Who knows? If it were as simple as someone wanting to defend Madame Devereux, why dispose of the body in such a needlessly dramatic way? I still think the fact he was dropped into the zoo means something."

"I forgot to ask! How was the publishing chat with the agent?"

"I had to postpone it," I confessed, hoping he wouldn't be too disappointed on my behalf. I wasn't that worried about missing it.

"Well, you've got to help your friends out, haven't you?" he allowed.

I took another sip of my wine. "Speaking of friends…

Lowell, I heard a rumour in the village earlier. A rumour about you," I invented.

He deserved to sweat for what he'd done.

"Oh?" he said, his eyebrows shooting up.

"I'm not sure if I overheard it correctly, but while you were supposed to be cooking a three course dinner, one of the locals saw an attractive redhead enter this cottage and not come out again." I took another sip of my wine, enjoying the genuine concern and conflict on Lowell's face. "I must admit, I wasn't sure if I was going to come back to a microwaved ready meal but now I find out that you're not only a brilliant cook, you also found time to entertain another woman while doing it! It's really quite an achievement."

"That's not... It's not what you think," Lowell blustered, running both hands through his dark hair and making it stick up in tufts. "I didn't..."

He stopped talking and narrowed his eyes. "You don't seem very angry about this."

I grinned, knowing he was starting to cotton on. "That wasn't the only gossip I heard either. The next door neighbour told me they saw the same woman leave this house clutching a wedge of euro notes! I'm sure you can understand the conclusion they drew from that. The whole village will be in uproar!"

Lowell's mouth set in an unimpressed line, but his eyes still held a spark of amusement. "You saw, didn't you?"

My grin widened. "I came back from my walk a little early," I confessed. "Tut, tut... paying someone to make the dinner for you." I took another sip of the wine. "To be honest... I'm impressed. Some men might have tried using YouTube videos and made something passable but you skipped that stage and did something really impressive."

"Well, I said you'd be surprised." A smile was just starting to creep onto his own face.

I pouted. "Where's my 'well done' for being a good detective and catching you at your game?"

Lowell shook his head. "I suppose I only have myself to blame there, although I think you were already pretty good at sticking your nose where it didn't belong before I came along."

"How dare you," I said, smiling into my wine.

"I don't know what you paid her, but it was worth it," I confessed, finishing the last of my duck. "Hey, maybe she could give you lessons so you could do it yourself!" I tilted my head hopefully, but he shook his head.

"Why bother when you can cut out the middle man?"

I rolled my eyes. "I knew it was too much to hope for, you cheat. What's for dessert?"

"I have no idea. It's a dessert. I really should have paid more attention when Anise told me what all of the courses were," he confessed.

"Ah well, my favourite kind of dessert is dessert, so we should be okay," I told him with a grin.

4

SECRET ADMIRER

The sun shone down on me when I walked through the zoo on Monday morning. The weather hadn't blipped once, despite it being September. Even the locals were surprised but they were all betting it would end soon. I smiled. It wasn't just the British who were pessimists when it came to the weather.

"Bonjour!" I called to every member of staff I met on my way to the little staffroom. Today, I planned to tackle L'airelle's collection of reptiles and amphibians - something that I now felt surprisingly confident about, thanks to my last job. I also doubted that the animals at L'airelle would be anywhere near as deadly as the ones at Dracondia Manor. Before I got on with that, I'd made plans to drop in and see Luna and Adele. After all, I was sure Adele would have news to share.

"Hey! How are we?" I said, walking in to the familiar smell of coffee. Adele and Luna were sat on the sofa with a couple of espressos, having finished feeding their charges breakfast.

"I'm good," Luna said, and Adele echoed the same sentiment.

"How are the animals?" I enquired, knowing this would undoubtedly get a longer response.

"The three brothers have calmed down and seem back to normal," Adele began. "They've been arguing ever since… the body." She cleared her throat. "They're back to normal now, at least. Tiana and Lawrence are fine, too," she said, referring to the parents of the three bengal brothers.

"Lions are all good. I tried them with a block of that ice you suggested. It's been pretty hot and they really seemed to go for it. I'm looking forward to figuring out some of the other toys you've planned," Luna said.

"The rest of the clan are all doing fine," Adele said, referring to the various felines they collectively cared for.

"Where's Justin?" I cautiously asked.

Adele's mouth quirked up at one side. "He's at home, but don't worry… it's not because we're getting a divorce and he's moving out."

I breathed a dramatic sigh of relief and she laughed. "I came clean about Jolie and guess what? She ran out on him, too! So now we have no idea which time it was that she had her fling."

"Equal guilt… hooray!" I said, pleased it had worked out so fortuitously.

"Justin stayed home because we think there's not long to go until Jolie pops. We're both taking our holiday leave one day at a time. I'm not sure if the lucky one of us will be the one who's at home or here when it happens," she said, thoughtfully.

"I can't wait to see them. You're sure you'll let me have one?" Luna piped up.

"You can have them all if you like," Adele joked with a wry

smile. "Don't commit too soon. Who knows? She might have done it with a Dachshund!"

A knock on the wooden slat door of the hut cut off our conversation. A man in a uniform stepped into the room. "I've got a delivery here? I'll just pop it down on the counter," he said.

"Who's it for?" Luna asked.

The man shrugged. "No idea! The instructions just said to bring it to the hut where the big cat keepers hang out. You'll have to fight over it."

He turned to go, but I moved to block his exit. "Wait a second, you really don't know who sent it?" I asked.

"Sorry, Madame. The company I work for just does deliveries. I don't know where the package originally came from. We work for loads of different businesses."

I moved aside and let him go.

We all converged on the table, looking down at what had been left.

"Chocolates. Nice ones, too," Luna observed, lifting the ribbon and looking at the assortment we would find inside.

Adele reached for the gift label, which would normally contain a message. "It says 'For you, beautiful'," she read.

"Maybe Justin sent them for you as a surprise?" I suggested but she shook her head.

"No... I love Justin, but he wouldn't know a romantic gesture if it slapped him in the face. How about your guy?"

"He paid a local woman to cook a three course dinner for us yesterday. I think he's all out of romantic gestures," I said.

Adele's expression melted into a smile. "Aww, that's really sweet!"

"He paid her to come and cook it at the house and told me to go for a long walk... so he could pretend he cooked the whole thing himself," I continued.

Adele's smile was replaced with a smirk. "He's a sneaky one. I hope you got him back?"

"I did," I reassured her, thinking back to the line I'd spun Lowell. It had been more than fair payback for his little trick. In the end, who was I to complain? It had been a truly fantastic meal.

"Luna? Do you have a new beau we don't know about?" Adele said to the lion keeper.

"No," she said, although I noticed she was blushing a little bit. "No one's sending me chocolates," she reaffirmed and I believed her - although maybe not that part about not having a love interest on the table.

Adele and I exchanged a look, both of us silently promising we'd get to the bottom of that later on.

"Don't," I said, when Luna tore a little of the packaging open.

"But…"

"I know," I answered. I really did. "They're probably fine, but you've got to admit it's weird. A man falls from the sky right over the zoo and now a box of chocolates with no intended recipient and no clue as to who they're from arrives. I'm not saying we need to throw them away, but let's think a bit first, okay? Let's all try to get to the bottom of who sent them. I'm sure whoever it was wanted it to be a surprise but… it's better to know for sure."

"Okay, we'll leave them right here. It's only the cat keepers who come in here anyway. Start researching, ladies," Adele said with a grin.

"I'd better be getting on. Lots of animals to see, lots of health and safety issues to butt heads over," I said.

"Have fun," Luna mocked.

I stuck my tongue out at her before turning and walking out the door. Or at least, I tried to. Someone was blocking my way.

"Good morning, Ms Amos," the familiar voice said. I squinted in the sunlight that streamed through the doorway and realised I was uncomfortably close to Mr Flannigan. I spared a thought to wonder where his partner had got to. I hoped she wasn't after Lowell. He'd told me they'd had work history but he hadn't been much more forthcoming.

"Who's the lucky lady?" Mr Flannigan asked when he walked in uninvited and eyed the chocolates on the counter.

"We don't know," I said and hastily pushed the conversation onto a fresh topic. "You're here to ask questions, right?"

"Yes. It's good the three of you are here together." he said, smiling brightly and falsely at each of us in turn.

He dragged a bar stool across the tiled floor and sat down in front of the sofa. I moved over and perched on the arm of the sofa.

"So... you both knew the victim, correct?" he said, addressing Adele and Luna.

They nodded.

"But, Miss Fleur, I believe you had problems with Monsieur Devereux for years? Was there some sort of a grudge?" He zeroed in on Luna.

"If you know about 'my problem' with Monsieur Devereux, then you'll also know that he had a vendetta against my father and the reason for it," she responded, coolly.

"Do you know how to skydive?" he asked, quite out of the blue.

My mouth fell open in shock. He wasn't really suggesting...

"No, I do not," Luna replied.

"Really? I thought the majority of locals would have at least tried it, especially when there's a facility so close by." Mr Flannigan wasn't dropping this easily.

"I'm scared of heights," Luna told him with a thin smile.

"I've done it before," Adele admitted.

The agent's attention snapped to her. "How recently?"

"Not for a couple of years," Adele replied, but I noticed a crease appeared between her eyebrows. *And with good reason!* I thought. I couldn't believe this man persisted in being so rude. I wondered if he behaved the same way around his wife.

I surreptitiously cast a glance down at his ring finger and noticed it was bare. No surprises there. When I looked up, I found Mr Flannigan's eyes fixed on me. I turned away, not wanting him to make the wrong assumption.

"Are you certain?" he pressed, returning to interrogating Adele.

I found I'd already had enough. "Are you seriously trying to imply she had something to do with the incident? She was right on the ground with Luna and me when it happened. We all saw the paragliders fly over."

"I'm just establishing the facts," Mr Flannigan droned without meeting my gaze.

"You have access to all of the information the police took from us on the day it happened, right?" I knew he must do from the facts he'd already seemed aware of. "Everything we saw is in the statements we gave."

"I'm just checking there's nothing that you might have remembered since," he said, expression unchanging.

He pointedly turned away from me and returned his attention to Luna. "What was your relationship with Monsieur Devereux?" he asked.

"I didn't have one," Luna said. "He was bitter about some money he perceived he missed out on and he took it out on me and my father in petty ways. Like I told the police, it went on for years, but he stopped recently. I guess his age started to catch up with him."

Perhaps his drinking, too, I privately thought.

"When was the last time you saw him?" Flannigan asked.

"I don't know. He lived in the village, so I'm sure I saw him around occasionally, although we never spoke. I did my best to stay as far away from him as possible."

Flannigan nodded, like she'd just said something significant. "Ms Nice, you're married, aren't you? How about you, Ms Fleur?"

I bit my tongue and then couldn't hold it in any longer. I'd had enough. "Mr Flannigan, I'm afraid we all have our own jobs to be returning to. I know Luna and Adele were about to attend a rather urgent situation with one of the cougars when you came in. I don't think it can wait any longer," I invented.

Adele and Luna had probably planned to have a longer break after the early morning feed, but they both stood up eagerly. An invented emergency was infinitely better than putting up with Flannigan prying into their private lives.

"I'll be in touch if there are any more questions," Flannigan said, as if he'd decided the interview was over.

It took all of my willpower not to offer him a chocolate on the way out.

Once he was definitely gone, I turned back to Adele and Luna and breathed a sigh of relief.

I suddenly realised they were both looking at me like I'd sprouted horns.

"What was that?" Luna said, a smile slowly taking over her face.

I looked from her to Adele, confused. "What was what?"

"That! The way you gave him the boot. It was like a fluffy Chihuahua throwing a fit and giving someone a bite that needs stitches!" Luna clarified.

I frowned at the 'chihuahua' analogy and pouted when I remembered she'd also called me 'fluffy'.

Unfortunately, they were too busy laughing to notice.

"That's exactly what it was like," Adele said, much to my annoyance.

I tried to shrug it off. "I just don't see what right he has to ask all of those irrelevant questions. I don't know why he was trying to turn the suspicion on us. We were on the ground when it happened! We told the police everything when we gave our statements, right? As far as I'm concerned, that means we're done. Or at least… it should be the police asking further questions, not someone with a hidden motive." I frowned again when I thought about that. Lowell had said the agents came from the British government, but why were they here? Was this all to do with witness protection, as he suspected? Or was it something else?

"Let's go on a walk, just in case that awful man is watching us from somewhere," Adele said.

"Oh, I'm meant to be working," I said, but they both tilted their heads at me imploringly. I rolled my eyes heavenwards. "Fine. I'll just take it out of my lunch break."

Now that I was self-employed, I got to schedule my work hours. It meant I had more freedom, but at the same time, I didn't want anyone to think I was lazy. I was determined to give my employers their money's worth.

"Everyone will think you're working if you're walking with us," Luna tried to reassure me.

I shook my head with a rueful smile. "Anyone with eyes knows we're thick as thieves. Let's get going, or I'll have no lunch break left at all."

We walked out of the tiki hut into the already warm sunshine. I'd been right to think it would be another beautiful day when I'd arrived at the zoo. Summer had not yet breathed its last sigh.

Visitors were already milling around the zoo, but Mondays were not one of L'airelle's busiest days - especially now we were at the end of the summer season.

"Luna, are you still okay to take Matti home with you when the action kicks off?" Adele enquired. "Matti's my dog - a Dogue De Bordeaux. He's a big softie, but we aren't sure how he'll react to puppies," she explained for my benefit.

"It's no problem. Bring him round if you even suspect something's happening. You know I love looking after your dogs. Hopefully it will convince you that I'm the right choice to be one of those puppies' new mum," Luna said, waggling her eyebrows.

Adele laughed. "Wait until you see just what we've got on our hands."

"I know I'll love them," Luna said.

"Me too," Adele agreed. "Maybe so much I won't want to share," she said with a twinkle in her eye. "Thank you for saying you'll look after Matti. Even if you're doing it as some sort of bribe..."

"How dare you suggest it's a bribe! It's actually more of a hostage situation. I'll be keeping a hold of Matti until I get my puppy," Luna joked. She sighed happily. "It's nice to talk about something that's not to do with Pascal. How long do you think his death will be hanging over us?"

"As long as it takes to either solve, or exhaust all avenues of enquiry," I replied, automatically. "I think the police are stumped. They're probably waiting to see if anything else happens."

"Anything else?" Adele queried.

I gave her a brief account of Lowell's suspicions about the witness protection programme. I was glad I'd never been trusted with a secret like that. It would probably slip out in no time at all.

"That's interesting," Adele commented. "I think everyone in the village is realising they didn't know Pascal as well as they thought they did. I wonder who else that's true for," she mused.

"Hey, speaking of weird things… you've both got phones in your house, right?" Luna asked.

Adele and I nodded, although no one had called us at our rental property.

"Have either of you been getting junk calls recently? I keep getting those funny ones that when you answer, someone just hangs up. It's so annoying!"

"Have you reverse dialled the number?" Adele asked.

"It was private," Luna replied.

"I just get the usual solar panel and life insurance sales people. They never give up," Adele said.

I just shook my head at Luna. To be honest, I wasn't even sure if the phone was actually plugged into the wall.

"Awww!" I said, unable to resist going up to look through the window at the Pallas's cats. They mostly spent their days inside the artificial caves and burrows. I knew they tended to come out at night. The southern French weather was too warm for them with their thick coats.

Today was an exception. One of the short legged cats had made an appearance and was rolling around in the dust of their enclosure. There was something very appealing about their large eyes, wide spaced ears, and stocky bodies. They were one wild cat you'd love to have a cuddle with, although the cat itself would definitely have a thing or two to say about that.

These cats were another group of animals at the zoo that I really wanted to engage. Their enclosure had been beautifully thought out. L'airelle Zoological Park gave them some good space, but in the wild, the cats would be hunting during the day. Interestingly, as well as hunting rodents and birds, the cats had also been known to hunt spiders and insects.

There was a lot of debate within the zoo community over whether or not live prey should be allowed for carnivores. There was a European regulation against giving zoo animals live prey, as it caused stress to the prey species. However, although it sounded harsh, I knew that visitors didn't mind nearly as much if a live insect was dropped into a snake's vivarium, as opposed to a fluffy mouse. Adding a few more spiders than might be strictly natural to the Pallas's cats enclosure might give them something fun to do that also resulted in a nutritious (albeit gross) snack.

We were all still watching the solitary Pallas's cat when I noticed both Adele and Luna flinch. I was about to ask what was up when someone started talking at us.

"What a surprise. You zookeepers think you run the place! Never working, always skipping work. You disgust me. I'll be reporting this to Francois," the woman said, using the zoo boss' first name.

I turned around and found myself face to face with a frizzy-haired woman. She had darkly tanned skin and a mouth that looked like it remained permanently pursed.

"They're with me. I needed to ask their opinion on an idea I have to liven up the Pallas's cats' lives a bit." I tried a smile but it was like smiling at a block of marble.

"You're the one claiming to be able to solve all of our problems, aren't you?" she replied, looking me up and down. Whatever test she was running, I could tell I hadn't passed.

"I've never made a claim like that. Perhaps you're thinking of someone else," I said, knowing my politeness was becoming strained.

"No, it's you," the woman said.

I waited for a second but she seemed to have reached the end of her spiel. "Okay, well I'm glad that's all cleared up." I turned away and she started talking again.

"I'll be reporting your laziness to Francois. I want him to know exactly what you're doing with time he is no doubt paying you far too much for."

"Knock yourself out," I said and then wondered if that

little phrase might translate to a literal threat to someone for whom English wasn't a first language. *Oh well, it's not bad advice,* I thought.

The mystery woman spun on her heel and clip-clopped away, leaving me to wonder if she tiptoed everywhere until she found someone she deemed to be not doing their job properly. That would explain why none of us had heard her approaching until it was too late.

"Who was that?" I asked, baffled by what had just happened.

"Constantine," Adele and Luna replied in unison.

"She hates me," Luna confided.

"She hates everyone," Adele amended, rolling her eyes at Luna. "She's the assistant manager of the restaurant but she seems to have far more free time than she accuses us of having. She patrols the zoo like it's her personal mission to find anyone wasting the zoo's money by not having their nose glued to the grindstone. She'll run off and report it to Monsieur Quebec."

"We think she's doing it because she thinks he'll give her a promotion to be his second in command. I don't know why she doesn't see that if you make everyone at the zoo dislike you, when you do make it to the top, people will still hate you. It's just stupid," Luna cut in.

"Still, we'd better all get back to work," I said and they nodded. I automatically felt for my folder of notes and realised it must still be in the staff hut. I shut my eyes for a moment, wondering what my brain had been doing these past couple of days.

"Oh no!" Adele said, as soon as she walked back through the door of the tiki hut.

"Adele! I just came by to ask you something."

A young man I thought I recognised from the caretaker team was stood next to the counter. I looked down at the box of chocolates, which was now fully unwrapped and open. A few of the chocolates were missing.

The young man followed our collective gaze and blushed. "Oh, sorry. They were already half opened. Did you mind?"

"No, it's fine," Adele said when no one else spoke. "Do you feel okay, Nathan?"

"Yeah, I'm fine, thanks for asking. I was just wondering if you're doing the tour later today? Justin was supposed to, but as he's taken today off…"

"Oh! Sure, that would be fine. Thanks for letting me know. I'd have completely forgotten," Adele said, flashing Nathan a smile. I thought he seemed to glow with the praise.

"See you later!" he said, nodding to each of us in turn.

I waited for him to leave the hut. "At least we know the chocolates are probably not poisoned," I said, glad for Nathan's sake that they had turned out to be innocuous.

"Good, that means I can get stuck in!" Luna said, grabbing a couple.

I was sorely tempted to join her, but even I wouldn't be able to come up with a good enough tall tale if Constantine or Mr Flannigan were to walk back in. It was time to tackle the reptile house.

5

ATTACK OF THE KILLER EMUS!

I sketched out a new A4 page storyline for my comic. Lucky was on an adventure and the ducks were conspiring to make their escape, with the goal of world domination. I smiled at the scenes in front of me. The zookeepers in *Monday's Menagerie* were going to have their work cut out for them.

The publishing agent had emailed me back and had agreed to reschedule. They'd been really understanding and had even reiterated how brilliant it was that my art reflected my life. Apparently it would make a great selling point. I still had my doubts about the wisdom of revealing my identity by slapping my real name (a rather unmistakeable one) on the front of a book. My comics were never truly based on real people, but some of the characters I sketched certainly drew inspiration from real life. I was worried people might come to associate the comics with what really went on at Avery Zoo. I was certain Auryn would never forgive me if I unwittingly managed to give the zoo a bad reputation!

I shook my head. I was getting ahead of myself. I hadn't even had a discussion with the agent yet. I had no idea what they were offering. All I knew was that they seemed genuinely interested in my comic. It was nice, but I knew full well that even if the book was picked up by a publisher, there was no guarantee it would be successful. Being popular on the internet was one thing, but I wasn't naive enough to think that my small success online would translate well into print when shown to an audience who hadn't tuned in every few days to read the new comic.

"We'll see," I said, making the final touches to a fully coloured comic and then bringing up the upload page.

I checked my inbox and quickly replied to the regular fan emails. There had been far more recently, even than the steady increase I'd started to expect. I suspected it was all to do with the crowd funding campaign. Speaking of…

I clicked to the comic's crowd funding page and felt my breath catch. It was 200% funded already and it still had time to run. I looked at the amount of money and felt a bit faint. I knew that some of it was taken as a fee and I'd also calculated just how much it was going to cost for me to be able to produce all of the rewards and the stretch goals. I rubbed a tired hand across my temples, wondering if I should design a whole new tier of stretch goals if it funded another 100%. I actually hoped it wouldn't come to that. A small, limited print run was one thing. I didn't want to have to set up my own factory to post endless comic books.

I shook my head and returned to the fan emails, reading and replying to every one. When that was done, I still had one more task to do.

I braced myself and opened Tiff's email. She'd somehow found time to set up my Etsy shop, whilst holding down her job as the commercial manager at Avery Zoo and also creating and selling her fantasy maps.

I clicked to the shop apprehensively. Tiff had already given it the same name as my comic and had also used my comic's logo as the shop's logo. She'd written in the email that all I needed to do was use the photoshop templates she used to sell her maps and paste my comic sketches into the gaps. I had long admired Tiff's presentation of her maps and I knew it was a great favour that she was letting me use her templates, but I thought it was all so posh for my rather, well... 'sketchy' sketches.

I opened a template and gave it a try.

"That does look pretty good," I admitted to myself. I quickly knocked up ten sketches for sale and sent them all back to Tiff. At least it would get her off my back about it. As a little footnote she'd added 'Don't forget to link to the shop on your comic site'. I stifled a groan. She'd thought of everything.

I sent off the email and then made the changes to my website. *There*, hopefully now she would be happy. I'd already included some of my original sketches as rewards in my crowd funding campaign, but I wasn't convinced they'd sell in real life. Especially not at the price Tiff had suggested! She'd reminded me how long it took me to make each one, and that they were original works of art. Her side-business was producing prints, so she could run them off quickly and affordably.

I just worried that my comic fans would think I was out to get their cash. All I'd ever wanted was to have a fun hobby I could use to express my creativity.

I sighed and shut the computer. Lowell was in another room of the cottage, working on some remote detective cases (I hadn't asked beyond that). I tapped my fingers on the case of my laptop for a few seconds, before I decided to go and see if I couldn't persuade Lowell that he was done with work for the day...

The clouds were crowding overhead two days later when I walked up the hill to L'airelle Zoological Park. It was the first sign I'd seen of the approaching autumn, beyond the leaves beginning to turn copper and scarlet. It seemed rather fitting that the weather should be reminiscent of good old rainy England when I visited the zoo's collection of farm animals. It was almost enough to make me feel a little homesick.

"Bonjour!" I said, popping into the staff hut.

To my surprise Adele and Luna were so engrossed in their conversation that they didn't even notice me come in. It was only when my shadow fell across them that they both looked round and jumped.

"Is everything okay?" I said, concerned that something serious must have happened.

"It's fine..." Adele said and then looked across at Luna. "We think it's fine... probably."

I sat down on a chair opposite the sofa.

Luna lifted her face and I immediately noticed that it was lined with worry. It was Adele who spoke first.

"Do you remember that I asked Luna to look after our dog, Matti, if Jolie showed any signs of the puppies coming?"

I nodded.

"Yesterday evening, Jolie started getting a bit more agitated and we thought it would be better to take Matti away because he seemed to be getting stressed. Luna took him home."

Luna nodded and continued the story. "I took him for a walk, fed him, and so on. Later that evening, I let him outside to do his business. He was taking a long time, so I just left the door open while I sorted out some washing. I must confess, I did leave it a little longer than I should have done before I checked on him, but when I called out the back door he came back right away." She hesitated and I knew she was about to get to the point of her story. "Someone had painted a pink heart on his back."

I blinked. "What?"

"A heart! In some pink paint. Don't worry, I washed it off right away and then called Adele to let her know. I don't think it was toxic paint. It's just really weird." Adele bit her fingernails and then thoughtfully lowered her hand. "My garden is enclosed by walls and a fence. There is a gate they could have come through, but I don't know... I've looked after Matti before and he's usually talkative when it comes to strangers. I was only just inside the house and I'm really surprised he didn't bark his head off when whoever it was got out their paintbrush." She shuddered. "I don't know why, but this really creeps me out. Why would anyone do that to Adele's dog?"

I shook my head. I really had no idea what would motivate someone to do that. Was it some kind of threat? A sign that, whoever it was, was able to get around Adele's largest and scariest dog with ease? I didn't know. "Do you think he might have been drugged so he didn't bark?" I asked.

"Ha!" Adele cut in. "More likely, someone bribed him with food. Everyone around here knows Matti's putty in your hands when you give him a treat. Justin and I specialise in dogs who have bottomless pits instead of stomachs."

"I'm really sorry," Luna said, and it sounded to me like she'd already said it a few times.

"It's okay, honestly it is," Adele reassured her. "I just wanted to find out the details. I never wanted you to think that any of this is your fault. It's some weirdo's."

"Adele, you said that anyone who knows Matti would have known that he'd stay quiet for a treat. Doesn't it stand to reason that whoever did the painting knows you personally?" I suggested.

"Sure, but that's pretty much everyone in town, Madi," she replied, with a knowing smile.

I nodded. I'd momentarily forgotten how village life differed from town life, where only a handful of people knew who you were.

"It was probably just some local pranksters," Adele said, with a shrug.

"Maybe." I privately thought that it wasn't the first strange, unexplainable thing to happen around here lately. However, there wasn't enough time to dwell on it. I had an appointment with the zoo's mini-farmyard.

Half an hour later, I'd written so many notes I thought my wrist might be about to fall off. I'd toured the entire zoo on my first day, but it had really only been a glance around. Since then, I'd been rationing myself a bit of the zoo a day, gradually working my way around. Today was my first proper look at the area meant as a petting zoo.

My first impression was that it wasn't entirely finished. I vaguely remembered the zoo boss saying something along those lines. I'd mentally noted it and assumed that it was an attraction that would be coming soon. It turned out, the petting zoo was open, but almost hilariously half done.

The area was penned off with a gate, which was lucky, because the goats had escaped their own little area of the petting zoo and roamed where they pleased. I wasn't convinced that the zoo had made the best choice of a child-friendly goat breed either. These goats came up above my waist, had long, curling horns and if you dared to walk into the farmyard without any popcorn with which to distract them, you found out what it was like to be butted by those horns. As someone who stood tall at five foot nothing, I thought I was probably a better judge than many as to what might be found intimidating by children and other tiny adults.

"Did no one stop to think, 'Hey, maybe pygmy goats would be a better choice?'" I muttered when I received another painful bump to my rear that nearly sent me sprawling.

Goats could be tricky to handle. If I'd been willing to bribe them with food, I would have had no trouble at all… until the food ran out. Beyond bribery, there weren't really any tricks. All I could hope was that if I kept ignoring them, they'd get bored with trying to eat my t-shirt. I found myself praying that a family with some plucky kids would come along and distract the herd. Unfortunately, I seemed to be the only one crazy enough to even set foot in the half-done farmyard.

I sighed as the goats started to masticate my shorts and wrote down another a paragraph.

At least the majority of the other animals in this part of the zoo had remained in their enclosures. That was pretty much the only positive thing I could pick out. It was clear that while the vision for the farmyard was interesting, the execution hadn't yet happened.

"Why open it?" I said, feeling exasperated.

I walked over to an enclosure holding a very large ox and found the double safety barrier stopped halfway down the enclosure, making it a pretty pointless exercise. Worse still, whoever had built the enclosure had decided that the inner fence only needed to be a two bar fence. So anyone who was small and not entirely under the control of a watchful parent could slip into the ox's enclosure before you could say 'trampled to death'.

I felt faint even thinking about it. "If this were in Britain," I muttered to myself. But the same rules just didn't apply here. I really hoped L'airelle would make the changes I put forward, both for the animals' sake and for their visitors' wellbeing, but I wasn't sure it would happen anytime soon.

The half completed nature of this area was evidence enough of that. The fencing was new, but there were no signs that the builders intended to return.

I sighed again and moved on, wondering if I would be wearing a crop-top by the time I left.

At least the pigs are happy! I thought, until I saw the felled skeleton of what was supposed to be another fence and realised the pigs had invaded the ducks' enclosure. The ducks themselves now floated forlornly on top of the pigs' water trough. Their own little lake had been turned into a mud bath.

I made another note and moved on.

The rest of it wasn't so bad. The donkeys were perfectly happy, as were the sheep. Half of the chickens were where they were supposed to be. The others were fighting it out with the goats in the main yard, but in the grand scheme of things, I could overlook that.

My loop of the farmyard had nearly come to an end when I met the emus.

"What kind of farm are you supposed to be from?" I said, eyeing the pair warily. They stared straight back and I didn't have to look far to realise what they wanted. The zoo's paper maps were strewn around the interior of the emus' pen. As were a number of other miscellaneous items including; sunglasses, sun hats, and even a wig. I tried not to imagine how the latter had ended up on the other side of the fence.

"Safety fence needed immediately," I said, writing it down. I raised my eyes to the emus, who both seemed to stretch their necks out expectantly. "Not going to happen," I said, smugly waving my folder at them from a prudent distance.

It was at that moment, the goat who had been worrying my t-shirt got bored and decided to butt me hard and unexpectedly. I fell forwards, turning for a second to glare at the goat.

It was a second too long.

The emus pounced, their beaks seizing my sheaf of papers and scattering them in a snowstorm of A4 flakes.

"No!" I yelled, running forwards without even thinking. I was not going to write all of this out again! I'd already spent what felt like an age inspecting the farmyard and that work was not going to be wasted because of a conspiracy between a goat and a couple of emus.

I'd love to say I vaulted the fence and chased the emus down.

In reality, I rolled over the barrier like a limp noodle and then flailed around the enclosure for a while, waving my limbs at the emus without really achieving much at all.

It was of course at this moment that every single one of the families who were visiting the zoo that day decided to visit the farmyard. Years later, I would still occasionally wonder how many family photo albums 'the emu chasing lady' cropped up in.

Eventually, the emus got tired of my flailing and instead went to see how many small fingers they could bite. I was able to gather up both my papers and my last few shreds of dignity and retreat from the farmyard.

I was wrong to think my day could only improve. I was on my way to a well-deserved lunch break when I bumped into Constantine and nearly dropped my papers again.

She looked down her nose at me. It wasn't a very difficult feat for most, due to my short stature, but it was very difficult for me to not stare at her proliferation of nose hair.

"I heard you were attacking the emus. I'm just on my way to report it to Francois. I doubt he'll be impressed when he hears that his animal expert is actually an animal abuser,"

Constantine informed me, even going so far as to make a note on the clipboard she was carrying.

I was saved from saying something that would have actually justified me losing my job by Luna coming up behind me.

"That's enough, Constantine! You walk around this place, calling everyone out on not doing their jobs while neglecting your own. I can't believe no one has ever told you this before, but keep your nose out of other people's business! You're not the boss' little pet," she said, turning into a highlighted firework of fury.

Constantine gave me a look, as if she expected me to contradict everything Luna had just said and also admit to being an animal abuser.

"That sounds like a fair evaluation to me," I said with a thin-lipped smile. "Come on, Luna, I think I owe you lunch," I said, walking away with the lion keeper, feeling a lot cheerier.

"I can't believe you told old Constantine to keep her nose out of other people's business!" Adele said, when she'd stopped howling with laughter.

Luna sat at our lunchtime picnic bench and looked grim, despite the burger I'd bought her. "She's probably going to go and tell Monsieur Quebec," she said, referring to the animal park boss.

Adele snorted and shook her dark mane. "When have you ever seen Monsieur Quebec intervene on anything Constantine has reported? I don't even know if she actually speaks to him, or if it's all just talk." She tilted her head. "It has to be talk. Anyone sane would have fired her by now, if she really does report on everyone's misdemeanours every few hours."

"Don't worry about it, Luna. I'm glad you stuck up for me. Other people are, too," I added with a grin.

Luna had been congratulated by no fewer than three

other zoo staff members on our way to lunch. Gossip at L'airelle spread just as quickly as it did at every other zoo I'd visited. Luna's little exchange must have been overheard.

"You're the zoo hero," I told her.

At least it got her to smile.

To my surprise, I was summoned to the main staff building, above the restaurant, later that day. My mind immediately jumped to Luna's words with Constantine and I wondered if she'd managed to escalate things. A meeting of the entire zoo staff sounded incredibly extreme.

I nodded at Luna and Adele when I entered the room above the restaurant a few minutes after the runner had found me. The place was already full, but I managed to wiggle my way through and stand next to my friends. I had a feeling I'd be needing their translation skills.

The air smelt of dust and despite the clouds, the day was a muggy one, which meant the atmosphere in the room wasn't an incredibly enjoyable one.

A few wooden feed boxes had been pushed together at the front of the room and I recognised Monsieur Quebec, my employer, when he stood upon them to raise himself above his audience.

"Hello! I'm sorry to gather you all on such short notice," he began, and Adele hastily whispered the translation in my ear. I could hardly expect a staff address to be in English.

"I hope this isn't Constantine," I heard Luna mutter.

"I have a couple of announcements to make. The first is that the family of Monsieur Devereux will be visiting at the end of today to get some closure." Mr Quebec looked unsure when he said those words. Visiting the tiger enclosure where a member of your family crash landed and was then ripped up by tigers didn't seem like a very logical way to seek solace.

"I would ask you all to be courteous and respectful during this time..." he continued.

I might have imagined it, but I thought he eyeballed Constantine when he said that bit.

"I also have some other news. You'e all aware that our head primate keeper, Victor, was away on sickness leave. He has decided not to return to the zoo. In his place, I would like to introduce you all to Monsieur Alcide Reynard, who will be stepping in as our new head primate keeper."

There was a smattering of applause, that I couldn't help but notice mostly originated from the female staff members. I couldn't say I blamed them. Alcide Reynard was rather easy on the eyes. He had dark blonde hair that seemed to naturally flop over his forehead in a side parting. There was also something that reminded me of Indiana Jones in the sideways smile he possessed and those sharp eyes, that seemed to already have taken everyone's measure.

"He is just... wow," Luna said, next to my ear. I noticed Adele nodding along before she hastily corrected herself.

I smiled at Luna and turned back to the front, only to find that Alcide was looking in our direction.

"Did I say that too loudly?" Luna whispered in horror. I shook my head. Unless he had the hearing of a bat, he wouldn't have picked up on her words amongst the hubub of other zoo staff probably saying very similar things. He was probably looking our way for another reason all together.

My hypothesis proved correct when Alcide walked into the tiki hut at the end of the day.

"Chocolate?" I said, offering him the nearly empty box, while Luna tried to quietly cough up the chocolate she'd accidentally swallowed whole when he'd walked in. Adele had already rushed home to see Justin and Jolie.

"No thanks, I don't really eat sweet things," he said, flashing me a white grin.

I'm afraid I immediately marked that as a point against him.

"So, you're the new primate keeper. I'd love to talk to you about the primates, in particular…"

"…the squirrel monkeys?" he finished for me.

I raised my eyebrows at him.

He leant forward, placing both his hands on the counter in an amazingly relaxed way. I privately wished I was so at ease with strangers. "I know they're a bit of a handful," he began and I started nodding along like an idiot. "I've been told they escaped their enclosure and are now living wild and free around the park. Obviously, this is not what was intended and might pose a risk."

"Exactly," I said, pleased he was getting it.

"But, have you ever seen a happier group of monkeys?"

I opened my mouth to contradict him and then bit my tongue. He was right.

He nodded when I didn't answer. "I think the best thing to do is to simply let them carry on. Give the public fair warning about the risks of aggravating them, but other than that, leave it as it is. Nothing bad has happened yet, right?"

I struggled to find the right words to answer him. I loved animals and the whole idea of this job was to do right by them and give them the best conditions possible but this… this was a conundrum.

"If someone gets attacked, the monkeys might have to be put down, or L'airelle could face a lawsuit," I protested, somehow feeling like I was the bad guy in this situation.

"As I said, we'll give the public fair warning, but you can't deny they're happy," he said, those sharp eyes seeing everything they needed to see, written on my face.

"I can't deny that," I admitted, wondering for the first time if I was in the wrong here.

"Look, I understand the job you have to do and your responsibilities. I promise that this decision will be my own and shall never come back to haunt you. Anyway, what's a few scratched faces and bitten off fingers when you're talking about complete freedom?" Alcide said.

I fixed him with my own sharp-eyed gaze. "I hope you're not planning to let any of the other primates try a taste of freedom?"

He flashed me a grin. "I promise I won't let the gorillas have a wander about, if that's what you're worried about. Even a liberal thinker like me has his limits."

"Hmm," I said, still not utterly convinced. "If you want an example of how things can go wrong when animals escape and run rampant, just pop down to the farmyard and visit the goats."

"Ah, is your t-shirt not supposed to be like that? I thought it was fashionable," he said, with a straight face.

I gave him a 'don't try to kid with me' look and decided that Luna had probably regained her composure by now.

"Alcide, I'm guessing you haven't yet met Luna? She's a big cat keeper and lion specialist." I gave her a supportive grin.

"Nice to meet you," she said, sticking out a hand. Alcide dodged it and kissed her on both cheek, leaving them glowing.

"It'll be great to make some friends around here who know the ins and outs of the place. I'm so glad I've met another keeper," Alcide said, charm turned up to the maximum.

"I'll be happy to help in any way I can. You can come by here for coffee any time," Luna said, surprising me with her smooth talking.

"I might just take you up on that," Alcide replied.

I suddenly felt like the third wheel, watching him look into her eyes for several seconds too long.

I waited for him to get a good distance away from the tiki hut before I turned to Luna.

"Well, that went really…" I trailed off when she flopped down onto the sofa.

"I feel sick," she confessed.

"Butterflies in your stomach?" I asked.

"More like spiders with trampolines."

I snorted. "Ah, love. Such a joyous thing."

6

INCY WINCY SPIDERS

"Don't pretend you're sorry. One of you killed him!"

Those were the words I heard shouted across the village square the next morning. I'd been on my way to buy a baguette and had noticed a small crowd gathered outside the boulangerie. The reason soon became clear when the villagers shuffled off.

A man in his early forties stood on the steps leading up to the shop, clutching a roll of Sellotape and some posters. A single glance at the picture told me they were posters announcing the date and time of Monsieur Devereux's funeral. From the angry words I'd just heard, I assumed this must be a relative of Monsieur Devereux, perhaps even his son. While I could sympathise with his anger that a murderer was still walking free, I couldn't help wondering if he had also known about Monsieur Devereux's drinking habit and his behaviour towards his wife. If he'd been aware, why hadn't he put a stop to it?

I decided to keep my judgements to myself. Who was I to know what went on behind closed doors in this man's family? Unfortunately, the irate relative wasn't so silent with his own views.

"What are you, a tourist? Come to read all about my father's funeral have you, tourist?" he said, moving towards me aggressively.

As I didn't have size on my side in any confrontational situation, I did the only thing I could.

I shocked him.

"Actually, I saw your father fall from the sky. I work for L'airelle Zoological Park."

His mouth opened and shut for a moment. I could tell he couldn't figure out the correct emotional response and I didn't want to give him time to get it right.

"Au revoir, Monsieur," I said, brushing past him into the boulangerie. To my relief, he didn't follow. A moment or two later, he stalked off in the direction of the convenience store - probably to yell at some more people.

"I see you met Nicholas," the baker said, parcelling up my daily baguette. "Unfortunately, he takes after his father. You can tell by the temper. His sister is better. She is more her mother, but sadly, she is not strong enough to stand up to the others. Still, perhaps now she will do it, no?"

He picked up a chocolate studded croissant and put it in a paper bag, before handing it to me with the baguette. "Here. A little something for standing up to that bully. It's time someone did."

I was pleased to bump into Adele on my way back to the cottage. She was taking another day off at home with Jolie.

"She looks ready to burst!" Adele confided when I asked her how Jolie was. "Honestly, I can't thank you enough for convincing me to go to the vet. If I hadn't, we'd probably be starving poor old Jolie right now, thinking she was getting porkier by the day." She shook her head.

Adele brushed her hair back from her face and her

expression grew thoughtful. "Are you coming to the funeral? You must have seen the posters around town."

"I met the man who put them up, too," I said and briefly explained what had transpired between me and Nicholas Devereux.

"Sounds like you handled it well. I've seen Luna spin around and walk the opposite way when she used to see him around the village. He believed every word his father spouted. When he's not angry, he's pleasant enough. But that temper!" She shivered a little. "It scares me."

"I don't think I should go to the funeral. I didn't know him," I said, but then realised I may be attending anyway. "Lowell knew him, so maybe I will after all."

Adele nodded. "You were there when it happened and you provided comfort to Madame Devereux. I know she'd want you to come."

She seemed to dither for a moment instead of continuing on her way. "There's something I need to tell you. I have to get it off my chest. I just don't know if I should have told the police…"

"What is it?" I asked, curiosity immediately piqued.

"It's about the day when Pascal gave me that parking ticket. We argued, but once I'd calmed down and accepted that the old bat wasn't going to bend, he started trying to chat to me about Luna. He was asking questions about how she'd been and what she was up to at the moment. I thought he was either being a creep, or he was planning to start up his stupid vendetta again. I told him to forget it. I wasn't going to tell him anything but… do you think I should have said something about it? I didn't want to mention it in front of Luna in case it freaked her out. She's put up with enough of his nonsense already and I'll be damned if she still has to deal with it after his death!"

"I can't see how it would affect the case. No one thinks

Luna had anything to do with it," I reassured her. I didn't count Mr Flannigan, who seemed convinced we were all guilty of something.

Adele nodded. "Thank you, you've put my mind at rest. Well, I hope you have a good day! Perhaps Alcide will come over for the cup of coffee Luna told me she'd offered him," Adele said with a twinkle in her eye.

I was willing to bet Luna had rushed right over to Adele's house after work to discuss the details of the encounter. Their friendship reminded me of mine and Tiff's. I missed her a lot, I realised.

My phone buzzed right on cue. I looked down at a whole new bunch of Lucky pictures. He was still having a whale of time with Tiff's collection of animals. I hoped it wouldn't be too long before I'd be able to take him on my travels with me again. I hated missing him grow up.

"See you soon," I said, both to Lucky and Tiff.

"It's happening! It's happening!" Luna ran around the corner of the orang-utan enclosure, waving her phone. I'd been deep in conversation with Alcide discussing the best ways to challenge the intellects of the apes when she arrived.

"The puppies! Jolie's just started having contractions," she explained, so excited she didn't even think to be bashful in front of Alcide.

"Where's Justin? Does he know?" I asked.

Luna nodded. "Yeah, he's already running home. Monsieur Quebec said it was fine, as long as you were okay with taking over his duties for now. You don't mind, right?" she said, struck with a sudden case of doubt.

"It's fine. It'll be nice to be a keeper again," I said.

I turned back to Alcide and threw him an apologetic

smile. "We'll have to have this discussion another day. For what it's worth, I think L'airelle is lucky to have you as their head primate keeper.

"Definitely," Luna agreed and it took all of my self control to not laugh at her strength of agreement.

"All right, you'd better show me a few of the ropes so I can be keeper for the day," I said, nodding goodbye to Alcide.

"Hey, how's Matti doing after the painting incident?" I asked while we were walking across to the big cat area of the zoo.

"He's fine. He sleeps all day on my couch. Adele or Justin have my spare keys, so they go in a couple of times and let him out to go to the bathroom. No one's tried to use him as a canvas since," she said.

I was glad that nothing further had happened to the dog.

"Oh, I forgot to say! The order of live spiders you wanted arrived today. How about we go and dump them in the Pallas's cat's enclosure and see if they like them?" Luna asked, brightly. "They're really big and black." She shuddered. "There's a reason why I chose cats, not critters, to look after."

We popped by the food store and grabbed the delivery box before making our way to the cats' enclosure. Luna and I walked in through the gate, knowing that the cats themselves were both notoriously shy and mostly nocturnal. I hoped that this might give them an excuse to do a little hunting in the daytime.

"Here we go!" Luna said tilting the box away from us and upending it. A sea of black poured out of the box, running across the grass as fast as their eight legs could carry them.

I was rather shocked by how many of them there were. "I hope the cats decide they like them, otherwise they might be evicted from their caves!"

Luna grimaced. "We'd better keep quiet about this experiment until we know it's a success." She shot me a grin. "At least this enclosure won't have a fly problem anymore!"

All the big cats had issues with flies due to their carnivorous diets. It was a constant worry to zookeepers that the animals in their care might pick up all sorts of fly-borne diseases.

"Okay, so I think I've briefed you on everything. If you handle the tigers, the ocelots, and the servals, I'll stick with the lions, the leopards and panthers, and the Pallas's cats. I've also got to do a guided tour later today, but give me a shout if you need anything," Luna said.

"No worries," I told her, secretly excited to be working as a zookeeper for larger animals than I'd ever personally dealt with before.

During my last couple of jobs, I'd spent plenty of time with keepers who looked after animals like tigers, and I thought I knew the kind of work that went into it and the precautions that needed to be taken. I'd even experienced firsthand what happened when you abandoned common sense and went for a wander through a lion pride's territory. It wasn't something I ever wanted to repeat.

As Justin had already done the morning feeds, I was left to go round and check the enclosures for any maintenance that might need doing. It was also a great opportunity for me to personally put together and test out some of my animal engagement ideas. Adele and I had ordered some large, hard rubber balls, filled with holes. One hole was larger than the rest and the idea was that whatever was put inside the ball would only fall out through this hole. What to put inside of the balls had been the topic of much debate. Today, I wanted to test out one idea.

The tigers at the zoo had a good diet. They were fed carcasses, rather than prepared meat. This not only gave them an activity to do, it also helped them to maintain their health. However, the internal organs were not always given with the meat and I thought that was a shame. It was grisly, but I was planning to stuff the rubber ball with some offal - hearts, kidneys, livers. They were all great ways to enrich the tigers' diets.

Once I'd prepared the ball, the next step was to get it into the enclosure. Keepers usually fed the tigers by placing the food in a penned off area and then letting the tigers in to eat. There were several different penned off spaces within enclosures, so that keepers would never be foiled by a tiger hanging around in a pen that had been left open from an earlier feed. The tigers also usually liked to drag carcasses deeper into the enclosure, often up onto the wooden platform, where they could feed and fight over it in peace.

As well as seeking to engage the big cats, my ideas were also intended to benefit the visitors. So, instead of placing the ball in the usual feeding zone, I decided to take a walk up to aerial viewing pathway. A few visitors watched me curiously, and I was glad the zoo had insisted that I wear the L'airelle uniform from the start. Otherwise, people may have been a little perturbed to see a person carrying a giant rubber ball stuffed with organs.

The visitors watched with interest when I flung the ball with all my might over the side of the enclosure. The tough rubber bounced, but as luck would have it, it hadn't turned the right way in order to dispense any of the gory goods inside. It wasn't long before a tiger came running over to investigate, followed by his two brothers. The visitors began to point and take photos as the tigers patted the ball around and brawled over who got the opportunity to try their luck at persuading the unyielding rubber to give up its contents. Interestingly, it was the smallest tiger of the three who gained the most rewards. He seemed to understand that the ball needed to be pushed along in order to get something to fall out of it. His brothers preferred to bite at the rubber, which - to my relief - defied their strong jaws.

I grinned and left them to play as more visitors flocked, drawn by the excitement happening in the tiger enclosure. I glanced at the time on my phone and thought I could probably make up a few more of the balls before lunchtime. I knew that chasing a ball around wasn't akin to a real life hunt - something which was very definitely prohibited - but it gave the cats something to do. They had to exercise problem solving skills and stop lazing around on their wooden podium in order to get a tasty treat. It was definitely a step in the right direction.

I hoped it wouldn't just be the largest cats who benefitted. The Pallas's cats already had their spider experiment, but there were smaller rubber balls for the ocelots and servals. I was planning to treat them to a bit of offal, too - albeit chopped into smaller pieces. Fish was another thing that could be a great and unusual treat for the cats, but that would have to wait for a cooler day. Even though the weather hadn't looked bright for several days, it was still too warm for fresh fish to be left lying around.

I was on my way back to the food store when I saw Constantine walking towards me. She looked like she had murder on her mind.

"Going for a nice stroll?" she said, despite the fact that she was doing the same thing herself.

"I'm on my way to the food store. I'm working as a big cat keeper for the day," I told her.

Constantine threw me a doubtful look. "That doesn't sound right to me."

"Feel free to bring it up with Mr Quebec. He was the one who okayed it," I said, feeling my temper start to fray.

She bristled. "Well, aren't you a know it all! Anyone can

call themselves a consultant. I don't know why Francois would employ someone who is so obviously a quack."

I raised my eyebrows, surprised that she'd had the guts to say it. I thought about suggesting that she and 'Francois' get a room, if they were as involved as she clearly imagined they were.

Instead, I took the high road. "That's it. I've had enough of you insulting me and others with the idea that you're better than everyone else at the zoo. You have no right to do that." I inwardly allowed myself some grim satisfaction over my next words. "I'm going to see Monsieur Quebec about this right now. You are welcome to come with me. I think it's the only way to reach a proper solution."

I thought Constantine's permanently angry expression wobbled a little but she soon steadied herself.

"Fine," she snapped.

Off we went to speak to Monsieur Quebec about one of the most petty and nonsensical things I'd ever experienced. I hoped he would take the same view I did and also not blame me for the inevitable waste of time.

Ten minutes later, we were both sat in front of the manager's desk. There was a stale smell in the office that reminded me of school, and the occasion didn't help much either. I tried not to giggle as I compared the situation to two naughty children being sent to the head teacher because they'd got into a fight in the playground. Unfortunately, I would need to show composure if I were to be taken seriously.

"What seems to be the problem?" Monsieur Quebec asked, looking at us over his horn-rimmed glasses.

Constantine dived straight in. "I have constantly witnessed Madame Amos wasting time and doing nothing that resembles work in the slightest. She spends her day fraternising with Madame Nice and Madame Fleur instead of doing the job you are paying her to do. She is wasting the zoo's resources. I hate to see you taken advantage of in such a horrible and shameless way."

I thought her eyes even misted over a bit with emotion. It took all of my self control to not roll my eyes.

Monsieur Quebec looked at me expectantly.

I spread my hands over the arms of my chair. "I haven't been at L'airelle Zoological Park for long, but during that time, I have been impressed with the courtesy, kindness, and quality of the staff you employ. Constantine is the unfortunate exception. I am not usually one to tell tales, or even escalate something so petty, but in this case I had to make an exception. Constantine is a bully who does everything she can to criticise the work of her colleagues. I believe she works in catering?"

Mr Quebec nodded.

"And yet, she seems to spend most of her time wandering around the zoo, threatening people. I find it unfortunate that she believes me to have not been working, but she is mistaken. A lot of observation is necessary in order to correctly identify areas that can be improved upon. I also believe she might have made a mistake today, being unaware that I am currently acting as a big cat keeper," I allowed, figuring I'd cut the tyrant a little slack.

Constantine shook her head. "I know what I've been seeing. They're having too much fun to be working."

I shot a disbelieving look at Monsieur Quebec, who looked like he'd aged another ten years during the conversation.

"How is your work going, Madame Amos?" he enquired.

I happily filled him in on the progress that had been made. The only part I neglected to share was that of the spider invasion Luna and I had unleashed that morning.

He nodded when I'd finished. "That sounds very promising. I'm looking forward to receiving your final report. Thank you for stepping in at such late notice to help out with a staff shortage. I do appreciate it."

"You're welcome," I said, trying not to look smug.

Constantine looked like she was sucking on a lemon.

"I'm sure you are right, Madame Amos, when you said that this was all just a misunderstanding. Thank you both for bringing it to my attention. I hope we are all on the same page now," he tactfully said.

"I'm sure we are," I agreed, smiling sweetly across at the other woman.

"Excellent. I hope both of you have a productive rest of the day," Monsieur Quebec finished, with just a hint of grit in his voice. I knew it was a warning of what would happen if he were bothered by something so trivial again. In spite of that, I thought it had been worth it. Even more so when we exited the office and Constantine stormed off in the opposite direction without a word.

Nathan walked over to me, brushing his dark comma of hair back from his forehead. "What did you do to her?" he asked, half in awe.

"We had a disagreement, so I did the sensible thing and brought it under the jurisdiction of Monsieur Quebec," I explained. "It's all sorted now."

"You called her bluff! That's brilliant!" He grinned.

I threw him a subtle smile. "In my experience, that's the only way to deal with people like her. You can fight her face to face as much as you like, but it will never make a difference. You have to appeal to the only thing she respects - authority." I pushed my wildly waving hair back from my face. "Despite everything she says about reporting to Monsieur Quebec, I don't think she's ever done it. Perhaps take her claims with a big grain of salt in future," I said. While I didn't think Constantine would take me on again after today's warning, I doubted she would be changing her spots anytime soon.

"I can't wait to tell everyone what you did," Nathan told me with a smile and I knew the gossip would be all over the zoo in no time at all. I wondered if I should feel sorry for the deeply unpopular Constantine, but until she changed her ways, she was never going to find friendship. Perhaps if I were a permanent employee at the zoo, I would have worked harder to find a way to get beneath all of her bitterness and find out what made her behave so obnoxiously. But I was only here for a few weeks. The most I could do was to stop her from wasting any more of my time, which I hoped I'd achieved with today's intervention.

"I was actually looking for Adele. Have you seen her?" Nathan asked, just as the zoo's insect specialist walked over.

"Hey, Nathan, how's it going? You still seeing Sage? I'm amazed she hasn't thrown you off the side of a mountain yet," the newcomer said, flashing a set of uneven teeth at me.

I raised an eyebrow at the unusual comment.

"Sage helps run the paragliding school with her dad," Nathan said, for my benefit. "In answer to your question, Julian, I'm still seeing her. So you can keep dreaming," he added with a grin. It was meant to be cocky but it somehow didn't suit Nathan, whom I had down in my books as a slightly sensitive young man.

"I don't know how someone with a face like yours gets to be so lucky," the other guy joked. "See you around!"

I was left alone again with Nathan.

I suddenly remembered he'd asked a question before Julian had come along. "Adele's at home. Her dog is giving birth," I explained.

"Wow! That's great. I wonder if she'll let me have one?"

"Probably! I know she's going to be looking for homes for them but - fair warning - we also have no idea what the dogs will be like. Jolie's a Labrador but the father remains a mystery. The only thing we know for sure is that it wasn't Matti."

Nathan nodded. "I'm sure they'll be just great. Just like Adele. She's great too, isn't she?"

A couple of things slotted into place for me when I saw the misty look that came into Nathan's eyes. To be fair to Adele, although she was past the first flush of youth, she was still a very attractive woman. One who had inadvertently put young Nathan under her spell.

"She is great. Her husband is nice as well. Do you know Justin?" I said, wondering if I was being horrendously unsubtle.

Nathan nodded a little hesitantly. "Yeah, he seems like a good guy. Anyway, I'd better be getting on before Constantine catches me," he said, with a twinkle in his eye.

"I'll see you around," I said and watched him walk away. I wondered if I should mention his little crush to Adele, but I was sure she already knew. Nathan wasn't nearly as subtle as he thought he was. I just hoped he gave as much attention to his actual girlfriend, although if he were looking at other women…

I smiled and shook my head. He was in his early twenties and clearly trying his luck. He'd probably get knocked down for it at some point and then he'd learn.

I returned to my new duties of caring for the big cats and the rest of the day passed without any further accidental declarations of love or shouting matches.

"Did you have a good day?" I asked Lowell when I arrived back at the cottage.

"Yeah, it was great. I'm working my way through the local

mountain walks. It's tough, but I think I'm already a bit more in shape. This is turning out to be a really great holiday," he said, walking over and wrapping his arms around my lower back before giving me a kiss.

I smiled up at him and raised an eyebrow. "Despite the mysterious murder?"

"Yes. For once, I haven't been dragged into the whole mess. It's a relief," he said.

I noticed a slight flicker in his eyes and suddenly remembered there was something I'd wanted to ask him for a while. "Have you seen the other agent around? The female one?"

She'd been missing when Mr Flannigan had conducted his incredibly rude interview.

"We did bump into each other in town a couple of days ago. She asked what I was up to and I asked her the same. That was it, really."

"You didn't happen to discuss the case, or why, exactly, they're both in town?" I queried.

"It didn't come up," Lowell said and reached past me, picking a bottle up from the counter. "I bought us some wine from a local vineyard I stumbled upon. Isn't that great?"

I decided to let the sudden change of subject slide. "Did you taste some first, or did you let them sell you a bottle of vinegar?"

Lowell threw the wine bottle a doubtful look. "I guess we'll find out."

"Before we do that, can we walk over to Adele's house? Jolie started to give birth earlier and I haven't heard an update since then," I said.

We grabbed a bottle of wine (one that wasn't so risky) and walked across the village towards the house. The night was still and quiet, and in the peaceful surroundings, I really did find it hard to believe that a murderer could possibly live close by. All the same, a killer lived beneath one of the rooftops and no one had a clue who they were.

My pensive mood ended when we reached the house and rang the doorbell. It was Luna who answered. She saw my anxious face and smiled.

"Come in! It's all fine. She's done so well! Come and see the puppies."

We walked into the building and followed Luna through to the open plan kitchen and dining room area. Adele looked up and smiled from her place on a tartan rug. Next to her, Jolie lay on her side, looking tired but happy, with her tongue lolling out. Justin nodded to me from behind the kitchen counter, and I could just make out a little bundle of cloth in his hands.

"I'm just rubbing this one to make sure his breathing's okay. Although we thought Jolie started having contractions this morning, she didn't actually give birth until later in the day. This little chap was the last one out, but I think he'll be just fine," he said. He lifted the towel up and I walked forwards to take a look at the little puppy.

Despite being the runt of the litter, he looked like a pretty big puppy to me.

"Look at the size of those paws," I said, reaching down to lift one of his white feet. The rest of his body was a curious mix of black and white. "He's a harlequin," I observed, surprised by the unusual colouring.

"Four of them are. The other two are nearly all black and then there's an almost white one, too," Adele said, gesturing to the row of puppies.

"Seven puppies," I breathed and then grinned. "The size of them, too! Well done, Jolie."

Adele laughed. "I know! The poor old girl. That's what she gets for sneaking out and flirting with Madame Louve's Great Dane."

"Great Dane?" I repeated and realised it made sense. I had never seen puppies this big before.

"Are you going to tell the owner?" I asked.

Adele, Justin, and Luna all gave me 'are you mad?' looks.

"No! Madame Louve doesn't even let that poor dog sniff either of ours. Can you imagine if she found out what had gone on?" Adele let out a very un-Adele-like giggle.

"Not to mention the sort of fee she'd charge us for using him as a sire," Justin added with a shake of his head. "We're not going to hide the puppies' breed, it would be unfair on their new families. We'll tell them the father is a Great Dane, so to expect big dogs when they grow up. We just won't say which Great Dane."

"Won't everyone figure it out?" I said, thinking about the way word spread like wildfire through the small village.

"Oh, sure. No doubt Madame Louve will know the truth by tomorrow, but she won't ever want to admit that her precious pedigree dog had contact with someone as rough and ready as our Jolie. We think her pride will mean that we're safe," Justin said.

"Come and see Georgette. She's my one," Luna said, pulling me over to the pups. "Isn't she beautiful?" She pointed to the nearly white one, who wriggled around a bit and then flopped onto her back, revealing an unusual black splat on her chest.

"She's adorable. They're all lovely," I said.

To my surprise, I found my face was being washed. I turned to face the tall, tan culprit. "Matti!" I said, somewhat surprised.

Adele stood up and ruffled the Dogue De Bordeaux's ears. "He started creating a fuss, so Luna brought him over. It's almost as though he knew something was happening with Jolie. He's been a dear with the puppies, and Jolie is the most laid back mum I've ever seen."

"Well, congratulations!" I said. "I didn't have any doggie treats, but here's something for the both of you," I said, handing over the wine we'd brought with us.

"Have you eaten yet? We should all celebrate," Adele said.

"We'd love to," Lowell replied, before I could say anything different. Thoughts of getting more work done on my comic flew out of the window. I chided myself for being so selfish. It was nice to spend time with friends.

Adele opened the fridge and swore. "This week's flown by. We've all been so worried about Jolie that we forgot to get the shopping," Adele said with a smile.

"Oh, don't you worry about that. I've got plenty at my place. I'll go bring some over," Luna said, standing up.

"I can bring some things, too," I said, eager to get in on the charming village tradition of sharing food.

"The shop's still open right? I'll grab some other bits," Lowell contributed. I smiled gratefully at him.

"You guys are the best. We'll see you back here soon then!" Adele said and we all went off on our separate missions.

The rest of the evening was spent in good spirits, as we tucked into the strange but tasty assortment of food and snacks we'd rustled up and toasted Jolie's achievement.

I only wished the good times could last forever. Little did I know, they would end as soon as the next morning.

"Morning, is Jolie still okay?" I greeted Adele when I walked into the tiki hut the next day.

She blinked blearily at me. I took a moment to rub some more sleep from my eyes. Our celebrations had gone on a little late, considering that we all had work the next day. I was currently envying Lowell, who was still tucked up in bed.

"She's fine. Justin and I are going to pop back home on our breaks and check in on her. We're taking the puppies to the vet just as soon as they're old enough to be moved, so he can look them over. We think they're all healthy though, even the little one."

I thought about the size my kitten Lucky had been when I'd rescued him. Now, you'd never know he was the runt of the litter. "I'm sure the little one will soon catch up," I told her.

"Boy, did we get carried away last night!" Luna said, walking into the hut, looking just as worse for wear as the rest of us.

"How exactly did you get carried away?" A serious voice asked.

We all turned to find that Detective Prideaux was stood in the doorway. Detective Girard hovered apologetically by his side.

"Adele's dog gave birth. We all went round and had a bit of a celebration," I explained. "Do you have some more questions about what we saw?"

"No," the detective said, walking into the hut and looking disdainfully at the all but empty chocolate box. "I'm here because last night Madame Duval was stabbed so badly, it is uncertain if she'll survive her injuries. She was found in Angoux outside her house in the early hours of this morning."

"Constantine," Adele said, making me realise exactly who the police were referring to and exactly why the detective was currently examining each of us, as though we were potentially deranged killers.

"We're all sorry to hear the news, Detective. Is there

anything we can do?" I said, knowing that courtesy was not going to save me from suspicion this time.

"Madame Fleur and Madame Amos, you've both had grievances with Madame Duval. Isn't that correct?" Prideaux enquired.

"I had a difference of opinion with Constantine yesterday, but we both agreed to take the matter to Monsieur Quebec. It was solved," I told him.

"What about you, Madame Fleur?"

"I just told her what I thought of her always walking around pretending she's better than everyone. That's all. It's not a crime," Luna said, showing pluckiness at entirely the wrong moment, in my opinion.

"I was right there when it happened. There was never any violent intention whatsoever. You can't possibly be implying that we had anything to do with this horrible crime!" I protested.

Detective Prideaux didn't meet my gaze. "We are just…"

"Furthering our inquiries," I mimicked, frustration getting the better of me.

"Where were you last night?" he asked.

Relief washed over me. "We were all at Adele and Justin's house for the whole evening," I said, triumphantly.

"What time were you there?"

"From about six in the evening to midnight," I said, suddenly anxious as to when the attack had occurred. If it was after midnight, I would have Lowell to give me an alibi, but Luna wouldn't have anyone.

"Were you together for the whole evening? Were there any times when you weren't in each others' company?" the detective pressed.

I felt my heart drop what felt like a million miles. "Lowell, Luna, and I all went to get some food but we were only gone for about…. half an hour?" I guessed.

The detective nodded, looking grimmer by the second.

It had been the wrong answer to give.

Angoux was only a ten minute drive away. It was therefore plausible that one of us could have popped over and stabbed poor Constantine before returning to the dinner party, laden with food. I remembered the impressive spread Luna had managed to rustle up and somehow doubted anyone would have the time to do both - not that I was even contemplating it for a second. It was ludicrous that we were under suspicion.

"I'd like both of you to come to the station for further questioning. Some facts need to be established. Make your way there as soon as you have informed your employer," Detective Prideaux said. He swept out of the tiki hut before we could say another word. Detective Girard threw us all another apologetic look before scampering out after him. I thought she was the one I pitied most of all in this situation.

I shrugged at Luna when we were alone with Adele again. "I guess we'd better get going. For what it's worth, I know you didn't stab her."

I waited patiently.

Nothing happened.

"That was your cue to say you know I didn't do it either," I told Luna.

"Oh! Yeah, of course. I don't see how anyone would believe that you'd be able to stab Constantine," Luna said, looking me up and down a little too much.

I sighed.

We were both excused by Monsieur Quebec. I noticed he seemed to be getting steadily more exasperated. The poor man was having to excuse people from work left, right, and centre. It was a miracle the place was still running.

"I'll come down to the station after my break to make sure they let you go again," Adele reassured us both.

I took a moment to pen a text message to Lowell, letting him know where I was going and to come and spring me if I wasn't home in time for tea. I hoped it wouldn't come to that. A spell of incarceration in a French prison probably wouldn't help my employment prospects.

Stepping inside the police station was like stepping into a 70's cop show. There was oiled teak wood everywhere and a haze of cigarette smoke that I was certain defied EU workplace regulations. But then, Britain had always been the only country to take the rules to heart.

"We're here for questioning," I informed the woman at the reception desk, feeling faintly ridiculous.

"Oh no," Luna muttered, when a gendarme I estimated to be in his thirties approached us. He had fair hair that sat on his head in a fluffy haze and a pleasantly soft face, which lent him a babyish look.

"It's my ex," Luna just managed to hiss before he arrived within earshot.

I kept my raised eyebrows to myself. I couldn't even begin to imagine the complications of breaking up with someone who lived in the same little village as you did and having to bump into them forever more. It was bad enough when that happened to work colleagues, but you could always leave the job. Moving house was a bit more drastic.

"Luna, please come with me," the gendarme said, completely ignoring me.

"Is someone going to see me?" I asked.

The man looked blankly back.

"I'm Madigan Amos," I prompted.

"Someone will come," he said, in the vague way of a man

who has no clue about what is really going on, but is loathe to admit it.

Instead of waiting in the middle of the surprisingly well-staffed room, I decided to follow Luna and the gendarme.

The next room was comprised of cubicles formed from padded boards, presumably intended to afford those inside some privacy. The gendarme sat Luna down and then disappeared, allowing me ample time to sneak over to her.

"This is a nightmare!" Luna whispered to me. "I used to date Enzo Argent last year. He then cheated on me with another woman, knocked her up, and had to marry her," she confided.

"Wow, a shotgun wedding in the heart of France," I said, unable to stop myself grinning at the unusual setting for such a thing.

"It was quite a scandal, but hush… his wife is a few cubicles down behind you. She's already looked over here once." Luna glanced that way and then ducked her head again. "Oh no, now she'll think I'm talking about her! I don't want anything to do with this. The word is that they're about to get a divorce. Quick! He's coming back," she fast-whispered, and I slid around the corner of the cubicle and managed to get back into the main room without Enzo spotting me.

"There you are," Detective Girard said, making me jump. "Come on, I'll make this quick."

I noticed she looked over at officer Argent's cubicle and shook her head in disgust. After what I'd just learnt about the man in a very short space of time, I couldn't blame her. There were usually two sides to a story but a man who'd cheated on Luna and was now trying to use her to antagonise his soon to be ex-wife - the very woman he'd cheated on her with - didn't sound like a decent person to me.

Detective Girard gestured to a seat behind a wooden desk and flipped open a folder with a sigh.

I sat down and waited.

"How would you describe your relationship with Constantine Duval?" she asked.

"We didn't really have one. I only met her a couple of times. Both of those times she was antagonistic towards both me and my colleagues, but I hear that was just her way. I think I might have been the first person who took our grievance to the zoo manager, Monsieur Quebec. After we had a discussion, I felt that the matter was resolved," I told her.

Detective Girard nodded and I had the distinct impression that she wasn't really interested in tales of petty disagreements.

"Okay, thanks. What time would you estimate that you and Luna went to get food and were unaccompanied?"

I thought about it. "I suppose it was probably quarter past seven or so. We'd just been in to see the puppies and then decided to stay. What exactly happened to Constantine?" I asked.

"We aren't completely sure, as she hasn't regained consciousness so far and no one saw it happen. She was on her way to visit her sick mother, who she cares for, when it happened. We asked her mother and she thinks that Constantine may have been robbed," the detective informed me.

I felt my heart drop as I thought about her poor mother, who had most likely lost the daughter she both loved and relied upon. I wonder if it was this hidden burden that had made Constantine so abrasive. Perhaps she had resented anyone she perceived as having it easier than she did. It was tragic but some small part of me was pleased that there was something redeeming about Constantine after all.

"That's terrible," I said.

"I know. I can't believe something like that happened

around here. Thank you for your help. That's all for now, I think,' Detective Girard concluded.

I hesitated for a moment, surprised it had been so simple.

The detective noticed and managed a tired smile. "Detective Prideaux likes to do things by the book. He only appears to accuse everyone of the crime in question," she told me.

"I have a question," I said, feeling that a barrier had been broken down. "L'airelle is a small village, but the police station here seems pretty big to me. Is there really enough crime around here to warrant it?" I asked, wondering if I should be concerned.

The detective laughed a little. "No, crime around here is usually very rare. This police station covers L'airelle and the surrounding villages and also Angoux. I suppose it's strange that it's based here and not in the town, but it's just the way it's always been. I suppose at one time all of the villages were the same size, but Angoux grew."

"Thanks," I said, interested to learn this piece of local knowledge.

I nodded goodbye to the detective and then walked back across the room, stopping to peer around the corner into the second room where I'd last seen Luna. She was still in the cubicle, seated in a chair facing my way. She looked up long enough to pull an exasperated face. I leant against the wall, hoping my presence would show some solidarity for Luna.

Her ex was conducting his interrogation in a low voice, designed to be impossible to overhear.

"Could you speak up?" Luna repeated in a tired way. The gendarme had leant almost halfway across his desk while Luna looked like she might be about to fall backwards off her chair.

"I said, what is your association with Madigan Amos?"

I blinked in surprise, immediately feeling that I shouldn't be watching. There was an empty cubicle adjacent to the wall and I slid inside it, knowing I now couldn't be seen by Enzo Argent.

"She's here to review L'airelle Zoological Park. Monsieur Quebec hired her to improve the breeding programme and animal welfare standards. We're friends," she finished.

"Are you aware that she has been involved in two cases of black-market animal trading?" he enquired.

I frowned. That wasn't even true! Lowell and I had stopped the illegal sale of zoo animals at Avery Zoo and there hadn't been any black-market trading at Snidely Safari and Wildlife Park. The police had seized some venomous snakes being kept without a licence, but that hardly amounted to black-market trading. My mouth set in a grim line, as I wondered where he'd got his information from. Perhaps there was more about me on police records than I knew, or, more likely, the two mysterious agents who had come to town had done a background check and shared their information.

I bit my lip, wondering just what else they knew. If this was the light I was going to be painted in...

"I'm sure Madi would never have anything to do with something that promoted animal abuse," Luna said, stoically. I silently sang her praises.

Enzo sighed and I thought I heard the chair creak as he finally gave up on the leaning forwards tactic to get Luna to confide in him.

I silently wondered why he'd ever thought he'd be a good choice of person to get information from Luna. I thought she'd probably rather talk to a pile of bricks than spend time in his company.

"Luna, for your own safety, you need to tell me the truth. Is Madigan Amos dangerous? We've been told she has violent tendencies. Do you think she might attack someone who angered her, or perhaps someone who was nasty to you?

You've admitted that you're friends. Do you think she might have done it because she cares about you?" Argent asked in his softest (and unfortunately, most annoying) voice.

"Are you crazy? Madi's not violent at all! Anyway, she's tiny. Who is she supposed to have beaten up?" Luna asked, sounding genuinely curious.

I tried not to feel a bit miffed by her belief that I couldn't be a violent criminal if I chose to be, but at least she was defending me.

"Fine. I suppose that's all there is to say for now. Be careful around her, Luna. She hasn't told you the whole truth about herself," Argent finished.

I just knew he'd got that line from a film.

"Let me walk you out," he said, just as softly.

There was jaw tensing sound of a chair being scraped against a hard floor. I stuck my head around the edge of my cubical and watched the woman, whom Luna had told me was the ex-wife, stalk off.

It didn't come as much of a surprise that Enzo Argent lost interest in making conversation after that. He stood up and made to lead Luna to the door. What actually happened was that he ended up trailing her like a puppy while she managed to keep up a spectacular pace all the way to the door. I reappeared from my hiding place and jogged after them.

Adele was waiting in the foyer with a cup of iced coffee in her hand and a bag that smelt like it was packed with doughnuts.

"Hey guys," she said to Luna and me, pointedly pretending that Enzo Argent didn't even exist. "I took my lunch break early and drove over to Angoux to pick up some pastries. I thought you might both need them after being interrogated for no reason at all," she said.

"Thanks, Adele," Luna said, reaching into the bag and coming out with a sugar coated bun.

"My car's in the police station car park. I'll drive us all back to work," she said.

We all did our best to ignore Enzo Argent, who continued to trail our group, even out of the door.

"Here we go." Adele flashed her keys at the blue Citroen. "Oh!"

We could all see what it was that made her say 'oh'. A brown leather bag had been left on the bonnet of the car. A few of its contents had even spilled out across the paintwork.

I had a bad feeling about the bag.

I glanced over my shoulder and found that Enzo was mercifully distracted. I took the time to gently open the bag and came out with a purse. What I found when I opened it was of little surprise.

"This is Constantine's purse and her bag, I reckon," I told Luna and Adele, who both looked at me aghast.

"What is it doing on my car? How did it get there?" Adele shook her long, dark hair back from her white face.

"Detective!" I shouted, determined to avoid bringing Luna's ex back into the equation.

Detective Girard looked up from the cigarette she'd been smoking outside.

I beckoned her over. "We came back out of the police station with Adele and found that this bag had been left on her car. We think it belongs to Constantine."

"Did you see anyone, Fae?" Adele asked.

Detective Girard shook her head. "Sorry, Adele. I only just came out for my break. I'll go and get someone to gather the evidence. You'd better all wait here." She threw us an apologetic look - something she seemed to be an expert at - and disappeared back inside the building.

"Do you actually want to be locked up?"

I didn't have to look at Luna to know she was frowning. Enzo Argent had been listening in on our conversation.

"Excuse me?" Luna said, taking the bait.

"Is this all some kind of way to get some attention from me? You stab a woman who got on your nerves and then when we still fail to arrest you, you decide to leave her bag on your car," Enzo said. He had a nasty smirk on his face.

"I've been inside the whole time, right up until Adele arrived to pick us up. It's not even my car, you moron," Luna bit back and then looked a little panicked. "Adele was inside waiting. It clearly wasn't her either."

"Is there anyone who can corroborate that?" the insufferable gendarme asked.

"The receptionist was there the whole time," Adele said with a shrug.

"Clearly someone is trying to frame one of us," I cut in, just as Detective Prideaux arrived. I suppose I should have expected that he'd be the one that Detective Girard ran to get.

"We're collecting the bag for evidence now. Please come back inside to answer a few questions."

"No thank you," I said, my fuse finally burning down.

"Excuse me?" the detective asked, looking for all the world as though no one had ever refused him anything before. Ever.

"We have work to be getting back to. Anyone with eyes can see that the bag was planted while Adele, Luna, and I were all inside the building. There is nothing to ask questions about. Either arrest us, or let us go," I said, feeling tired. It was only halfway through the working day but I felt like I'd been passed through a wringer.

"We'll be in contact if we have any further questions," Detective Prideaux said, pretending that he was the one who'd dismissed us.

I decided I could live with that.

Now the bag had been removed, we all got into Adele's

car as fast as possible. There was no telling when another piece of evidence might crop up in the wrong place.

The interior of the car was uncharacteristically silent as we drove back up the hill to L'airelle Zoological. I knew each of us were lost in our own thoughts.

As I thought back over everything strange that'd happened I was only able to reach one conclusion: someone was out to get one of us.

Before the bag incident, I hadn't thought it was a malicious campaign. Adele's dog being painted, the chocolates… they seemed like pranks designed to confuse, rather than intimidate. But the bag being planted was a different matter.

I chewed on my lip and wondered if any of this was somehow connected to Pascal's strange murder. The targeting of the zoo and the eventual landing spot of the paraglider - was it telling? I just couldn't be sure that it was all related.

"I think someone's out to get me," Adele muttered, and I wondered if she was right.

7

THE BODY IN THE ROAD

"I hope your day was better than mine," I said, when Lowell rocked up, clad in shorts and hiking boots. It wasn't a look I was used to him sporting.

"It was great! I walked up past the paragliding place and then across another couple of valleys and up some more of the mountains. I almost wish there was a job I could do that just involved walking over mountains," he confessed.

"That's great," I said, but my voice clearly lacked enthusiasm because he threw me a sharp look.

"What happened?" he asked.

I told him about the attack on Constantine and my subsequent questioning. I then explained about the bag found on the bonnet of Adele's car.

"I think someone may be trying to cause trouble for Adele. First they send chocolates from a secret admirer - perhaps to try to cause problems in her marriage. Then they paint her dog, and now they leave a piece of evidence on her bonnet," I said.

"But why would they attack Constantine?" Lowell queried.

"I'm sure there are no shortage of people at L'airelle Zoological who've thought of doing exactly that. Perhaps one of them cracked enough to do it and thought they could frame Adele at the same time," I suggested.

"Maybe," Lowell said. "I'm surprised I haven't been brought in for questioning. I was unaccounted for at the same time you were. What if you'd told me about Constantine being nasty and I decided to take her out for you?" He raised a dark eyebrow, but I just rolled my eyes at him.

He did have a point about the conspicuous lack of being dragged in for questioning.

I thought back to what I'd overheard of Luna's interview. "The police seem to know about what happened at Snidely and Avery. As I've never been arrested, there shouldn't be any record of it all. Am I right?"

Lowell nodded in confirmation.

"I think your agent friends have been sharing a few details," I said, grudgingly.

"Probably," Lowell admitted. "They'll have offered an information trade in order to further their own enquiries."

"So, what... you slipped the net because you're mates with them?"

"We're not mates," Lowell said, with a grin. "Stop sulking. Your history just looked worse than mine because you don't have an official reason to be sticking your nose into trouble."

"Stop being so smug, or I'll make you cook dinner again," I told him. "On second thoughts, you'd better not. I'm not sure if we can afford it."

"At least they didn't arrest you, right?" he said, still grinning.

"I still think you need to make it up to me. What's the point in having contacts if you can't get me out of the police station?"

"Will a hot chocolate with cream and marshmallows be

penance enough?"

"Maybe," I said, narrowing my eyes at him as I thought of a few other ideas.

I looked over at the kitchen window, hoping to see the last few rays of sunlight disappearing beyond the fields. My eye caught on the clunky phone that hung on the wall. A little red light was flashing.

I walked over and realised it was the answer machine saying we had a new message. While Lowell busied himself with heating up a pan of milk, I pressed play.

"I got this number from… It doesn't matter. Is Mr Adagio there? I need to speak with you. I will call another time," a female voice with a French accent said before hanging up.

I turned around to find Lowell had stopped stirring the milk and was looking at me with just as much surprise as I felt.

"A new mystery. Just what we need!" I said, trying to make light of the unusual call.

"I haven't made any friends who sound like that," Lowell promised me. "Other than saying 'bonjour' to the entire village, I've only had a decent conversation with the farmer who works up in the mountains. In fact, it's hard to get him to stop talking. I think he misses life down in the village, but he can't get up and down the hill as often as he used to. Trust me, he doesn't sound anything like that."

"I suppose we'll have to wait and see if she calls again," I said, neutrally.

My initial reaction had been suspicion as to why another woman would be calling Lowell at home. I'd since realised it hadn't sounded like that sort of call. Instead, this woman had seemed nervous.

I wondered why she needed to speak to Lowell.

The hot chocolate did a lot to boost my spirits. After we'd

eaten a big salad for dinner, we both went our separate ways to work on our hobbies and jobs.

My job of the evening was not one I was hugely anticipating. A series of webcast interviews were a part of the campaign rewards and I needed to make a start on recording them.

I sat down in front of my laptop and procrastinated.

First, I answered the slew of daily fan emails and then I uploaded a new comic to the site. I also saw I had an email from Tiff. I weighed up the potential content of the email versus recording the webcasts and picked the email. I wondered what task Tiff had set for me now...

Hi Madi,

Hope everything is going well in France. The weather here is rubbish, so you definitely dodged a bullet. Just writing to let you know that your Etsy store has sold out of all but one of the original sketches and quite a few prints besides. It should all be in your PayPal account by the end of the month. Are you okay to package and ship them? I've sent you your login for Etsy, so you should be able to find all the details.

Let me know!
Tiff

I read the email a couple of times in amazement. We'd priced the original sketches at £50 each! I couldn't believe I'd already sold nine out of ten.

Then I swore. I was stuck in France while the rest of my portfolio was back at home. I also had no access to a printer, or the supplies needed to produce a good quality art print.

I bit my fingernails for a second or two and then emailed Tiff back, offering to split the profits with her if she would go round my house and send everything off - just this once.

I also figured I owed her something for setting up and dealing with my Etsy shop. I'd never really taken it seriously until now, but I was amazed by how successful it had been. I'd known I had fans, but I was truly surprised that they were so voracious they wanted to own my original, scrappy sketches. Despite the evidence in front of me, I still felt like I was somehow cheating them. I'd started this comic for a bit of fun and now it was taking off.

On a whim, I clicked from my Etsy store over to Tiff's. Her sales had jumped by at least a hundred since I'd last visited her shop. I smiled, pleased that her own side business was going from strength to strength.

After the surprise success, I found I was more motivated to record these webcasts. I popped to the bathroom to briefly repair my make up and attempt to do something with my hair, before I returned to the laptop and set up my camera. I brought the list of interview questions up on screen, gritted my teeth, and promised myself I could do hundreds of takes, until I didn't feel quite to ridiculous talking to a camera.

"I hope no one I know ever sees this…" I muttered and pressed record.

The nights were getting cooler as autumn finally got a grip on southern France. That still didn't stop me from being unable to sleep that night.

I woke up at four in the morning and found that the first light of dawn was already beginning to lighten the horizon. I knew I wouldn't be getting anymore sleep, so I decided to get up and go for an early morning walk.

The village was quiet apart from the few tweets of some

early rising birds. The tourists had been steadily declining over the past week. The village wasn't incredibly busy at the best of times, but now it was completely deserted. I walked through the houses, feeling like a ghost, whilst inside everyone continued to sleep.

I decided to take a circuitous route back and walked down the lane where Luna and Adele lived. My eyes struggled to see clearly in the gloom of the early morning, but I spotted something up ahead. I squinted and kept walking, wondering what the lump in the middle of the road was.

Two steps later, I realised it was a person.

I broke into a run and then dropped to my knees by the body. I recognised the brown hair as I felt for a pulse.

It was Justin.

A wave of relief crashed over me when I found a pulse - albeit a faint one. I daren't roll him over, so I couldn't tell if he had any hidden injuries, but blood was still sticky on the side of his face. His hair was also matted with the stuff. I thought he'd probably been hit on the head with something.

"What were you doing out here, Justin?" I said, before realising I needed to do something. I should call the ambulance and the police, but my French just wasn't good enough. It would only waste valuable time.

I did the only thing I could and ran to the nearest house, which happened to be Luna's.

I banged on the door and was relieved when she answered a few seconds later, wearing a dressing gown.

"What's happening?" she said, blearily.

"You've got to call an ambulance. Justin's out in the street. He's been hurt," I said and then rushed back out to Justin without waiting for an answer. I knew Luna would do her part.

Justin was still breathing when I returned and he also

seemed aware that I was there. He started to mutter something unintelligible.

"What happened, Justin?" I asked.

"Don't remember," was all I could make out. At least he'd understood me.

Luna rushed by a couple of seconds later, giving me a thumbs up. She'd called the ambulance and now she was heading to wake Adele up.

"Don't worry. The ambulance is on its way. It's all going to be okay," I reassured Justin, who had worryingly become silent again.

I hoped the paramedics weren't too far away.

I'd just finished dragging a fresh carcass in for the paired tigers and opened the panel to allow them access, when I saw Adele walk past.

"Adele!" I called, surprised to see her back at the zoo so soon. She saw me and blinked a couple of times before walking over.

"Sorry, my head is on a different planet today," she explained.

"What are you doing back at the zoo? I thought you'd still be at the hospital."

I hadn't had a chance to speak to Adele about finding Justin early that the morning. The ambulance had pulled up just as Luna had managed to rouse Adele and she'd jumped inside the ambulance straight after they'd loaded him in.

It was Saturday, and technically my day off, but I'd known it was more important to step into the breach to help a friend.

"Justin is actually doing okay and we've both missed so much work recently. I can't really afford another day off," she said with a wan smile. "He's fully conscious now, although he says he doesn't remember what happened." She sighed. "Matti's been playing up since the puppies were born. We think he may be feeling ignored because the puppies need so much attention at the moment. I went to bed pretty early yesterday evening, so I have no idea what happened. We think that Matti might have managed to slip out of the house and run away. Luna found him in her back garden this morning, so at least he's safe. We just have no idea how he got there." She ran a hand through her dark hair. "Justin probably went out to look late at night and someone attacked him. I'm just so glad you found him. Thank you."

"I couldn't sleep, so I went for an early morning walk," I explained, knowing Adele would probably be wondering just what I'd been doing strolling down her road in the early hours, but was too polite to ask.

"I thought it must be something like that. We're lucky you found him," she repeated.

"I just hope he gets better soon and remembers what happened."

"I just can't imagine why anyone would want to attack Justin," Adele said.

I nodded in agreement, but inside I thought I had a pretty good idea. If someone was running a strange campaign against Adele, attacking her husband would be a pretty good fit. *Who's obsessed with her and what is their goal?* I wondered.

"If you're okay to work, I'd be happy to go back to doing my review," I said, unsure how much Adele would be able to handle today. Now I was at the zoo, I may as well stay for the day.

"I think I'll be fine. Thanks though, Madi," she said.

"Oh, have you seen Luna around?" I asked her. We'd agreed to do the same rounds we'd done when I'd covered last time, but that had been right after Justin had been taken away in the ambulance. I hadn't seen her since.

She shook her head. "No, I haven't. I'll let you know you're looking for her."

I nodded and left her to finish off the morning rounds. It was only when I paused to think about it that I realised I didn't have much left to do before my review was complete. There'd been so much going on, I hadn't noticed that my time at L'airelle was coming to an end.

All I had to do now was finish my observations and suggestions for some of the large herbivores and a few of the smaller animals here and there and I'd be ready to hand it all in. In spite of everything that had happened, I would be very sorry to leave the quaint village and the firm friends I'd made. I hoped that this trip wouldn't be the last I made to L'airelle.

I went back to the hut to pick up my review worksheets and then made my way across the zoo to the macaws.

I'd been putting off visiting this particular enclosure, because I already suspected it would be a problem.

It turned out I was right.

When I approached, I found a keeper with a macaw on their arm. They were encouraging visitors to come up and stroke the large bird and also allowing some of them to hold the parrot and have a photo taken with it.

My lips set in a thin line at what I was seeing. It wasn't that it was a bad thing to regularly handle birds - especially macaws - but I got the impression that this went on all day. Education was one thing, but continual exploitation for the sake of a photo opportunity I wouldn't stand for, and I just knew my observations were correct. The macaw should have had a bright and colourful plumage, but instead he seemed drab. I also noticed some bald patches on his chest, where he'd been pulling out his own feathers. All in all, it wasn't a happy sight.

The macaw's fellows weren't much better off. Their enclosure was bare and covered with sand. The only interest being the large, dead tree, where a couple of other macaws and an African grey parrot perched. I noticed they all had leather thongs around their legs that kept them from flying.

I shook my head. How could a zoo who had such a laissez-faire attitude to monkeys running around loose treat their birds like prisoners? Even if they weren't confined, the enclosure was inappropriately sized, designed for viewing rather than animal happiness.

I filled out the sheet with every criticism I noticed and then placed it firmly at the top of the pile. I made a promise to myself that I would not be leaving the zoo until these poor parrots were guaranteed a proper aviary, with space to fly around. Any educational up close viewing should only be during a specific time slot daily, and the birds should always be rotated and rewarded. Animals were not our slaves.

When I looked up at the parrot enclosure again, the keeper holding the bird met my gaze. No words passed between us, but I thought he knew my judgement all the same.

I walked away to move on to the next animal on my list. None of this was personal. I had a job to do.

A strange sound distracted me on my way to see the hippos. I backed up and looked down the small side alley, blocked off by a staff access only gate. The noise sounded like giggling. I wondered if a child had somehow managed to crawl under the gate.

Any normal sized person would probably have been able to climb up on something and peer over the top to satisfy their curiosity. I was reduced to lying flat on my face and peering underneath the gap.

All I could see were two pairs of shoes. It took me a moment, but I realised I recognised them both. The giggling continued and despite my face being pressed against damp concrete, I smiled.

Luna had obviously sought comfort and found it in the arms of Alcide, the primate keeper. I pushed myself back to my feet and walked back the way I'd come, silently wishing Luna a better relationship than the one she'd gone through with Enzo Argent. She deserved someone nice.

I walked on with a spring in my step, pleased that something good had come out of today.

My good mood evaporated when I heard a loud chorus of 'Eeeeeew!'.

Concerned, I hurried towards the source of the noise and discovered that a large group of children had gathered outside the Pallas's cats enclosure. Some of their faces were pressed up against the glass. I spared a thought for the poor caretakers who'd have to polish it later.

I got closer and stood on tiptoe to see what was causing the children so much disgust. The few adults around had similar expressions of distaste on their faces.

My first impression was one of surprise. The Pallas's cats were up and about in the open. They were even looking pretty active. They kept jumping about and patting the ground with their paws. Then they'd bite at the floor and… oh.

I'd forgotten about the spiders.

Another delighted 'Eeeeew!' went up, as one of the cats caught a many legged creature and crunched down, clearly enjoying it immensely.

I looked at the crowd again and noted that the children's disgust was definitely the fascinated kind. The adults just looked like they wanted to be sick. I grinned.

Perhaps conventional wisdom was that it was the adults

who paid for the entry and their opinions should always be considered, but I knew that kids held a lot of sway, and they loved gross things like cats munching on spiders. I decided I would be sharing the spider experiment with Monsieur Quebec when I handed in my final review. Despite the somewhat unappealing spectacle, it was great to see the normally reclusive cats getting active. I was glad we'd bought the 'right flavour' spiders.

I was surprised when my phone rang on my way to lunch break. I checked the screen and discovered Lowell was calling me.

"Hi, is everything okay?" I asked. Perhaps it was paranoia, but I couldn't help but wonder when the next dreadful thing would happen. Constantine had been attacked in Angoux, but Justin's attack had taken place practically down the road from us. I wasn't sure who was next on the madman's list.

"Yeah, everything's fine. I'm at the hospital with Justin. I thought I'd check in on him and make sure he's in good hands," Lowell said.

I frowned at the handset. Lowell was a great guy and had shown me he could be caring at times, but visiting hospitals to check a man he barely knew was okay? It was definitely unusual.

"He's lucky he's got so many visitors. Mr Flannigan's just dropped by and we're all having a nice chat," Lowell said.

I snorted into the phone and hoped it wouldn't make Lowell grin. So that was why he was at the hospital. He wanted to find out if the agents were on to something.

"Talking about anything interesting?" I asked.

"Yeah, we're having a great time. I'll see you later," he said and hung up.

I smiled, knowing that Lowell would be sure to dish the dirt when I saw him that evening.

I'd just entered the restaurant and was browsing sandwiches (I hadn't expected to need lunch) when Luna came up behind me and tickled my ribs. I laughed and my arms reflexively shot up, unfortunately launching the brie and ham baguette I'd been holding, halfway across the room.

We both turned away as it landed on the head of a parent, who already looked like he was having a hard time controlling his brood. I contemplated the blank wall in front of me and heard a child shout 'food fight!'. A few wet splunches followed, encouraging me to look round.

"How about we walk down to the village and grab something?" Luna said, dragging me out of the restaurant before the whole place went into melt down. I hoped they wouldn't look back at the CCTV.

We walked down the tree-lined road that led down to the village. Orange leaves fluttered by every time the breeze blew. I smiled as I watched them fall. Autumn was my favourite season.

"Did you spend some time with Alcide this morning?" I asked, casually.

Luna turned scarlet. "We, um..."

"Had a moment?" I suggested with a smile.

Luna nodded happily. "He's going to take me out for dinner tonight. Isn't that great? I was feeling so down after that horrible trip to the police station and Enzo being Enzo," she said, disgustedly. "I was just talking about it all to Alcide. I also said how what had happened to Justin was so terrible. I got pretty upset, to be honest, but he was really great. He just let me talk and then said some really good things and we kissed." She blushed again. "I just can't believe he's interested in me."

I frowned at her. "Luna, you're great! Don't you dare

think you aren't just because of the way Enzo treated you. You are more than worthy of a wonderful partner," I told her.

"Thanks Madi," Luna said, all happiness and light.

A cloud crossed her face. "Before all the good stuff happened, I was hoping to find you to ask your thoughts on something. I had a weird call yesterday evening. I answered it and this voice on the other end whispered 'are you alone?'. It really freaked me out, so I hung up and went out for a walk."

"You didn't recognise the voice?" I asked.

Luna shook her head. "It just sounded husky. It's hard enough recognising people on the phone without them whispering."

"Hmm," I said, thinking about the strange answer machine message we'd had yesterday. I wondered if these odd calls were unrelated to everything else that was going on, or did they somehow tie in? I felt like I was caught up in a storm that was throwing everything left right and centre without a clue as to where it had all come from.

We walked into the boulangerie and snagged the last two cheese and ham puff pastries.

"These are my favourite," Luna confessed, as we walked across the square and sat on the edge of the fountain.

"I'm glad Justin is okay," I said, referring back to the morning's events. It felt like they'd happened on a different day.

"Me too," Luna agreed. "It's so weird how Matti managed to get into my back garden. The gate was shut, so he must have jumped it. Maybe he's only athletic when no one's looking, the big lump," she said, fondly.

"Do you know how Jolie and the puppies are?" I asked, anxious to hear how they were doing. I hadn't wanted to bother Adele when we'd bumped into each other by the tiger enclosure. I was sure she already had a lot on her mind.

"They're doing great. The little one's being bottle fed, as

Adele and Justin don't think he's getting quite enough from Jolie, but the others are behaving just like puppies. Matti got a bit too close and was nipped for his curiosity. That's why Adele thinks he ran away. He was in a bit of a sulk," Luna explained.

I giggled. Dogs could be such drama queens. I hoped one day I'd be able to have a dog of my own. At the moment, I simply didn't have the time to spend with them. Cats were more independent and also liked to spend most of the day sleeping. I had high hopes that Lucky would love life on the road with me.

"Hey, are you busy tomorrow?" Luna asked.

"You mean for the village party?" I wasn't even sure why the village was having a party. In France, there always seemed to be a celebration going on. However, I wasn't complaining. I thought it was charming that the village had events which brought its residents closer together.

"No, before then," Luna said.

"I haven't made plans," I replied, thinking of the lack of time spent with Lowell and feeling a bit guilty.

"There's an errand I need to run and I could really do with some help. Could you meet me by the bridge out of the village first thing tomorrow?"

"Sure," I said.

"Great! Thanks."

I thought about asking what we were going to be doing but I had my suspicions it wasn't entirely above board. Otherwise Luna would have surely already told me. I'd just have to hope that she wasn't trying to trick me into coming to the edge of the village alone so she could kill me.

A couple of weeks ago, that would have been funny. Now I wasn't so sure.

The sun was shining the next morning when I set off for my rendezvous with Luna. Preparations for the village dinner and party that night were already underway, and I walked beneath several strings of bunting that were being put up. The square itself was a sea of activity with long tables being brought in and a bonfire set up right in the middle of it all. I couldn't help but be reminded of the scene at the end of every *Asterix and Obelix* comic, where the whole village gathers for a feast of roast boar. Tonight's menu was more of a potluck affair, but I had no doubt it would be wonderful. After all, Lowell and I had already sampled the culinary talents of one of the village's homespun chefs.

I walked past the preparations and it wasn't long before I arrived at the bridge on the way out of the village. Luna was already waiting next to her car.

"So, what are we doing?" I asked, curiosity getting the better of me. Why had she needed to drive out of town to meet me?

"There's just something I want to figure out," she began. "The police don't seem to be doing much but I'm fed up of all this. First Pascal, then Constantine, and now Justin. I've been thinking about it and I thought if we can just figure out how Pascal came to be in the paraglider, we might learn something. At least, it may give us a hint as to who was responsible." She shrugged and looked away. "I asked you because you know a thing or two about investigating."

"Lowell's the private detective, not me," I warned her. "But, I have been known to dabble," I confessed.

Usually at my own expense.

"Great!" Luna's face lit up and I realised she'd been expecting me to say it was a stupid idea.

"I don't know if we'll find anything. I don't even know where to start looking," I confessed looking up at the surrounding mountains. Which way had the paraglider come from? I tried to remember.

"Don't worry, I've already figured out where to look. I think the police have been so caught up with the new attacks, they haven't put any time into this. I know they tried to find the spot where the other paraglider landed but I don't think they thought much about where they jumped from. They might even have jumped from the paragliding school," she said.

I frowned. "You think? Surely they have someone watching everything all the time."

Luna nodded. "Well, probably… but that's what we're going to find out. Now get in!"

I opened the car door and sat in the passenger seat, wondering how this was going to work. Luna started the engine and her car chugged its way up the side of a mountain. Sign posts let us know that the paragliding school was at the top, and it wasn't long before we pulled in to a gravel car park.

Luna killed the engine and turned to me. "I've lived here my entire life and this is the only mountain with a road leading all the way to the top. Perhaps whoever killed Pascal Devereux managed to get him to walk up one of the other mountains, carrying the paragliding gear, but…"

"… They probably met up here. Or he may have been killed elsewhere and brought up here," I finished and looked around the car park. There were relatively few vehicles around and plenty of scrubby bushes for cover, but I still couldn't imagine the murder taking place in such an open space. "I bet he was already dead when they went up the mountain," I mused, wondering if we were currently sitting in the same spot as Pascal's killer.

"Yeah, exactly," Luna agreed.

"If this is all true, it means that dropping the body into

the zoo was definitely supposed to send a message," I said, having all but confirmed that in my mind anyway.

"Yeah," Luna said again, looking worried for a moment. "Do you think it has something to do with Constantine and Justin? Do you think they knew something and it was like a warning?" Luna shook her head. "I could imagine Constantine hiding something, but not Justin. We've known him for years! He moved out of Paris to get some rural peace and quiet. Then he met Adele and they fell in love." She sighed, happily.

I nodded but inside I wondered... was Justin the person in witness protection? Or did he know the identity of the person who was? What about Constantine? I shook myself. None of this made any sense and going round in circles wasn't getting me anywhere. It was time to give Luna's idea a shot.

"What's the plan?" I asked, realising she'd skipped that part.

She gave me a smile I didn't much like and popped the boot open. We both walked round to back of the car and she lifted the lid to reveal...

The largest sack of dog food known to man. It was probably a little shorter than your average person, but definitely more squat.

"Are you stocking up for when you take your puppy home?" I was confused.

"Nope. This is one of the bags for Matti, Justin brought over. It's about 40 kg, so not as heavy as a body would be, but I figured it would give us an idea."

Luna's plan started to take shape in my head.

"We're trying to find out if it's possible to get past the staff and launch yourself off the cliff with a dead body?"

Luna nodded. "Yep! The paragliding booth looks out over the jump site, but I bet they don't watch it all the time. As soon as September starts, they lay off their summer staff. It's just Sage's father, Alex, running it at the moment. Sage works in town during the autumn and winter," she explained. "So, I'll go in and chat to Alex. He loves to gossip. You try to get this bag to the jump spot and pretend you're about to jump off."

"Right," I said, not failing to notice that I was the one stuck lifting the stand-in body.

"I would have flipped a coin for it, but Alex doesn't much like to speak English. Also, I'd have to look at the drop and you know I have an issue with heights. Okay, good luck!" Luna said, waltzing off to chit-chat with the paragliding school owner.

I scanned the area before making my move. There were signs that people had come up to the top of the mountain this morning, but no one was around right now. There was a small shed and a rack full of gear that seemed to be for hire. I wondered about tandem jumps, which were often offered by instructors. I didn't know for sure, but I guessed Sage usually worked as an instructor, but must not be booked anytime soon. I shrugged. That wasn't part of this test anyway.

With a sinking heart, I looked down at the big bag of dog food and seized it by its plasticised corners. I grunted and tugged and the bag flopped out onto the floor, nearly making me fall over backwards. I grumbled for a couple of moments about Luna picking the easy job. Unfortunately, complaining didn't get the job done. I sighed and started dragging the bag across the car park.

By the time I reached the building, I was sweating. The sun had decided to drench the valley and mountains in a final burst of summer warmth and I was suffering for it.

I tried to imagine someone dragging a body all the way up a different mountain to a private jump site and couldn't see it. However, there was still the possibility they'd tricked Pascal into going up to the top himself.

I shrugged and kept pulling, dragging the bag of dog food past the hut where Luna was chatting away animatedly. I wondered what her contingency plan was if Alex turned around right now and saw me with a bag of dog food. I sincerely hoped it wasn't to pretend she didn't have a clue who the crazy dog food lady was.

I kept dragging and pretty soon I neared the outcrop of rocks, between which people ran and flung themselves into oblivion. I tried to imagine it, but found my legs were starting to turn to jelly. The breeze whipped up over the rocks and provided a welcome relief from the heat but it did nothing to distract me from the long drop just a few feet away. Figuring I should do the job properly, I moved the food bag so that it was just a metre back from the edge and then risked a peek over the brink.

I pulled back, feeling dizzy. I didn't share Luna's fear of heights, but we were a heck of a long way up. What made it even worse was the thought that someone had not only flung themselves over the edge, they'd strapped themselves to a corpse when they'd done it.

I sat down with a bump, the dog food bag standing more or less upright - a sentinel watching over the orange roofs of the village and zoo at the bottom of the valley. Now I was up here, the whole happening seemed even more surreal. Someone had planned to drop a corpse into the zoo. While I now felt sure Luna and I had the execution all figured out, I still had no idea why they'd done it.

I used a hand to push myself to my feet and experienced a strange feeling of shifting gravity. Too late, I realised the bag of dog food was teetering away from me. I lunged and then thought better of it at the last moment. Instead, I was forced to watch as the 40kg bag of dog food pitched forwards and flopped over the edge of the precipice.

I closed my eyes and stayed with my hand outstretched for a second. A treacherous voice in my head whispered 'at least you won't have to carry it back to the car'.

I walked back towards the vehicle, pausing by the booth to give Luna the thumbs up from behind Alex's back.

A minute or two later Luna joined me.

"How'd it go?" she asked.

"I think you were right. The jumper definitely could have taken a corpse right by here, put on their gear and jumped, if Alex was distracted. Perhaps they even put the gear on in the car park and rushed straight by," I hypothesised.

Luna nodded. "Well, I asked him if he saw anything and he said he hadn't. He said the police had been by and asked that, too, and he'd told them the same. I did find out one interesting thing though." Her eyes sparkled. "Pascal Devereux was the one who hired the tandem gear. He did it over the phone a few hours before. Alex said he thought it was a little odd because Pascal hadn't jumped for years, but he figured friends or family must be in town and they wanted to have a go and Pascal had agreed to take them. He left the gear on the rack for him to collect. A few hours later, it was gone, and Pascal fell from the sky above the tiger enclosure."

"He must have lost the gear, I guess," I said, thinking about the sabotaged parachute cord and then what had happened in the tiger enclosure.

"Yeah, he's not best pleased about that. Tandem harnesses and the 'chutes themselves are expensive. They're a small, family run business, so it's a blow. But, Alex said Detective Girard let him into the evidence locker and he looked over the 'chute and it's not actually in bad condition. The lines just need to be replaced."

"Well, that's something at least. What about the killer's gear?" I said, thinking of the 'chute that had popped up from the backpack they'd been wearing.

"The police actually asked Alex's view on that and passed on the descriptions we all gave. It was his daughter, Sage, who figured it out. She said it had to be a BASE jumping parachute. They fit in small backpacks and it's kind of a given that you'll open them close to the ground. That's how the killer was able to jump ship so late. It also means they'd have known they'd be able to make a precision drop," Luna said and bit her lip. "Madi, do you think they were targeting the zoo on the whole, or was that body meant to end up in the tiger enclosure?"

I shook my head. I thought if we knew the answer to that question, it would be half the mystery solved.

"I don't suppose anyone around here knows someone who does BASE jumping?" I asked, knowing it was too much to hope for.

"Nope, but visitors have been known to come in and do it from near here. According to Alex, with paragliding, you don't free fall, so you jump from a place that's high up, but it doesn't have to have an immediate vertical drop. With a BASE jump, the real thrill seekers want to fall for as long as possible before deploying the 'chute. I don't know if you looked down, but there's quite a drop off here. Some people do BASE jump off the ledge, but mostly they go elsewhere to jump." Luna brushed her fine hair back from her face. "Anyone can get hold of the gear to do it and even train themselves. It's a dangerous hobby, but that's part of what draws people to it."

"Too bad no one in the village is boasting about being a secret BASE jumper."

"Is it ever that easy?" Luna asked with a grin.

"Not in my experience," I confessed.

We leant against the blue car in silence for a couple of moments.

"So, did you already load up the bag of food?" Luna asked.

"No," I replied, knowing I was about to face the music for the accident I'd had.

"Oh, well where is it?"

"Waiting for us about halfway down the mountain," I confessed.

In the end, Luna saw the funny side and was happy I hadn't followed the bag over the edge. We both kept out eyes peeled on the drive back down to the village and lo and behold, halfway down, a flash of white caught my eye. Luna stopped the car and we got out to investigate.

"Well, it doesn't look damaged," I said.

Luna nodded. "Too bad it's halfway up the only tall tree on the entire mountain."

We gave the bag of food up as lost. Although I offered to replace it, Luna let me off, saying it had been her idea to run the little experiment in the first place.

On the way back to the village we lapsed into silence. I knew we were both thinking through what we'd learnt that morning and how it hadn't been the light bulb moment we'd been expecting. The only grain of information gained was that Pascal Devereux had been the one to hire his own corpse's unorthodox method of transportation.

I wondered if when he'd been forced to make that phone call, he'd known he was going to die.

It was nice to finally have time to properly catch up with Lowell. The extra work I'd been drafted into doing and Lowell's new penchant for long walks had meant we'd hardly seen each other. Fortunately, today he'd decided to take it easy and we'd managed to meet up for a long lunch.

"Lowell, have you ever seen anyone BASE jumping on your walks?" I asked, suddenly inspired.

"No, I haven't," he replied, much to my disappointment.

I'd told him what I'd done that morning, including the inadvertent mountainside littering with a 40kg bag of dog food. I wondered what would happen when it eventually fell out of the tree. Perhaps some lucky dog owner would gain free meals for their pooch. I thought it more likely that the local fauna would work their way in. With the winter approaching, having a big bag of food lying around could be a big help to them. That was what I tried to tell myself, anyway.

I'd also told Lowell about Pascal being the one to hire the gear and my theories on how the perpetrator had grabbed the paragliding gear, returned to the car park, and then walked right back past the kiosk with a corpse attached to them. It still sounded so grisly I couldn't imagine why anyone sane would want to do it. But then, when you considered the frenzied attack on Constantine, and what had befallen Justin, it hardly painted a sane picture. That was, if you assumed the same individual was responsible for all of the happenings.

"What are you wearing tonight?" I asked, tired of thinking things over and getting nowhere. I would focus on something I could work out in a logical manner.

"My dark blue suit trousers and a white shirt with my red paisley tie," Lowell said.

I racked my brains to think of something that would go with that combination and came up blank. Perhaps logic wasn't going to help me after all.

"Madi, I know you've been busy with work and I've been off, well... having a great time, but it's going to be really nice to spend this evening together. I'm not sure if I've already said it, but thank you for inviting me to come out here with you. It's the best holiday I've ever been on," he said.

"I'm glad you're here. I don't know what I'd do if you weren't!" I told him, first thinking about the murder and then about how nice it was to have someone to share my days with - someone who was interested to hear about them. I'd been single for a long time but even when I'd been in relationships, they'd never been like this. What Lowell and I had was attraction rolled into a friendship. I thought it was the perfect mix.

"I'm sorry it's coming to an end," I said and filled him in on how little work I had left to do.

Lowell smiled and shrugged. "Don't worry about it yet. Let's enjoy it while we're still here. Where are you planning to work next?" He shot me a curious look.

"I'm not a hundred percent sure," I confessed. "Snidely and the zoo here were the only two big jobs I had on the cards. I think I may be hopping up and down the country for a bit to help some of the smaller zoos out with echidna breeding." My success with Avery Zoo's echidnas was what had garnered so much interest in my services as an animal breeding and welfare consultant in the first place.

"Well, whatever it is, I'm sure we'll find a way to be okay. You know…" he started to say, but I never got to find out what he'd been about to tell me because there was a knock on the door.

Lowell got up a little too fast to answer it, and I was left wondering just what I'd missed.

"Hey, look! Justin's out of hospital!" I heard him say and turned around to discover that the man I'd thought might be lying dead on the pavement was now upright and walking around.

"I'm so glad you're feeling okay," I said, standing up and

going over to greet them both. Justin had a pretty fat bandage wrapped around his head where he'd been hit by a blunt instrument, but other than that, he looked remarkably good.

"I hear that it's because of you that I'm in such good shape, relatively speaking," he said. "Thanks for finding me."

"It was completely by chance," I admitted. "I couldn't sleep and went for a walk, but I'm glad I did. I'm only sorry I wasn't around to see who did that to you," I said, nodding at the bandage.

Justin's smile vanished for a moment. "I'm not. Whoever did this knocked me out and left me in the street. I don't think they cared whether I was alive or dead."

No one knew what to say to that, but fortunately Adele stepped into the breach.

"We're both coming to the village celebration tonight and wanted to make sure you and Lowell knew to come find us and sit with us. We've reserved a spot next to Luna and her guest and added you both to the seating plan," Adele said with a twinkle in her eye.

I thought I had an inkling who Luna's 'guest' might be.

"I didn't even know there was a seating plan," I confessed.

"You haven't lived here your whole life. It's our responsibility to make you welcome," Adele informed us. "Are you bringing anything along? Perhaps something British?"

Despite being ignorant of the seating plan, I had known that some baking would be required.

"It might not sound British, but we did actually come up with the dish I've made. It's called chicken tikka masala," I told her.

I didn't miss the apprehensive eyebrow raise, but I couldn't blame Adele for being unsure. I only hoped I'd done the surprisingly British dish justice.

"I also made a blueberry cheesecake," I said, not knowing where that particular dessert had originated from.

"We will be sure to try it," Adele bravely promised me.

I tried not to roll my eyes at the typically French belief that English food was terrible. It wasn't all pot noodle and sausage rolls!

The sky was a deepening hue of lilac when we left the cottage that evening.

Lowell and I had spent the afternoon on the sofa, watching a TV series about a couple of supernatural detectives. It had been fun trying to guess who the killer was, only to find out it was a monster lifted from the pages of history. All things considered, we didn't have it too bad in the real world. At least no one got eaten by a wendigo.

I looked up at the pink and orange streaked sky and wondered what it would be like if summer lasted forever. The last time I'd wanted to extend a summer for so long was back when I'd been a kid on a family summer holiday that had felt like every day was a new adventure. As an adult, I was surprised the thought had crossed my mind but I understood why. The smell of woodsmoke and the gentle hum of the local musicians in the town square definitely gave me the sensation that all was right in the world, even if my adult self knew it wasn't.

A leaf from a sycamore tree floated down and landed on the cobbled road. I looked down at it and reflected that autumn was already here. Inside, I knew I welcomed the change of seasons and the call to a fresh adventure.

"Madi!"

I looked up in time to see Lowell's exasperated expression. "Sorry, I was just thinking," I said with a grin.

"You can think later. Let's get going or we'll miss all the good food," he said, inclining his head.

"Hey, the good food is right here!" I said, lifting my foil wrapped dish containing chicken tikka masala. A bowl of cooked basmati rice balanced precariously on top and my only regret was that there weren't any pappadums.

"Oops!" Lowell teased, pretending to drop the cheesecake.

"Don't you dare," I told him and strode on ahead, forcing him to hurry to keep up.

"Whoa, what's the rush?" he said with a grin.

"You reminded me that there's food on offer," I replied. "I know it's bad manners but... someone has to be first in line for the buffet, right?"

"Oh, Madi," he said, with that funny look in his eyes again. "Never change."

Adele waved us over as soon as we walked into the square. The place was packed and it was clear that the entire village had turned out for the celebration. I recognised Madame Devereux, her son who'd been so distraught the other day, and a woman who must be the fabled daughter. I exchanged nods with various faces I recognised from the zoo when I walked through the crowd to leave my offerings at the vast table of food.

"Wow, this is going to be a good night," Lowell said, echoing my thoughts exactly.

I placed my dishes down and looked up into his dark eyes. The last streaks of colour in the sky made them light up and I before I knew it, I found myself kissing him.

When I pulled away I turned to see Mr Flannigan staring at us.

"They really did invite everyone," I muttered, less than thrilled that he'd turned up.

I pointedly walked into the crowd with Lowell by my

side. Unfortunately, I didn't think Mr Flannigan understood such subtle means of being told to stop being a creep.

I nodded at Detective Girard, who returned the greeting with a thin-lipped smile that hinted to me that not a lot of progress was being made down at the police station. Then I said hello to Nathan and his girlfriend, Sage. Having briefly seen her father through the window of a booth that morning, I couldn't really see the resemblance. Alex wore thick-lensed glasses and had an impressively thick moustache. Sage had neither of these things.

Her hair had a reddish hue that I wasn't sure was natural, but was incredibly pretty, and her nose turned up just a little at the end, which made her look cute. Despite her appearance, there was something in her eyes that let me know this was definitely a girl who liked to throw herself off high places. She was wild, and I wasn't entirely convinced that Nathan had got the memo.

"They're meant to be next to be engaged, you know."

I turned to find Madame Myrtle - the woman I'd met when Luna, Adele, and I had paid our condolences to Madame Devereux - standing there.

"That's interesting," I said, politely, thinking of Nathan's wandering eyes. I doubted he was ready for a commitment as big as marriage. I thought Sage would probably feel the same way, although perhaps for different reasons.

"Oh my gosh! Don't look now, but Enzo is here with another woman!" Luna said, coming up behind me and grabbing my arm.

Despite her warning, I turned and looked. The gendarme had just walked into the square with the daughter of the boulangerie owner, who often worked in the shop with him. I'd always thought she looked like she was still in her teens, so I was surprised to see her with Enzo. She was also wearing the shortest miniskirt I'd ever seen. It made me nervous every time she took a step.

"I wonder what his wife thinks of that," Madame Myrtle contributed, clearly delighted that there would be some new gossip around town tomorrow.

I turned back to Luna, but Alcide had arrived and they were already pretty engrossed in each other. I wasn't the only who noticed. Madame Myrtle let out an 'ooh!' of interest and when my gaze returned to Enzo and his date, I thought he looked ready to come over and punch Alcide. I hoped Luna had seen fit to warn her new beau about her awful ex.

After Luna and Alcide had broken apart with glowing faces, we all went in search of Justin and Adele and found them already sitting at the table.

"Come on, grab a plate! Everyone's still chatting and someone needs to get the eating going," Adele said.

I thought I might be about to faint with happiness.

"Oh wow," I kept saying, over and over, as I opened dishes and lifted foil. There were so many amazing looking foods - most of them heavy on the butter, cream, and cheese. It was heavenly.

Adele asked me to point her in the direction of what I'd brought and she spooned a bit of chicken tikka masala out onto her plate, looking at it doubtfully. "It smells nice... a little spicy," she said in surprise.

I hid my smile, remembering that the French tended to think we Brits only cooked bland food. My tikka masala had a little more of a kick than it usually did.

Justin stuck a fork into Adele's portion, prompting her to shout 'hey!'.

"That's pretty good," Justin admitted.

"Would you care to put that in writing and publish it to

the world? 'Frenchman admits Englishwoman's cooking is 'pretty good'," I joked.

"Whoa now, they'd take my citizenship away!" Justin joked back.

People had noticed us diving into the offerings and now a queue of people formed behind us. I finished serving myself a little bit of everything interesting, wishing I had a bigger plate.

We sat down at the long table. Nathan and Sage arrived a few moments later with their plates piled as high as mine and sat down next to Lowell and me. I couldn't help sneaking a look at Adele to see if she was aware of Nathan's deliberate seating choice, but she wasn't looking my way.

"Thanks for visiting my dad today. He really enjoyed speaking to you," Sage said to Luna, who blushed. I avoided making eye contact.

"That's okay, I just fancied a trip up the mountain, you know?" she said.

"I thought you were scared of heights. All these years I've never been able to get you to go paragliding. Have you finally conquered your fear?" Sage asked with a twinkle in her eye.

Luna shook her head. "No, but that's why I went up there. I wanted a small dose of fear to conquer," she blustered.

Sage nodded, but I wasn't convinced she didn't have a shrewd idea of why Luna had really gone up there.

"Oh, Luna, you must try it! It's amazing! Sage has been teaching me and I did my first solo jump the other day. Enzo jumped at the same time. It was great!" Nathan said.

Sage jabbed him in the ribs and his face morphed into horror. "Sorry! I didn't mean…"

"It's fine," Luna said, remarkably casually considering the way Enzo had made her gnash her teeth at the police station. "I deserve better than him and I've finally found my perfect match," she said, smiling at Alcide who looked fondly back.

I realised that Luna was someone who was quick to love. I only hoped that Alcide was the same and that he wasn't the kind of man who messed women around. From what I knew of the man so far, he seemed decent and passionate about what he did. *Sometimes to a fault*, I mentally added, thinking about the way he'd made it hard for me to argue that the squirrel monkeys should be returned to their enclosure.

"Huh!" I said, having a sudden thought.

"What is it?" Lowell asked but I shook my head at him.

"Nothing, it's work. I just suddenly thought that if the squirrel monkeys stay on the loose, their enclosure could be converted into an aviary for the macaws and African grey parrots," I told him and then apologised for bringing it up when we were supposed to be having some time off.

"Inspiration strikes where it may," Lowell said, lifting a hand to brush back one of my wild tendrils of blonde hair.

"The plot thickens," Adele said, sliding into the chair next to me. "I just saw Juliet Argent walk in with Detective Prideaux. Wonders never cease! I thought the man was married to his job."

I thought back to my exchanges with Detective Prideaux and had to agree with Adele. I wondered how Juliet had managed to distract the detective from his job long enough to get him to agree to attend with her. I also wondered if Detective Prideaux knew that he was just a pawn in the sparring lovers' games.

"This is actually not so bad," Adele told me after she'd made a suitable amount of fuss over taking a bite of the curry.

"Told you we can cook," I said, feeling slightly proud to be British.

Unfortunately, Enzo chose this moment to walk in front of our table and throw a suspicion filled look Adele's way.

My culinary success was forgotten when she swore under her breath.

"He's got it into his head that I'm guilty of something. He thinks I might have been the one who stabbed Constantine because her bag appeared on my bonnet."

"Lucky for us, he's not the one in charge," I said, thinking of the trouble Luna would be in, too.

"You're Madi aren't you?" A woman had come up behind me.

I nodded and looked questioningly at Adele, but she'd already turned back to her conversation with Justin.

"May I have a word?" The strange woman asked.

I threw Lowell an apologetic look as I pushed myself to my feet, but he was chatting happily with Alcide and didn't even notice I'd moved.

"What can I do for you?" I asked, when we were a little way away from the crowd in the darker shadows by the trees. For a moment, I was reminded that there was a killer on the loose… and I'd just walked off somewhere where I couldn't be seen with a woman I'd never met before.

"So sorry to take you away from the party like this, but I only thought it was fair to tell you."

The woman wrung her hands and I wondered what terrible truth was about to be sprung upon me.

"It's my neighbour, Ambre, she's been stalking your partner. I don't like to pry but I've seen her following him and then dithering around, like she's plucking up the courage to approach him. I just wanted you to know."

"Oh," was all I could think to say. It was odd enough that a strange woman had pulled me aside to let me know her suspicions, but even stranger to think that someone might be chasing Lowell in such an unusual fashion. I knew full well that Lowell was attractive enough to draw attention, but I couldn't fathom what he might have done to warrant a stalker.

"Perhaps I should have a word with her?" I ventured, but the woman looked stressed.

"What will you say? She'll know I told you!"

I didn't buy her concern for a second. She hadn't brought me aside to tell me this information out of the goodness of her heart; she wanted to start some drama.

"I'll think of something," I assured her, still unsure of what - if anything - I was going to do. "Enjoy your evening," I said, but the woman was already murmuring something about the raffle starting and drifted away before I'd finished.

I was left standing on the edge of the village square looking back in on the revelling villagers. I realised that the woman I'd spoken to hadn't exactly given me a clear description of who Ambre was. I shrugged my shoulders and figured there was nothing to be done about it. I'd warn Lowell that he might have someone after him, but he could look after himself. What's more, I trusted him, I realised. A lot had changed since we'd first met and he'd kept his cards so close to his chest it had nearly got him killed. We'd built a pretty decent relationship.

I walked back towards the festivities and arrived just in time to see Luna jump for joy when her raffle ticket number was called out. She ran up to the little stage that had been erected by the fountain and claimed her prize - a ridiculously large bottle of wine from the vineyard at the edge of the valley. By the laughter of some of the other villagers, I wasn't so sure it was a prize you wanted to win, but Luna seemed happy.

The announcer moved on to the next ticket number and I carried on making my way through the crowd. I walked past an elderly couple, eagerly holding onto their tickets, and happened to witness the moment when Luna walked straight into Enzo. I watched as his eyes slid up and down her body, before Luna tossed her hair and made to walk passed him. He reached out a hand and grabbed her arm, saying something to her. Even as I moved forwards to step in, she'd already shaken him off. I heard a sound of disgust from behind me and discovered I hadn't been the only one to witness the little exchange. The other gendarme, whom Luna had informed me was Enzo's ex-wife, shook her head. I thought about telling her that none of this had anything to do with Luna and everything to do with Enzo, but it seemed futile. All I could do was hope that she knew the man she'd married well enough to realise exactly whose fault it was that various women were being rubbed in her face.

I was nearly back at the table, where my food still waited, when someone grabbed my arm and made me jump.

"I didn't mean to startle you but please... I must talk to you," a woman with eyes as hungry as my belly said.

I resigned myself to it being the night of the wild women. "Are you Ambre, by any chance?" I asked and the woman turned white.

"Who told you? What else did they...?" She shook her head. "It doesn't matter. Please, I have to talk to you in private."

"Right now?" I said, trying to look around for Lowell. This was a woman who had been described as stalking him. I wasn't sure I wanted to go anywhere on my own with her.

"Please," she repeated, and there was something in her eyes that made me relent. This woman looked desperate, but not violent.

We walked away from the crowd, returning to the spot where I'd previously spoken with this woman's neighbour.

"What can I do for you?" I asked, still feeling a little nervous about her intentions.

"I've been trying to speak to the man you're with for a

whole week but no one ever answers your phone. He's a detective, isn't he?" Ambre burst out.

I immediately revised my opinion about her intentions towards Lowell. This was clearly about something else.

"He's a private detective but he's on holiday right now," I said, speaking carefully.

"He's definitely not working on a case?" the woman affirmed, looking harried.

"He's not. He'd have told me," I said, feeling ninety percent sure that it was true. I hoped it was true, anyway.

Her face flashed with relief for all of a second before she returned to looking concerned. "You saw Monsieur Devereux the day he fell, didn't you?"

I nodded. It was common knowledge in the village by now.

"Did he say anything? You know, before he died?" she asked.

Then it came to me in a flash of blinding reason. Ambre was the one in witness protection.

"He was already dead before he hit the ground, so nothing was said."

We made eye contact with each other and I knew she'd seen the knowledge I now held reflected in my eyes.

"It's not me, it's my husband. He committed a crime a long, long time ago. After he was released from prison, it became clear we weren't going to be able to have normal lives again. The hate against him was so extreme that the police gave us new identities. Paul and I both changed the way we looked as much as we could afford to and settled down here in L'airelle. We'd only been living here a couple of years when Pascal returned from working in England. He recognised us right away, as the case had been so big and he had all these connections. We were worried then, but he promised us he was a professional and would never reveal our secret. But when he died..." She trailed off.

"You thought he might have told someone the truth. Perhaps that was even the reason someone murdered him," I filled in, solemnly. "I can't vouch for what he said before he died, but for someone to kill him, I'd have thought Pascal must have made them very angry indeed." I left the implication hanging.

"Thank you," Ambre said. "You've put my mind a little more at ease. I just hope this all blows over. I like our life here."

"I hope it works out for you," I told her, still wondering over our strange conversation.

She nodded at me and then disappeared back towards the crowd, probably wanting to avoid being seen talking for too long, just in case. I wondered what it must be like to live in fear all the time and hoped I would never find out.

I wandered back towards the party.

This time I almost made it.

My eyes caught a flash of movement as something dark and tawny darted across the edge of the square.

Surely not, I thought as my eyes followed the movement. Unfortunately, my initial suspicion was proved correct.

"Alcide will have to see sense now," I muttered, before stalking off to find the primate keeper to let him know that the squirrel monkeys had escaped the zoo and come to join in the party in the village.

"Hey, where have you been?" Lowell asked when I appeared by his side, still searching for Alcide. He slid a hand around my waist and when I looked up, I thought his eyes looked warmed by the alcohol and something else, too.

I wished I was able to relax and enjoy the evening, but so far it hadn't exactly been uneventful.

"I've got to find Alcide. The squirrel monkeys have somehow got over the security fences and are now in the village," I quickly told him when he looked a little put out that I'd mentioned Alcide. It was bad, but I felt a little glow inside that Lowell cared enough to be jealous.

"So, where have you been?" he repeated, as we forged our way through the throng, both searching.

"I'll tell you later," I promised him, with what I hoped was a significant look. There were eyes and ears everywhere in the village and I didn't want to spill any secrets.

We located Luna and Alcide next to Justin and Adele, watching the live band, which consisted of an acoustic guitarist, a trumpet player, and a double bassist.

"The squirrel monkeys are loose in the village," I told Alcide, quite primly if truth be told.

"Bless them, they wanted to join the party," he said, flashing Luna a grin.

My triumphant mood faded a little.

He saw my expression and inclined his head. "I'm just messing with you. We should probably do something about it in a minute or two."

I was about to correct his use of 'we' when a loud screeching broke out. A woman ran screaming from the buffet table, while a monkey threw grapes at her retreating figure.

I looked back at Alcide.

"Okay, I guess I should go and do something now," he said, reluctantly slipping away from Luna.

I wondered what he had in mind to make the monkeys follow him back up to the zoo. They had all the food they ever wanted down here and I had a sneaking suspicion that they rather enjoyed preying on people, too.

I turned away with a grim smile. For once, it wasn't my problem. I'd already given my advice and it hadn't been taken.

Alcide didn't return, but the five of us who remained

had a great time dancing to the band. It felt like no time had passed at all when the band wished everyone good night and the village mayor took to the stage. He thanked everyone for coming and made a joke about the uninvited, furry guests. Then he wished us all goodnight and safe journeys home (ha ha!). I found I was able to understand almost all of this and wondered if my French was improving.

"Luna, have you seen Alcide?" I asked, walking faster to catch her when we started to make our joint pilgrimage home.

When I spoke, she looked up and I just saw the last few traces of distress on her face before they disappeared. I wondered what had upset her.

"No, I think he's still chasing the monkeys." She quickly smiled at me. "We had a great date up until then, and someone really does need to catch them."

I knew she was trying to reassure me that I'd done the right thing, but I could still hear the disappointment in her voice.

I opened my mouth to let her know I could see how much Alcide liked her, but when I looked up, she was on the ground with a man on top of her.

"Luna!" I said, getting down on my knees and reaching for her arm.

"I'm okay," she said after a few moments, looking at me with frightened eyes.

Something red and sticky dripped onto the cobblestones.

"You're bleeding!" I said, but she shook her head.

"I don't think it's mine. Can you help me up?"

I turned my attention to the man on top of her for the first time and realised it was Enzo Argent. His eyes were wide, but even as I tried to see what was wrong, he'd pushed himself up off Luna and onto his feet. He staggered backwards and Detective Prideaux was miraculously there to catch him.

"Call an ambulance!" I shouted, faintly realising what had happened.

"I'll go! There's a phone in the village hall," Nathan said, rushing away from the group that had quickly gathered.

While I pulled Luna off the road and checked her over, the detective barked out orders.

"Girard, go and radio the station," he told the long suffering detective, who hurried off towards the row of parked cars.

I looked across the street in time to see the second agent, Ms Borel, get out of a car. Had she been spying on us all night? I had no idea what she might be looking for, but perhaps she had seen something after all.

I left Luna with Adele and Justin, who'd both turned around as soon as they realised their friend might be hurt.

"Did you see what happened?" I asked Ms Borel, even as Enzo was hissing through his teeth while Sage applied pressure to the wound. The paragliding instructor evidently had a wealth of first aid training and was used to being cool in a crisis.

"Right - nobody leaves!" Detective Prideaux yelled, the most animated I'd seen him yet.

Everyone froze in place.

"I've called the ambulance. They should be here in two minutes," Nathan announced, reappearing at the front of the crowd.

Enzo complained loudly about the agony he was in, which I took to mean that he wasn't in mortal danger.

"Was he stabbed?" I asked Detective Girard, who was helping her other colleagues present to round up everyone who'd been in the vicinity. The boulangerie owner's daughter then appeared, making a dreadful fuss over Enzo, which he bore with all the grace of someone who is severely regretting picking the youngest and silliest woman he could find to make his exes feel jealous. I suddenly wondered why he'd been so close behind Luna without his date. Had he been about to make another pass at her?

It wasn't long before reinforcements arrived. Enzo was led into the ambulance and driven away, while the police searched the rest of us for the missing knife.

They didn't find it.

It was as if the knife had disappeared into thin air. The police took statements from everyone and we were allowed to make our way home, the party mood well and truly faded.

"You'll be okay?" Adele said to Luna, who nodded gratefully. Alcide had abandoned the monkeys and come running as soon as the news about Luna's fall had reached him.

"I'll look after her," he promised and we all wished one another goodnight.

"If I didn't know better, I'd say he set the whole situation up, just so he would have an excuse for not getting the monkeys back home," I said to Lowell when we were back over the threshold of our own home. "You saw Ms Borel, didn't you?" I added, suddenly concerned that Lowell had been awfully quiet.

He nodded. "Yes. Flannigan's been integrating himself with the community while she's been observing from the outside. It's a standard technique."

I raised my eyebrows at the description of Flannigan as 'integrating with the community'. In my opinion, he wouldn't win any medals for the job he was doing.

"Hey, you know those phone calls…" I began and quickly filled him in on what Ambre had told me.

"I thought there probably was someone hiding here," Lowell acknowledged when I'd shared the truth with him.

He rubbed his dark stubble for a moment. "Why attack Enzo Argent? He surely wasn't privy to any knowledge."

"Constantine can't have known either, if Ambre's telling the truth," I added, also thinking. "These attacks… they're not for information. They seem motivated by pure hate. What if the person responsible just likes hurting people?" I hypothesised.

Lowell shrugged. "Why come out of the woodwork now? Something must have changed. There has to be a catalyst."

"I hope it's nothing to do with us," I said, acknowledging the fact that, to my knowledge, everything had been just fine in the little village before we'd arrived. Since then, there'd been murder and stabbings galore!

There was also Lowell's history with Pascal Devereux to consider. Was this the work of a ghost from the past?

"It's probably not anything to do with us. You said you thought it was targeted at Adele, right?" Lowell commented, although I wasn't sure how seriously he was taking it.

"Yes, but Enzo doesn't really fit in with that." Then I thought about it. "She did mention he'd been hounding her about Constantine's bag, trying to get her to confess to the crime."

"Hey!" I said, suddenly having another thought. "Nathan said that Enzo had taken paragliding lessons at the same time as him."

"So we can add another potential murder suspect to the list of almost everyone in the village who knows how to paraglide. Anyway, I thought it was a different sort of parachuting that they were good at?" he said.

"Yeah, BASE jumping. I suppose you're right." I shook my head. "I'm just not seeing it right now."

Lowell walked over to the cupboard and pulled out a bottle of brandy. I grabbed some milk and heated it on the stove, before pouring it onto some hot chocolate powder. After a moment's thought, I added a dab of brandy.

"You just said that Nathan knows how to paraglide, too," Lowell said, playing devil's advocate, but it sparked a memory of something in my mind.

"Nathan mentioned he likes Adele. He also ran off to call the ambulance, so could have hidden the knife," I said, a feeling of dread setting in.

Was Nathan the coldblooded killer? I could see his motivation for the recent attacks, but the elaborate dispatch of Pascal Devereux still seemed a mystery to me. Also, if he and Enzo were both still taking lessons, it was more than likely that they weren't responsible for Pascal's plummet. Even now, I could still see the artful way the jumper had controlled the parachute and drifted away from the zoo to make their escape after the deed was done. There was, however, one person close to Nathan who definitely would have had the skill to do all of that…

"Maybe there's more than one thing going on here," I mused, taking a sip of my pleasantly spiked hot chocolate.

"All right, Nancy Drew. I'm sure the police are looking for the knife right now," Lowell assured me with a wry smile. "We'll know tomorrow morning if they find it."

I nodded, unsure what to hope for. If the police did uncover the blade hidden in the village hall, that would be it for Nathan. Despite the evidence pointing his way, I didn't want to believe that he could be responsible for all of the horrible happenings. I'd assumed he had a harmless crush on Adele, but had I deliberately ignored the warning signs?

8

LIVING IN FEAR

"You got the monkeys back," I said by way of greeting to Alcide.

We were both on our way to the weekly meeting of zookeepers. I was looking forward to telling Monsieur Quebec that I was practically finished with my review, but also saddened by the prospect of saying goodbye to the idyllic lifestyle and the new friends I'd made.

"Once the food from the party had been cleaned up, they were back at the gates asking to be let in. They know which side their bread is buttered," he told me.

I considered renewing my argument that the zoo should figure out a way to keep the monkeys in their intended habitat - both for their safety and the public's - but half of me agreed with Alcide. The small, furry devils were happy with their freedom. If the lax French laws meant that the zoo could get away with letting the monkeys roam, perhaps they should be allowed to carry on.

"Is Luna okay?" I asked.

"Yeah, she's fine. She was a bit shaken by someone getting stabbed right behind her. Although, after she'd had a few drinks to calm her nerves, she said she was just surprised it had taken someone so long to stab Enzo." He raised an eyebrow at me.

I figured Alcide would know as much as anyone about Luna's past relationship. That was the way things worked in the village. "I wouldn't blame his ex-wife if she was the one who did it," I confided.

"She wasn't anywhere nearby, apparently. From what I gather, she'd stayed back to talk with her neighbours when Detective Prideaux was near the action. I guess their date didn't go that well," he said, with a twinkle in his eye.

"Luckily for her," I agreed, thinking that she would definitely have been suspect number one if she had been in the vicinity.

We reached the restaurant and climbed the stairs at the back of the building to go into the large room above. It was a place that seemed to be perpetually stuffy and had the same smell as a school classroom.

Luna and Adele were already in there, along with a slew of other familiar faces. I felt another pang when I realised I'd be saying goodbye so soon.

"Hi," I said, moving to sit next to Adele, so Alcide could have the spot by Luna.

"Justin's home with the puppies today. Jolie's having a bit of trouble nursing them all and has a bit of a snuffle coming on. They've already grown so much! I can't believe it," Adele whispered, while Monsieur Quebec walked to the front of the room and paused to shuffle a few papers.

"Has the father been round to inspect his brood?" I quipped, remembering that the suspected father's owner would not be in favour of the rather unusual union.

Adele smiled. "No, but I have it on good authority that someone told her that the puppies look just like miniature versions of her dog. You won't believe it, but she's actually coming round to see about getting one! Wonders never cease. I just hope she's not going to charge us for the stud."

"I'm sure she wouldn't dare," I said, thinking of the wayward behaviour of dogs.

"If she does want one, I'll give it to her for nothing, of course," Adele said, willing to acknowledge that much. "I think her boy is already getting on. That's the problem with big breeds like Great Danes, they have such tragic life expectancies. Hopefully crossing one with a Labrador will make for a more hardy dog. I think that's why she's so interested. It's nice when people finally convert to looking beyond breeding."

"I hope many more people get to thinking that way," I said, reminded of the many health problems that a lot of overbred dogs faced. Even Adele's Dogue De Bordeaux had breathing problems. I knew they'd got him from a rescue centre, but it was surely time that others woke up and stopped breeding such negative traits, merely to create a desirable appearance.

Zoos faced the same problem. I was always horrified by the tales of white tigers in captivity. They'd long been bred for their looks, as any effort at conservation would be far more concerned by the animals' health. The gene pool was so small that many of their young died and others had grown up with serious deformities caused by so much inbreeding.

Monsieur Quebec finished shuffling his papers and we all lapsed into a near silence. He cleared his throat and looked around the room. Suddenly, I sensed that what he was about to say wasn't going to be pleasant. Hesitation hung over the usually forthcoming manager.

"I'm very sorry to announce that Constantine Duval passed away in hospital last night," he said.

The silence in the room now seemed cavernous. I felt as though someone should stand up and say something about her - share a fond memory perhaps - but I knew full well that there was no one here who had anything good to say. It didn't seem fair that someone who'd died so tragically didn't have anything to recommend her memory, but that was the way Constantine had chosen to live her life.

I spared a thought to think about her ageing mother and wondered who would care for her now Constantine was gone. I hoped that in the wake of her death, people would find out about the more caring side of her nature and perhaps understand more about why she'd behaved the way she had. Somehow, I doubted few would spend long on thoughts of Constantine.

Monsieur Quebec pressed on with the notices and that was all Constantine became - a small announcement at the start of the weekly meeting.

I hung back at the end to discuss a time with Monsieur Quebec where I'd present my review of the zoo and talk about ways to move L'airelle forward. When the moment came for me to walk out of the room, I found it wasn't as empty as I'd thought. Mr Flannigan was waiting in a chair at the back of the room and I could tell he wanted to speak to me.

"It's tragic about Constantine, isn't it?" I said, figuring that speaking about something sad was the only way I'd manage to remain polite with this odious man.

"Yes, it's a shame," he allowed. "I wanted you to know that we've moved Mr and Mrs Chanterelle."

"Ambre?" I asked, and he nodded.

"It seemed like the best thing to do. We've already spent too long in this backwater village. If you can't be certain of the truth, it's best to take every precaution."

I inclined my head to show agreement but I couldn't help but feel sorry for Ambre Chanterelle. She had told me that she liked her life in L'airelle and now she'd have to start all over again, someplace new. All because a man who'd known the truth had died.

"Did the police ever find out exactly how Pascal died?" I asked.

Mr Flannigan shrugged his shoulders. "Not really. The impact damaged the cadaver a lot. They think it might have been suffocation or strangulation, but it could just have easily been blunt force trauma to the head. It's complicated," he said, as if that settled it.

"I don't suppose anyone found the knife that was used to stab Enzo either," I said. I knew they hadn't. The gossip queens would have been all over it, and I hadn't heard a peep.

"No, but it's still being investigated. The crime scene was secured but several of the force thought it prudent that they investigate more thoroughly this morning," Flannigan skirted.

I took that to mean that the police had drunk a little too much last night.

"Mr Argent is already out of hospital," Flannigan continued.

I knew I should feel bad for not asking, but I'd seen every nasty side that Enzo Argent had to offer over the past few days.

I waited for a couple of seconds before I realised that Mr Flannigan had clearly concluded what he'd wanted to talk to me about.

"If you get the chance, wish Ambre all the best from me," I said, knowing it would never happen.

Flannigan nodded insincerely and I turned to leave.

"Did you find anything out at the paragliding place?"

I stopped walking and looked at him.

"I watched you and Ms Fleur. The dog food was an interesting idea. That was to represent a body, yes?"

"You were watching," I said.

It wasn't a question but Flannigan nodded anyway. "That's the job. We come in, and we watch and wait. Sooner or later, someone does something suspicious."

I threw him a curious look but there wasn't a trace of humour on his face.

"If you were watching, then you'll know we didn't jump for joy when we discovered who killed Monsieur Devereux. All we learned was that it was possible to drag a body past the paragliding kiosk and jump off without being spotted."

"It was the likeliest theory," Flannigan said and I tried not to bristle.

"Well, someone has to test these things," I said, shortly. I was actually rather annoyed that I hadn't known anyone was watching - especially when I'd managed to drop the bag off the edge of the mountain.

"So, you're with Lowell Adagio?" Mr Flannigan said, abruptly changing the subject.

"Yes," I said, hoping that keeping my answers short would end this uncomfortable encounter.

"You're aware he worked with Mr Devereux in the past?"

"Yes, he told me."

"Don't you think it's strange that Mr Devereux dies one week after his old colleague rolls into town?" Flannigan pressed.

"I think it's strange that anyone could be driven to murder another human being, but it still happened. If you thought Lowell was responsible, you wouldn't be here asking me questions, you'd be talking to him." I considered it for a second. "It looks to me as though you have too many maybes and no real answers. My advice would be to stop wasting your time talking to people and look at the facts you have on paper. Perhaps then you'll see the real picture."

That was the way I worked when I wrote my reviews for zoos.

"Interesting," was all Flannigan had to say. "You haven't known Lowell for long, have you?"

And with that ominous final statement, he nodded at me and walked out of the room.

I watched him go and didn't spot a single bead of sweat on his neck, despite the thick suit he wore and the stuffiness of the room. Mr Flannigan was a strange man indeed.

I wasn't sure what to think about what he'd just hinted about Lowell, but I knew it was going to be on my mind for a long time.

As I walked back through the zoo, stopping only to watch the Pallas's cats in their pursuit of the spider horde, a thought popped into my head. Could the agent be the one doing it all? He'd come to town after the first murder, but since then... the chocolates had arrived seconds before he'd turned up, and the paint on Adele's dog had been after he'd seen us at the vets with Jolie. Had he developed an obsession with Adele and thought leaving these strange offerings were the way to gain her interest?

I pulled a strand of wayward hair back from my face and hooked it over the arm of my red rimmed glasses. I didn't have much experience with all-consuming obsessions, but could Flannigan have really developed a fascination so instantaneously? *Unless he's been in the village for a longer time,* I suddenly thought... a conspiracy theory already forming in my mind. What if he'd been watching Pascal, the ex-detective, to make sure he wasn't up to anything? Lowell's coincidental arrival in the same village could have ignited suspicions that the pair were planning something that might jeopardise the secretive agency they'd both worked for in the past. Flannigan might have decided to eliminate one of the conspiring pair to stop the plot from going any further.

I walked past the ocelots without giving them a second glance, I was so distracted. Even if my wild theory was correct, why had Flannigan gone to such great lengths to drop Pascal Devereux's corpse in the tiger enclosure?

A thought I'd toyed with before hit me hard.

Offerings... what if he'd been around the village long enough that he'd known Pascal had given Adele that unfair ticket? He had needed to kill the man anyway, but delivering him to the tiger enclosure -where he knew Adele would be - could be his twisted idea of doing her a favour.

It was like a cat bringing their owner a mouse.

I chewed on my lip as I hesitated outside the tiki hut. Was this theory completely crazy? If Flannigan really had turned into some obsessive vigilante, Lowell would be the best person to speak to. With his connection to Ms Borel, he might be able to uncover the truth and stop things from going any further.

Unless she's in on the plot, too! I thought and something else occurred to me at the same time. If the agents had turned up long before Pascal's death, what if Lowell had known about that, too?

I sighed. These thoughts were running wild in my head. I didn't have a shred of evidence that suggested the agents were here for anything more than to investigate the risk to Ambre Chanterelle and her husband. Everything else was just conjecture.

Despite my return to rational thinking, I couldn't help but dwell upon Flannigan's last words about Lowell. Was it a strangely formed threat against my boyfriend, or was it a genuine warning about his past?

Either way, Flannigan's character and motivations remained opaque.

"Hi Madi, how's it going?" Adele asked when she came into the hut that afternoon.

I blinked and rubbed my eyes, suddenly aware of how much time had passed while I'd been working on my laptop. I looked at the screen in front of me and realised I was just one paragraph away from completing my review. I would be speaking to Monsieur Quebec tomorrow and then it would be time to go back to England.

"Pretty good," I said, replying to Adele. "How are things with you?"

"Okay, considering," Adele said, plumping down onto the sofa. I was suddenly reminded of Constantine's sorry fate.

"People are more concerned about the new threat of reckless violence than anything else," Adele said, following my train of thought.

"I don't think it's reckless," I told her and then regretted it when Adele threw me a sharp look. I'd forgotten that Justin had so recently been the victim of the same violence.

"I just mean, I think someone's doing it for a reason. They must have something against the victims," I said, as vaguely as possible. I didn't want Adele to think that she might be the reason these acts were being committed. I would hate for her to blame herself for what her husband had been through.

"No one has anything against Justin," she protested, looking sad for a moment.

I speculated that he may not be as fully recovered as the pair had presented.

"He remembered something more, you know," she said and I pricked up my ears. "It's not really significant, but he thinks he may have seen someone snooping around near the house. Perhaps he surprised them and that's why they attacked him." She shrugged. "It could have been an attempted house robbery. I'm just glad..." She trailed off. It somehow seemed in bad taste to be happy that Justin had escaped with his life when Constantine had lost hers.

"Have you heard anything more about what happened last night?" I asked, knowing Adele had been out and about in the zoo, while I'd been stuck inside working on the review.

"Well, I saw Nathan a bit earlier and he wasn't very happy. The police apparently gave him a bit of a hard time and combed the village hall. He was made to feel like suspect number one, which I think he took really hard. It is scary when the police focus their attention on you," she said, clearly thinking of the way she'd fallen under suspicion for the bag that had been left on her car.

"They didn't find the knife?" I prompted.

She shook her head. "No. They scared the life out of Nathan but they didn't find a thing. He's off the hook. He was so upset, I gave him a hug. He seemed a bit brighter after that," she told me with a twinkle in her eye that let me know she knew exactly how Nathan felt about her and knew how to handle it, too.

"Where did it go then?" I mused, thinking about the impossible vanishing act that had occurred.

Adele put her hands behind her head and looked thoughtful. "I was too far away to see, but the theory floating around is that Prideaux spent too much time checking Enzo was okay before he cordoned off the area. Someone could have thrown the knife far away before anyone noticed what had happened. Or perhaps they concealed it somewhere. Even if the police did find it, they have no way of knowing who it belongs to now. They've got away with it."

I didn't miss the anger in her voice. She was thinking about Justin when she said it.

"So, in conclusion, most people think that it's Enzo's fault for making a fuss?" I joked and was glad when it raised a smile.

"Like you wouldn't believe. Apparently, he's off work today but is hanging out in the café, waiting for the well-wishers to pour in."

"He might be waiting a while," I said with a shrewd smile.

Adele nodded, but her good humour was fading again. "I just hope this all gets sorted out, or L'airelle will be a different place. We aren't used to living in fear. I know it's old fashioned, but no one locks their doors here. I don't want that to change."

I nodded in agreement. I hoped that the perpetrator would be caught soon, too, but I had the feeling that the authorities were just as baffled as I was, as to who was responsible.

All we could do was wait and hope the culprit didn't kill again.

9

A GRAVE OCCASION

I'd forgotten that it was the day of the funeral.

Monsieur Quebec had reminded me when we'd scheduled our meeting at the end of the previous day. I'd been about to suggest the next morning when he'd reminded me that we'd all be going along to Pascal's funeral.

I still didn't feel as though I should be going along to the funeral of a man I'd never met, but Lowell had known him, and I didn't want to make him go alone. I knew what he'd told me of his shared past with Pascal, but I had no idea if they ever had been close.

I was also unwilling to let him go alone whilst I still retained my suspicions about Mr Flannigan. I hadn't had a chance to voice my concerns to Lowell, as I hadn't been able to think of a way to say it without bringing into question his past and my faith that he'd been completely honest with me.

I'd dressed in my one and only black dress, which I couldn't help but feel a little self-conscious in. It was a black cocktail dress and hardly appropriate funeral attire. I just hoped no one would notice me, hiding behind Lowell.

To my relief, we sat at the back of the little chapel, which was already packed with the rest of the village. It didn't escape my notice that no one seemed too upset by the occasion. I got the sense that the majority of people were here to witness any further drama Nicholas Devereux might have to dish out. Perhaps there were some well-wishers, too, but despite not knowing Pascal, I'd still got the impression that he hadn't been particularly well-liked.

Just like Constantine, my brain supplied, drawing parallels. Perhaps if it had just been Pascal, Constantine, and Enzo who'd been targeted I might have believed that all of this was just some long-suffering villager who'd finally snapped and decided some social cleansing was in order. But Justin, to my knowledge, didn't fit the remit. I sighed silently and tried to focus on what the vicar was saying.

Louis Devereux got to her feet and walked over to the lectern, delivering a few words in French. My knowledge of the language wasn't good enough to follow along but I could see plain as day that Louis Devereux was blooming. The difference between her appearance when Adele, Luna, and I had visited her after her husband's demise and now was astonishing. Her cheeks had colour in them and she'd lost the pinched, starving look which had marked her face.

I wondered what her children thought, knowing what they did about their father's drinking problem and the abuse it had brought with it. Did they now regret not stepping in after bearing witness to how much their mother had benefitted from their father's absence?

Nicholas Devereux got to his feet and a ripple went through the congregation as people sat up and hoped for a show. The frown line between Nicholas' eyes showed he knew it, too. The speech he gave can't have been what the villagers were hoping for as a lot of them returned to snoozing halfway through.

It was a relief when the service finally came to a close and everyone filed out of the church.

"Excuse me for a moment," Lowell said, touching my arm before moving through the crowd. I watched him go and my gaze collided with that of Ms Borel's. Something about her gave me the creeps. I wondered what Lowell was going to say to her and knew that Flannigan's words were still on my mind.

I turned to walk out of the church and found myself face to face with the agent himself.

"Do you have any more investigating planned for the rest of the day?" he asked. There was something I thought was meant to pass for a smile on his face.

I threw him a sideways look, unsure if he was making fun of me. "No. I'm handing in my review of L'airelle Zoological Park and then it'll be time to go back home," I told him.

"Back to not so sunny Sussex, eh?"

I tried not to think too much about how obvious it was that he'd investigated me. I'd known about it before, when the police had revealed their knowledge of my past brushes with the law, but here he was, flaunting his knowledge.

"Probably," I said, hoping it would end the conversation.

It didn't.

Instead, he continued to walk next to me out of the church.

"Could we go for a drink before you leave? I like you," he told me.

I was so surprised I made full eye contact with him.

"No thank you," I said.

"Is it because you're with Lowell?" There was something nasty in his voice.

"No," I said, astonishing myself with my frank answer.

"Okay," he said and I was equally astonished when he drifted off through the crowd.

This must be the reason why he'd chosen to single me out all the time. I'd thought he had something against Lowell, but really he'd just taken a liking to me.

I shook my head, mentally striking out my wild conspiracy theory about his fascination with Adele. I'd got the focus of his attentions completely wrong.

The autumn sun streamed down on the graveyard and I found myself wandering amongst the headstones of long gone villagers. I thought there was a certain sort of peace to be had, living in a village all of your life, knowing that even after your spirit left the earth, some part of you would forever remain in L'airelle. Surrounded by so many markers of the past, I spared a thought or two to wonder about what came after. Unfortunately, the only method to find out for sure was a very final one. It was one mystery I hoped I wouldn't solve any time soon.

"Lovely service," I heard the owner of the boulangerie say.

I looked round to find that Luna and Alcide had also just wandered into the graveyard. A few others must have also felt the call of the past, or simply the good weather, and were also dotted around. I spotted Detective Girard talking animatedly to Sage, while Nicholas Devereux was deep in conversation with Monsieur Quebec.

"I'm glad that's over and done with," Luna said to greet me, uttering the first honest opinion I thought I'd heard all morning.

"I'm glad for Madame Devereux," I said, and then bit my tongue, hoping I hadn't said the wrong thing.

Luna nodded. "So am I. I thought **my** life was made miserable by Pascal's pranks, but at least I never had to live with him."

"I'm glad I never met him," Alcide said, flashing a smile all round and managing to inject his usual positivity into the conversation.

I found myself hoping that Luna had picked right this time and that Alcide was everything he appeared to be. On the surface at least, I thought they might be made for each other.

"I'm giving my presentation to Monsieur Quebec later today," I said, my heart feeling heavy all of a sudden.

"You're leaving?" Luna said, looking suitably sorry.

I shot Alcide a shrewd look and he changed his own facial expression to match. We both knew he'd be happier when I was out of his hair. I also knew he would be unlikely to take too much of my review to heart. He was new to his job and had yet to put his own stamp on it. All the same, I hoped a few of my ideas would sneak into his subconscious.

Luna was just telling me how much everyone would miss me when I saw Alcide's expression change again. This time it went through disbelief before settling on guilt.

I turned around.

A squirrel monkey was perched on a carved coptic cross headstone, chewing on what looked like a grape - probably stolen from the local vineyard.

I looked back at Alcide who threw me an unabashed smile.

"I guess I must have miscounted," was all he said and then cleared his throat. "I'll get him back with his friends, I promise."

He moved towards the monkey, making soothing noises. I had a moment of thinking 'rather him than me' but I did appreciate him owning up to making the mistake. I thought there was definitely hope for Alcide.

"Do you want to come with me to Adele's house? I'm going to check on Georgette," Luna said, referring to her puppy.

I looked back towards the church in time to see Lowell walk out, still deep in discussion with Ms Borel.

"I'll see you back at the house," he called.

I watched as they walked to Ms Borel's car and got in before driving away.

"I'd love to come see the puppies again," I said, hoping to brush off what had just happened as nothing out of the ordinary.

Luna threw me a look laced with concern and sympathy but didn't comment.

"Okay, let's go then. I think Adele and Justin are probably already home by now. They didn't want to stay out too long because of the pups and Jolie. Matti's still in my backyard right now but we can collect him on the way. Bless him, he does mope about after a while without Jolie, Adele, and Justin. I think he thinks he's done something wrong but can't figure out what it is."

I nodded sympathetically. "I'm sure it won't be long before he can come back in and have a grand old time playing with the pups."

"Absolutely. He'll be a great big brother for them all… until they get bigger than him, anyway," she added with a little laugh.

I raised an eyebrow. "You really think that will happen?" Matti was definitely not small.

"Have you seen the size of Madame Louve's Great Dane?" She grinned. "I know they're only half Dane, but their feet are already massive and Jolie's quite a strapping Labrador. I reckon they'll beat Matti for size."

"I hope they all find loving owners," I said, privately thinking that seven puppies would eat Adele and Justin out of their home in no time at all. It was already pretty cosy in their little house with just Matti and Jolie!

"Well, I'm taking Georgette. Madame Louve has picked herself one of the boys. The vet's decided he'd like one too but hasn't picked yet, and the rest are being fought over by zoo staff. They're actually having to draw lots to decide who gets a puppy."

"That's great!" I said, thrilled to hear that there were so many people readily able to take on a new dog - especially one as potentially large as Jolie's pups.

"I know Adele's booked Jolie in to be spayed, just as soon as she's stopped nursing and the vet says it's safe," Luna confided.

I nodded, pleased that Adele and Justin had made that decision. If Jolie had escaped once, she'd no doubt be able to do it again and I knew that despite the puppies being welcomed into the world, Adele and Justin knew just as well as I did that there were thousands of homeless dogs all looking for homes. It wasn't fair to take those potential homes away by unnecessary breeding.

We turned to look back at Alcide. He was on all fours in front of the coptic cross headstone. The monkey was about two metres away from him on the grass, still eating its grape. It looked for all the world as though it was ignoring him, but I knew better. So did Alcide, but he grinned at us anyway.

"You two go along. I'll have this one back home in no time," he promised, although I could already see beads of frustration forming on his forehead. This squirrel monkey was clearly the wiliest of the bunch.

I thought Alcide might have just hit on a reason I hadn't even thought of for keeping the monkeys in an enclosure. They were quick learners. Left to live practically wild in the zoo, they'd learnt all of the tricks. Now Alcide was having to go up against all of that experience.

"Good luck," I wished him.

Luna and I walked back through the graveyard. The last few dregs of people were drifting away from the church. Luna waved over at Sage and Detective Girard, who also looked to be finishing up their conversation. I even managed to nod at Detective Prideaux as he swung out of the car park in his shiny BMW - despite living only half a kilometre away, Luna confided.

The late morning sunshine somehow already appeared old. I thought it might have something to do with the rust coloured leaves that frequently spiralled down from the tree-lined avenue we were walking down. It wouldn't be long before the winter chill moved in and the whole place battened down the hatches until the tourist season resumed once more. I didn't know why, but there was something sad about the end of the busy time. It was like turning the lights off after a show. But then, there was also a sense of peace. The little village and its inhabitants would live a quieter life, a life more similar to the rural France of the past. I thought there was something charming about that.

Perhaps the mood of the day had struck Luna, too, because we walked on in silence. It was a comfortable silence between friends, but none the less, I knew we were both wandering through our own thoughts.

My thoughts turned to the recent deaths and attacks, as they tended to do. No knife had been recovered. The more I thought about it, the harder I found it to suspect anyone in particular. All I knew was that there was something off about the whole thing. There was something I wasn't seeing.

As we turned the corner onto Rue De Jean, I tried once more to piece it all together.

The first thing I realised I'd become sure of was that the deaths and the attacks were intended as offerings. The mysterious chocolates, even the heart painted on Matti - it all felt like the work of an obsessed psychopath. Who else would believe dropping the body of a rather odious man into the tiger enclosure was a good idea? Everything had been carefully planned and considered. The killer was clever but also devoted.

There was only one thing I didn't understand.

The killer had done so much to impress and please Adele, all presumably with the rather twisted hope that she would appreciate the gestures. However, the most obvious barrier to the killer's happiness was Justin. Adele was married to him and it was plain for everyone to see that they were in love.

The killer had attacked Justin - which fit my theory - but he hadn't killed him. There was a chance that the killer had thought the job had been done. Perhaps if Justin had remained undiscovered until the morning, it would have been, but it still bothered me. The person responsible was a planner. They'd planned the body drop perfectly. They'd planned the anonymous chocolate delivery. Clearly, they were good at planning and execution. After all, it was a testament to their abilities that they hadn't yet been caught. They'd also proved they were capable of murder.

So why, when the opportunity to remove the biggest obstacle to their happiness presented itself, had they not finished the job in their usual perfectionist style?

Unless Justin wasn't the one who was in the way of their happiness after all, the voice in my head piped up.

"Oh no," I breathed, as several things jumped into place in my brain. It was like a sliding puzzle that finally slotted together. What had been nonsensical lines now became a fully formed picture.

I couldn't believe I hadn't seen it before.

It was the tiger enclosure that had thrown me off. If Pascal Devereux had crash landed in the lion enclosure, it would have been a different story. But he hadn't. The killer had their flaws after all. They'd made a mistake and it had fooled me completely.

The events of the past couple of weeks replayed in my head, changing to fit my new theory. Instead of casting Adele in the victim's role, I placed Luna there, and everything made a horrible sort of sense.

Enzo Argent had been stabbed because he'd been trying to drag Luna into the mess that was his broken marriage. It might also have been payback for the way he'd cheated on her when they'd been together.

Constantine and Luna had argued publicly enough that gossip about it had spread all round the zoo.

The paint on Matti had been applied when he was in Luna's yard. Perhaps the killer didn't know he wasn't Luna's dog, or more likely, they'd just wanted to be in her thoughts and knew she'd see their message. After all, they'd known to bribe Matti with food to distract him.

The chocolates must have been intended for her, too.

Then there was what had happened to Pascal Devereux. I'd figured out that the killer was leaving offerings but they'd dropped him into the tiger enclosure instead of into the lions' habitat, that Luna was in charge of. What I couldn't be sure of was whether the killer had missed their intended target when dropping the corpse, or if they'd only known that Luna was a big cat keeper and had assumed that meant all of the big cats.

If it were the latter, it would mean that I could exclude everyone who worked at the zoo as a suspect. Unfortunately, I couldn't rule out the parachute drop simply being less accurate than planned. I remembered the uncontrollable way it had spun round on the way down. I also remembered the person in the front harness struggling to be released in time. Pascal's final resting place could have missed the mark.

Justin's attack was the only one I couldn't understand. It had been an incident which had pointed to Adele being the heart of the matter. The only logical idea I could come up with was that it had simply been bad luck. Luna and Adele and Justin lived next door to each other. What if Justin's trip outside had happened to coincide with the murderer leaving another offering for Luna? They could have panicked and attacked Justin to stop him from seeing who they were. That would also imply that Justin knew the killer, but that much was surely already obvious. It was someone in the community who'd done all of this. Someone who wanted to be close to Luna.

My walk had slowed to a crawl. Luna tilted her head at me when I finally ground to a halt on the wide stones that made up the pavement. Something was stopping me from going forwards. It was as though my body knew something my brain hadn't yet caught up with.

Who is it? Who could have done it all? I thought desperately. My mind flashed over the many faces of the villagers, wondering who and how. I briefly toyed with it being Enzo. He had, after all, been learning to paraglide. He could have stabbed himself to allay the suspicion he might have thought was forming around him and he clearly still felt something for Luna. It wasn't anything good, but it was something.

It just seemed too hard to believe. I'd seen Enzo in action. He wasn't a subtle man. Turning up with that girl half his age last night was proof enough of that.

I also didn't believe he'd ever consider stabbing himself. Plus, I was sure someone would have seen him do it. Sneaking up behind someone and stabbing them before moving away was infinitely more subtle than reaching behind your back and attempting to jab a blade in.

There was also the conundrum of the missing knife. When Enzo was whisked off to hospital, they'd have taken his clothes and surely would have located the bloodied weapon.

Where else could it have gone? I thought, remembering the moment Luna had disappeared beneath Enzo's falling body. I tried to see the scene again, now knowing to discount

Nathan and Enzo. No one else had had an opportunity to get rid of the knife. Had it simply been flung away and luck was all that had saved the perpetrator from being discovered?

I didn't believe it.

With the exception of the attack on Justin, which I now thought I understood, this person liked to plan things. Flinging a knife away left far too much to chance.

Then it hit me. There was someone else who'd had ample opportunity to conceal a knife. Someone who would have been above suspicion.

I felt as though the bucket of spiders we'd released in the Pallas's cats' enclosure had been dumped down my back.

I knew who the killer was... and they were about to kill again.

"We've got to go back," I said, grabbing Luna's arm and pulling her around.

She trotted after me as I broke into a jog and then a run.

"What is it?" she asked, half torn between amusement and concern.

"It's Alcide. I think something really bad is about to happen to him."

She stopped talking and ran in step with me.

I only hoped we weren't already too late.

I motioned for Luna to slow down when we reached the border wall of the graveyard. I heard the loud shriek of a monkey and immediately knew that Alcide hadn't made it out. My heart dropped as my suspicions were confirmed in the worst way possible.

Grateful for my small stature for once, I crawled around the side of the wall and peered through the opening.

Fae Girard was standing with her back towards me,

facing Alcide, who looked dazed. I couldn't hear what they were talking about but I could tell from the way Alcide was shaking and stumbling that something bad had already happened to him.

I silently cursed myself for not having figured it out sooner. Of course Fae had been the only one with any opportunity to get rid of the knife used to stab Enzo Argent. I, along with everyone else, had overlooked her.

I saw it all replayed once more and vividly remembered Detective Prideaux telling Detective Girard to go to her car and radio the station. She must have known he would ask her to go. Or if he hadn't, I assumed she would have offered.

I wriggled a little further forwards, craning my neck to try to see what we were up against. In her left hand I could see something that sparked when she made a sudden movement. In her right, I could see a knife, still caked with blood.

My heart dropped. I'd been harbouring a slim hope that the knife had still been in Detective Girard's car, forgotten. Luna and I could have used it to at least have a fighting chance.

"What's happening?" Luna hissed when I pulled back from my reconnaissance. "That's Detective Girard, isn't it?"

I nodded. "She's the one who's been doing it all."

Luna's face lined with confusion.

I bit my lip, sorry to be the one to reveal the bad news. "I think she's been doing it all for you," I said, as carefully as I could.

Luna's expression grew mystified. "Why? Why would she do that?"

I noticed that Luna hadn't argued with my assertion that the crimes had something to do with her. Perhaps it had been on her mind, too, but she'd dismissed it as paranoia. After all, in a village as small as L'airelle, everyone is connected to everyone.

"I think she's developed an obsession with you," I told her, even more reluctantly.

Luna opened her mouth again but then shut it, choosing to nod gravely instead. Her face was several shades paler than it had been a few moments earlier. "She's going to kill him, isn't she." It wasn't a question. "What do we do?"

Her blue eyes turned on me and I found I was lost. We were hiding behind the wall of an isolated graveyard with no way of contacting anyone for help in time to make a difference. The woman we were up against was incredibly tough and had already proved she was willing to kill. There was nothing nearby that could be used as a weapon.

I opened my mouth to tell Luna that I didn't have a clue what to do when I stopped. Even if I couldn't see a way to successfully diffuse the situation, I still had to do something.

"Can you text the police?" I asked. It was so quiet out here that I knew a phone call would be overheard.

Luna nodded, a little doubtfully. It was good enough for me.

"Okay, I'm going to do something," I said, patting her on the arm and starting forwards.

I only wished I knew what that something might be.

Keeping low and out of sight behind the small brick wall, I skirted the graveyard and ended up in the car park outside the little chapel. The only car left behind belonged to Detective Girard. I wasted a moment wondering about the carelessness of that before I realised that this was another crime Detective Girard hadn't planned. Alcide had only stayed back because of the monkey, but Detective Girard had decided to take the unexpected windfall, despite the risk.

I was about to slide past her car and throw myself straight into danger when I hesitated. The knife may be gone, but what if there was something else I could use?

I gently tried the door handle, praying that I wasn't going

to set off an alarm. I was not entirely surprised to find that it was unlocked. Despite the dark motives of Fae Girard, she was still just as much a part of the village as any of the residents of L'airelle, where there was no need to lock your doors against thieves and criminals. Perhaps over the past couple of weeks, some of the inhabitants had revised their opinions, but Detective Girard of all people would have been the most likely to carry on with her old habits. She'd known she had nothing to fear.

I pulled myself into the passenger seat and threw a surreptitious look in the direction of the graveyard. The passenger side was tilted away from where Detective Girard and Alcide were still engaged in their inaudible conversation.

I looked around for something that might help.

At first, I considered the police radio. I'd told Luna to text for help but this would be an infinitely more direct way. I remembered how loud and crackly they always seemed in films and I also didn't have a clue how to use it. I gave it up as a bad idea.

Unfortunately, the rest of the car didn't yield the arsenal of weapons I'd been hoping for. Not even a baton had been left lying around, and I assumed that the knife Detective Girard had in her hand right now was one she'd grown rather attached to during her recent attacks.

I was about to give up when a flutter of dark material caught my eye. I hadn't closed the door, not wanting to make any sound, and a little breeze must have crept into the car and made it move. It took me a moment to remember exactly where I'd seen this type of fabric before. My hand moved beneath the passenger seat, tugging until a rather poorly packed rucksack slid out.

It was a parachute. The one that Fae Girard had used after she'd cut the cords on the paragliding 'chute and jumped free of Pascal Devereux's corpse.

I held it thoughtfully and almost put it down again before I stopped myself. No weapons had been yielded during my search, so this parachute was the only thing I had at my disposal. I slid out of the car and sank down into the dirt. My hands opened the rucksack and I tugged out the billowing material. Once it was free, I stuffed it together again into a more manageable bundle. There was just time to take a deep breath before I slid out from the relative safety of the shadow of the car and did my best to stalk across the open ground of the graveyard.

I hoped Luna would have better luck contacting the police than I'd had in my weapon search. I wasn't convinced there'd be a successful outcome to my flimsy plan.

Alcide saw me the moment I walked out into the open. To my relief, he didn't betray any reaction and the dazed look vanished for a moment. His eyes met mine and I did my best to look reassuring and as though I had an excellent plan for getting him out of here in one piece.

A second later, his eyes flicked back to meet Fae Girard's and he carried on listening to her monologue.

Now I was closer, I could hear what she was saying. My French was just about good enough that I could pick up the gist of it.

"You're just like the others. I know you don't see it but it's not right. I'm the only one who cares for her this much. I'm the only one," Fae Girard wheedled, as though she thought convincing Alcide of this would make him sink to his knees and bare his neck for the blade.

"I've told you, I really like Luna. I'm a decent guy. I know what that rat Enzo did, but I'm not like that. If you like Luna so much, why haven't you told her?" Alcide bit out and then looked surprised, as if he hadn't expected himself to ask the question.

"I have! She knows it. We're great friends," Fae said, sounding utterly convinced.

I took another deep breath and tiptoed forwards, ready to pounce.

I'd almost got into a position where I could throw the parachute over Detective Girard's head when the monkey screamed. I froze at the sound. To my horror, the squirrel monkey sat on the headstone next to Alcide jumped up and down, pointing right at me.

Detective Girard turned in what felt like slow motion. Her eyes widened when she saw me and the knife shot out, reflexively. I instinctively stepped to the side and the billowing fabric waved where I'd stood, half a second earlier. The knife tore through the parachute silk and I was left feeling like a second-rate bull fighter who'd bitten off far more than they could chew.

"Come on, Fae, you have to know that all of this has come to an end. The police know and are on their way here right now," (I hoped).

To my surprise, tears welled up in Fae Girard's eyes.

"I can still do this for her. I know she'll thank me for it in the years to come. One day... one day we'll be together."

I opened my mouth, hoping that some magical words would pop up - words that would get us out of this horrible situation. But it wasn't my words that would save the day.

"Fae, stop!"

All three of us turned and saw Luna running across the graveyard, her fair hair flying in the breeze. I felt Alcide's accusatory gaze land on me and wanted to tell him I'd done my best to keep her out of it.

"Luna!" Detective Girard said, her face morphing into a pleasant smile, as though she hadn't just been about to kill us both. "What are you doing here?"

"I came to tell you I want you to stop. You don't need to do this," Luna said, keeping her cool.

I held my breath and watched a furrow line Detective Girard's forehead.

"I do have to do this. It will make you happier, I know it will. I just want you to be happy," the detective said, smiling sadly at Luna.

"Thank you. I appreciate it, but what I really meant was you don't need to do this. I'm finished with Alcide. I was going to tell him right after the funeral today," Luna said, so convincingly I'd have believed her myself if I hadn't heard her waxing lyrical about how Alcide might be the one just a day before.

"You're done with him?" Fae Girard repeated, looking surprised but pleased.

Luna nodded, taking a step forwards. "Yes, I'm all done with stupid men. I just want for us to be friends, okay?"

The detective's eyes grew round and hopeful. "The very best of friends?" she said, sounding childlike for a moment.

If you forgot about the taser and bloodstained knife she held in her hands.

"Exactly," Luna said, although I thought her facade was going a bit wonky. "We can be together forever."

The line sounded weak to my ears but the detective was so far under the spell she'd constructed around Luna that she swallowed it.

"How long have you known it was me?" she asked. "Was it the phone calls? I was always too scared to speak. I wanted to tell you then that it was me who finally got rid of that idiot, Pascal. I knew you'd be happy but I just wasn't sure what you'd think. I didn't know if you'd trust me."

"I think I sensed it was you then, yes," Luna invented, endeavouring to focus on the detective and not meet my eyes. We both knew full well that she'd found out who the culprit was when I'd figured it out and told her, moments before we'd arrived back at the graveyard.

"You can put down the knife and the taser. Everything's going to be okay now," Luna chimed.

For a moment, I thought she might actually do it. Her grip on both weapons loosened but a moment later, her hands tightened again.

"You don't understand the legal system like I do, Luna. No one else will understand that what I did was right. Those people deserved what happened to them but the law won't see that. If we make these two disappear, we can get away. I think I can even make it look like they're the ones to blame for everything. I'll leave the knife behind. It's for the best, I promise," the detective said.

It made my blood run cold to hear someone so able to casually discuss the murder of two people.

Especially when one of those people was me.

"There's no need for that. We can just go now. Your car is right there! Come on," Luna said, but the desperation in her voice was now apparent, even to the detective.

Her mouth hardened. "You're too caring. Can't you see they've been using you? Look at them. They've been carrying on together behind your back all this time. He's just another cheat and she's a backstabber, not a friend."

I was relieved to see that Luna didn't believe it for a second. To my horror, she stepped forwards and reached for the knife. I didn't even have time to shout a warning before the detective jerked her hand away, the blade slicing across Luna's palm.

Bright red blood dripped onto the dusty ground. Time froze as the detective and Luna looked at it in horror.

Perhaps it was because he'd already been (literally) shocked already that Alcide was the only one who wasn't transfixed by the cut. He ran up behind Detective Girard, even as she stuttered to Luna that she'd never meant to hurt her, ever. Alcide's big hands made contact with the detective's lower back and he gave her such a tremendous push that she half-flew, half-staggered forwards and practically cartwheeled over a gravestone.

One hand splayed out when she fell and I saw the taser fly free and smash against another gravestone. Unfortunately, the knife remained in her hand.

I felt fabric between my fingers and realised that I was still holding onto the BASE jumping parachute. Wordlessly, I extended it to Alcide, who grabbed a corner. Together, we executed an unspoken plan, both operating on shared instinct that I hoped would be enough to save our lives.

Detective Girard was already on her feet by the time we reached the gravestone she'd fallen over. The knife slashed out wildly and one look at her face was all I needed to see to know that any slim hope Luna might have had of talking her out of killing us was gone. She had only one thing on her mind now... and it was murder.

Parachute silk parted like butter, but the fabric acted like a screen and both Alcide and I had feinted to the side. Despite the tear, we lunged forwards. The three of us fell to the ground in a tangle of cords and fabric. Detective Girard was beneath the cloth, still waving the knife around, but the angle was wrong for her to puncture through. Alcide grabbed a hold of her flailing arm and held it down.

I rocked back onto my haunches and breathed a sigh of relief. Running footsteps announced the arrival of the police.

At first, I thought Detective Prideaux was going to cuff Alcide, but Luna quickly explained the situation. He must have been having a few doubts himself, as he didn't disagree, and signalled for a couple of officers to restrain and cuff Fae Girard.

To my surprise, Nathan and Sage appeared in the graveyard.

Nathan noticed my puzzled expression.

"I was dragged in for more questions," he said, throwing Detective Prideaux a dirty look. The detective didn't even seem to notice.

The couple stayed with Luna, Alcide, and me after Detective Girard had been arrested and the police had collected all of the evidence they needed. One of the officers had promised Luna that she'd be put away for a very long time. The same officer had also mentioned that, with hindsight, it was pretty strange how Detective Girard had been basically running a hate campaign against Enzo Argent, ever since he'd cheated on Luna. He'd said that no one had really noticed because no one had been particularly impressed with Enzo's conduct anyway.

"I should have put two and two together. Fae has always been a big fan of paragliding, which is why I thought they put her on the case. It never crossed my mind that she was the one responsible," Sage said when we were all alone once more in the graveyard.

"It's not your fault, honey. You couldn't have known," Nathan reassured her.

She shook her head. "But I should have seen it! A few weeks ago, I saw Fae doing a super low flyby across the zoo, and it never crossed my mind again until now. I just figured she'd made a mistake that day. I didn't even speak to her about it because I was sure no one with her level of experience would deliberately do such a risky fly over when there's nowhere safe to land. I thought it had to be a rogue wind that had pushed her there."

Nathan just shook his head and patted her back, reassuring her that she hadn't made a mistake.

"I wasn't even certain what this whole thing was about

until today," I confided and shot a sorry look Luna's way. She still had a stunned expression on her face.

"At least things can get back to normal now." It was all I could come up with to say.

"Better get back home now everything's been cleared up," Nathan said and the couple excused themselves.

I was sure they weren't lying when they said they were going home, but I was willing to bet they were going to make a few stops along the way. The village's rumour mill would do the rest of the work. By tomorrow, there wouldn't be a single person in L'airelle who didn't know that Fae Girard had got so hung up on Luna that she'd murdered a couple of people and had tried to do in a few more besides. I just hoped the villagers were farsighted enough to see that none of the troubles were the fault of Luna herself.

Something touched my arm.

I jumped and looked down. A small, furry face looked up at me, dark eyes round and inquisitive.

"Still going to let them run free?" I asked, already knowing what Alcide would say.

"Of course," he said, summoning that same old lopsided grin to his face.

"Even after all of the trouble this fellow just got you into?"

Alcide shrugged. "Everything turned out okay in the end, didn't it? Better a graveyard in the sunshine than a dark alley at night. Who knows? This little monkey might have saved my life."

"Oh, thanks a bunch," I said, not entirely thrilled that the monkey was getting more credit than Luna and I were for helping Alcide out of a sticky situation.

He laughed and rested a hand across Luna's shoulders. "Thanks to you, too, Madi. If you hadn't figured it all out then maybe I would have ended up like Constantine or Pascal," he said a bit more soberly.

"Well, it all turned out okay in the end," I echoed. In my opinion, it was always best to reflect upon what had really happened, not what might have transpired. So much time was wasted contemplating things that never were.

We walked out of the graveyard together. Our appointment to meet the puppies again hadn't been forgotten. Despite the day's drama, life would go on as it always had in L'airelle.

We all waved goodbye to the monkey who was still sat on a headstone, eating another grape it must have stashed somewhere close by.

Alcide reckoned the monkey would return to the zoo when it got tired of the village and missed its mates. I was coming round to the idea that he was probably right.

After the events of the morning, giving my final presentation and handing in my review of L'airelle Zoological Park seemed anticlimactic. It was received with thanks and Monsieur Quebec had also commented on how many improvements had already been made during my time spent at the zoo. I thanked him for his kind words and then reiterated my main point, which was about the farmyard area that urgently needed addressing. France wasn't as tight on health and safety as England, but I still knew trouble when I saw it.

I walked back through the zoo at the end of the day, mentally wishing goodbye to the collection of animals I'd already grown to love. The lions and tigers were batting around rubber treat balls and the Pallas's cats looked healthy and happy, still hunting for the remnants of the spider horde we'd unleashed on their enclosure.

I made my way to the tiki hut where I'd left a few things.

Today, the end of the day quiet felt a little sad, and I sighed when I walked up the path towards the hut. All things must end and there was still so much I wanted to do for animals in other zoos. Although, I wasn't quite sure where I'd be going next.

I'll have to see what Lowell's doing, I thought and then frowned. I hadn't seen him since the funeral when he'd jumped in a car and driven off with that agent, Ms Borel. I'd tried calling him after the big showdown in the graveyard but he hadn't answered.

My mind drifted back again to what Mr Flannigan had said. I was starting to think that Lowell was hiding a thing or two from me after all.

I sighed, knowing there was going to have a to be a conversation later. I hated conversations like that.

I still had a frown on my face when I walked into the tiki hut.

"Surprise!!" a whole bunch of people yelled, jumping out from behind the kitchen unit and sofa.

My face must have gone through a truly startling array of emotions because when Luna and Adele popped out they were laughing.

"You didn't think we'd let you go without a little farewell party, did you?" Adele said, holding out a beautifully iced cake. It looked like it had a lemon glaze, dipped in chocolate at the bottom, with 'Au Revoir' written across the top in curling script. I recognised Adele's baking style and was even more touched.

"This is lovely," I said, looking around at the different staff members I'd come to know and like.

"No need to say anymore. Let's eat and drink!" Nathan said, when I struggled to find anymore words. He raised a bottle of prosecco and let the alcohol flow.

"Is everything okay?" I asked Luna, when we both had

slices of the cake and were sat on the sofa with only Adele close enough to hear.

"The police have been great. Enzo's still in hospital, which probably helped a lot," she said, dryly.

We both thought of her ex-boyfriend with less sympathy than we probably should have.

"Fae has tried to take back everything she said to us when she admitted she did it, but the evidence pointing to her is very strong. The parachute and the knife are more than enough for them to move forwards with. Detective Prideaux is sure that there'll be more evidence found when they search her home and go over her car with a fine-tooth comb."

The surprise must have shown on my face when Luna mentioned Detective Prideaux.

"He's not actually working on the case because of the personal connection, but he's being kept updated. A team from Saint Gerraire are in charge now."

"I'm glad it's over and that you're okay. How's Alcide?" I tentatively asked. He'd been tasered earlier on in the day and then threatened with a knife. Although he'd sounded chipper when we'd spoken after Fae Girard had been arrested, I wouldn't be surprised if the reality of what had almost happened to him had hit hard.

"He's back down in the village trying to convince the monkey to come home," she said, a little smirk pulling at her lips.

"What about that speech he gave about freedom and the monkey coming back when it wanted to?" I said in mock disbelief.

"Mmm… that was all well and good until the little devil stole an entire gateaux that Madame Myrtle had left out on her windowsill. After Madame Myrtle had a word with him, Alcide decided it was time for the monkey to go home after all." She raised an eyebrow at me and I giggled.

Alcide had met his match after all. He may not have been willing to listen to me but there would always be the villagers to contend with.

"All packed?" I asked Lowell, when he came back into the cottage after placing the last of our suitcases in the back of the hire car.

"I think so. Looks like the holiday's over," Lowell said with a smile, but I noticed it wasn't a particularly wistful one. He'd enjoyed the trip - that much I knew - but I also understood the hunger of returning to do a job that you loved. The only thing that bothered me was that I wasn't sure exactly what kind of job Lowell would be returning to do.

We'd spoken when he'd arrived back at the cottage the previous evening. I'd told him about everything that had happened in the graveyard. He'd been duly concerned and had lamented the fact that he hadn't been there, but all the same, I'd felt like he was half-distracted.

In turn, I'd asked him what his meeting with Ms Borel had been about. The only information he'd yielded was that she'd wanted to seek his professional opinion on something. Perhaps some people would worry that Lowell was being a cheat, but I didn't sense any of that and I'd learnt to trust my senses. That said, I wasn't convinced that 'seeking his professional opinion' was the whole truth.

Even as the morning sunshine illuminated the bright red paint of the hire car and I prepared to leave the cottage, I also waited for the right moment to question Lowell. Back when we'd decided we were going to be together, I'd warned him that any more secrets would not be tolerated. Unless I was much mistaken, he was well on his way to breaking that rule.

"There's something I want to ask you," Lowell said, when

we were five minutes down the road from L'airelle. I already felt the end of the long summer slipping away and had said farewell in my heart to the quaint village with its neighbouring zoo.

"Okay," I said, knowing I sounded nervous. Was this going to be about whatever he and Ms Borel had spoken about? What if it was something terrible? I braced myself.

"What do you think about us living together? We both rent, right? It would surely be more efficient if we made a decision on a house and moved in together."

"More efficient, eh?" I said, not incredibly impressed by the proposal.

Lowell's cheeks flushed a little and I suddenly regretted giving him a hard time.

"I just thought you might like to. I know I would like to live with you," he said, stumbling over his words. "We seemed to do pretty well out in France, so I just thought... It doesn't matter," he finished, giving up.

I bit my lip for a second before I replied. "I'd really like to live with you. I think it would be great. Of course, I might not be home much, depending on the cases."

"Me neither," Lowell cut in, gladly. "I travel a lot, too. That's why I thought if there was just the one place to rent, it would work out great."

"It does make sense," I said and then smiled at him. "I'd like to live with you, too."

Lowell's shoulders relaxed down. I hadn't even noticed how much tension he'd been holding in them.

"That's great," he said, a grin now etched across his face.

I returned the grin and settled down in my seat. Despite still having doubts about whether Lowell was hiding something from me, I really was looking forward to moving in with him. I liked Lowell a heck of a lot. I just hoped that my feelings weren't causing my normally excellent judgement to slip.

Time will tell, I promised myself and deliberately forgot about all of the questions I'd been about to ask him.

Only one little voice in my head remained, and it whispered: *what if that's exactly what he was hoping to achieve?*

EPILOGUE

I visited Avery Zoo the day after I returned from the South of France. My best friend, Tiff, had recently questioned my loyalty to my friends back at Avery and I was determined to prove that I was a good friend after all.

Both Tiff and Auryn had been very happy to see me, but I'd been even happier to see Lucky, my kitten. Tiff had been looking after him for me. The tiny kitten I'd saved after he'd been rejected by his mother didn't look so tiny anymore. He was nearly old enough to be at the stage where kittens were able to go to new homes. The milk formula was also in his past now. I was sorry to have missed a key moment in my little cat's life, but the time spent at Tiff's had been great for Lucky. He'd been allowed to socialise with her many other animals and Tiff reported that he'd made many new friends. It boded well for me potentially taking Lucky with me on my future work trips. He'd need to like other animals and have a healthy understanding of which animals were better left alone.

Unfortunately, Auryn's grandad was not doing nearly as well as Lucky. The elderly man had suffered a heart attack, which he wasn't expected to ever recover from. He was out of hospital, but bed bound and required carers. Despite the strain this put on Auryn, the young zoo manager looked healthier and happier than when I'd last seen him, several weeks ago.

I'd asked him how running the zoo was going but it had been plain enough to see when I'd walked around my old workplace. All of the animals looked healthy and happy. The information about them had been updated and some of the old exhibits such as 'how much weight can you pull?' had been resurrected. In my opinion, Auryn's father had been well on his way to turning the zoo into a theme park. His view had been that fun curiosities, that also provided an education, were things of the past. I was thrilled that Auryn clearly did not share the same view as his criminal father and had brought them back. I still couldn't pull as much as an ox, although I secretly suspected that this particular rope was not attached to a weight at all - simply tied onto something that wouldn't budge.

The young zoo manager had also taken my suggestion of making the running of the zoo a more democratic process to heart. Everywhere I looked, I saw posters advertising the many special events that were taking place at Avery. Auryn told me proudly that each of these events were being organised by individuals or groups of staff who had come up with the concept. He was giving everyone a chance to have their own project and I was sure that the success would speak for itself.

"How are things financially?" I'd asked, when we'd covered everything else. I'd known Auryn long enough that I knew he wouldn't mind me asking. After all, it was the zoo's financial situation that had allegedly driven his father, Erin Avery, to such drastic, money-raising lengths.

"I've found a great accountancy firm and they've put

together a debt repayment plan that should get the zoo back in the black within a year. Isn't that great? This month, the zoo made a fairly decent profit too and although it's early days, I think October is going to be even better."

"That's amazing," I'd said, meaning it. Auryn had taken what his father had called an impossible task and was making Avery Zoo into a business again.

"Are you staying here for long?" Auryn had asked.

I hadn't missed the wistfulness in his voice. I missed Avery Zoo a lot and was very tempted, but there were still zoos who wanted my help and I wanted to be able to give it.

I also happened to know that Auryn's desire for me to stay wasn't entirely animal welfare related. If I stayed, I wasn't sure my own motives would remain pure either. Auryn was several years younger than me but he was one of my closest friends and also undeniably gorgeous. I hadn't wanted to risk our friendship, so Auryn's wishes had never been fulfilled in terms of us giving a relationship a go. I was glad no one else, not even Tiff, knew about what had happened between us. They'd all think me crazy for turning down the most eligible bachelor around.

"I'll be back again before you know it," I'd promised Auryn after I'd spent a couple of weeks at the zoo to check on all of the animals and help Auryn out as best as I could. This time around, I hadn't really felt needed. It made me sort of sad and happy at the same time.

Avery Zoo was blossoming just fine without me.

I stroked Lucky's head and the kitten mewed and pushed against my hand. I had a feeling he was growing up to be a very affectionate cat, but also one who was full of trouble.

Since Lowell's suggestion of moving in together, we'd

discussed our options and as my place was more affordable and also (in my opinion) a cosier home, he was moving in with me. Lucky had shown his streak for mischief while Lowell was moving in. My poor boyfriend had been driven half-mad, believing he'd lost most of the socks he'd brought with him during the move. It wasn't until we moved the furniture in the lounge around that we'd discovered Lucky had hidden them all under the sofa.

Sock thief drama aside, things with Lowell had been going pretty well. Despite promising myself I'd let what had happened in France between him and the agents slide, I had kept a close eye on Lowell. I would never want to deny him independence, but we had made a deal not to keep any secrets from one another when we'd started our relationship. I just didn't want to be lied to.

Lowell had been working a few small, local cases since we'd been back home. I was more than willing to conclude that whatever had happened in France was over and done with. Lowell was back to his old job, working as a private detective, and seemed as happy as I'd ever seen him.

I tilted my head at the computer screen in front of me, looking at my latest comic and marvelling at the view counter. I had never expected my little hobby to turn into something so successful.

The crowd funding campaign had come to an end and had been 230% funded. Even when you took away the fees the site would claim, it was a massive chunk of money. My house buying deposit fund was certainly going to be looking a little more healthy. Of course, there was a vast amount of work that needed to be done, not to mention printing all of the books I'd promised to people who had pledged money. I had a hard task ahead of me and I'd be lying if I pretended it wasn't a bit daunting.

The publishing agent had also been in touch since I'd

skipped out on our Skype meeting. He was eager to set up another meeting and despite my concerns that a publishing deal would take up yet more of my time and distract from my main job - a job I loved to do - I had agreed to another meeting. The agent was so persistent I felt that I had to at least give them a chance.

I closed the webpage displaying my latest *Monday's Menagerie* comic (in which spiders intended for Pallas's cats had escaped and taken over the zoo!) and opened my email account. There was the usual growing slew of fan mail but there was something else, too. I reopened the email I'd received that morning and read it through again.

It was a plea for help.

A zoo in Cornwall had undergone a change of ownership and management after being so widely criticised by the public. The new owners were horrified by the conditions animals had been kept in.

When they'd taken over the zoo, they'd thought it would simply be a matter of building better enclosures and supplying better food and the animals would recover. They'd soon discovered this wasn't the case. The animals were damaged in more than just physical ways. They needed someone to help restore these animals' lives to the fullest.

The writer of the email, Jules Hemway, also claimed that despite the hard work they'd put in, people still avoided the zoo. Although I wasn't a PR coordinator, they were hoping that with my already growing reputation, I might be able to change minds and get people to take a chance on the zoo again.

"What do you think, Lucky? Shall we go to Cornwall?" I asked my little black cat. He raised a white paw and patted my chin.

"I'll take that as a yes," I said with a smile.

Jules hadn't tried to conceal anything in the email. I knew

I was accepting responsibility for an entire zoo's worth of abused animals. It was going to be heart wrenching at first, but I also had a strong feeling that it might be my most rewarding cause yet.

This was a chance to make a real difference, and I was going to take it.

EXCITING PREVIEW!

Read on for an exciting preview of the fourth book in the Madigan Amos series, Lions and the Living Dead!

LIONS AND THE LIVING DEAD

10

PRANK OR PERSECUTION?

Russet coloured leaves swirled in the breeze as I walked down the path that led from the car park to the village hall. I thought there was no place I'd rather spend the autumn than in Cornwall.

I'd just accepted a job working at Pendalay Zoo, situated quite close to Padstow. The zoo had recently been bought and taken over by the Johnson family. I'd met Mr and Mrs Johnson and their frenetic advisor, Jules, the previous afternoon and had immediately decided I liked them.

The Johnsons had made their money working as business consultants for some very impressive companies and they'd finally decided to try their hand at running their own business. A zoo hadn't been on the cards, but when Rebecca Johnson had turned on the news one night and witnessed a report on the squalor that the animals of Pendalay Zoo were living in, she'd found her calling. They'd bought the zoo and had thrown themselves into renovating the place.

That was when they'd realised it wasn't enough.

I'd been called in to help diagnose and rehabilitate the emotionally, and sometimes physically, scarred animals they'd inherited when they'd bought the zoo. It was only now that the Johnsons were realising they might have made a mistake buying when they had. With the truth about Pendalay out in the open, it wouldn't have been long before the animals were seized and distributed amongst better zoos. If they'd bought the zoo after that had happened, they'd have been able to start fresh with a group of animals who hadn't seen the worst that humankind had to offer. Instead, they'd done a deal with the unscrupulous previous owner and had bought the lot. It was their problem now.

I hated to think that the man responsible for so much suffering had made so much as a single penny from selling up, but it was unfortunately the way the world sometimes worked. He'd been let off with a slap on the wrist and it was up to the Johnsons and myself to pick up the pieces.

Well, it wasn't entirely up to us.

I wasn't the only expert Jules had hired. During the welcome meeting and yesterday's tour around the zoo, she'd revealed that I was going to be working as a part of a much larger team. She'd explained that Zara was the head of a team of PR experts. They'd started out specialising in bringing businesses back from the brink, or rebuilding reputations after a PR disaster, but more recently, they'd been working with family attractions. They'd helped out theme parks, farm experiences and (of course) zoos. That's why Jules had hired them.

In front of the Johnsons, Jules had waxed lyrical about how fantastic the company was. When we'd taken the tour minus the owners, she'd changed her tune a little bit. She'd confided that while the PR firm did have a great track record with turning businesses around, there were reviews that claimed the firm focused too much on the spin and not enough on the quality of the place itself. That was even more worrying in the case of zoos and farms, where animals were added into the equation. I'd assured Jules she'd made the right choice bringing me in.

I couldn't say I blamed the PR group for not paying attention to what they were promoting. After all, it wasn't really their job to worry about animal welfare. I did, however, blame the other zoos and farms for not hiring an animal specialist. I understood that tickets needed to be sold to keep a place open but I was a deep believer that animal welfare should always come first.

I only hoped that the head of the PR company would agree.

A leaf dropped onto my head and slid to the ground a second later when I shook my wayward blonde waves. I may like the Cornish climate in the autumn, but my hair wasn't quite so sure about the damp and salty air. It had rebelled by puffing out in an electric cloud around my head. Just what I needed before an important meeting!

Zara had contacted me as soon as Jules had passed on my number. Their team had been working on the project for a few days already, but she wanted me to come in, get introduced, and get involved. I hadn't been so sure about the last part. I had my own job to do and something about the woman's tone on the phone had hinted to me that she saw me as just another underling. *I'll put her straight right away,* I silently promised myself.

Before I could open the door that led into the hall, it was pulled open. A woman with a short, brown bob, designer glasses, and a couple of out-dated pencilled on eyebrows stood there. A second or two passed while both of us took the other in.

"Zara Banks," she said, thrusting a hand out towards me.

I gave it a strong shake and returned the introduction.

"I'm glad you could make it here. The meeting actually starts in ten minutes' time. I just wanted the opportunity to meet you myself and have a little chat," she said, attempting an encouraging smile.

"It'll be nice to get a few things sorted," I said, keeping my chat just as ambiguous as hers. The next ten minutes could go several ways.

To my relief, once we were inside the room Zara had introduced as her office, she warmed up.

"Right! We've got a lot of plans for this place and I basically don't want anyone on my team to tread on your toes. I'm also hoping we can keep each other updated on work that's done. That way, we should come up with the best final result," she said and this time the smile was more genuine.

"That sounds really sensible," I said, pleased that she wasn't treating me like one of her employees.

"Fantastic! Well, if you don't mind, I'll get you to introduce yourself in the meeting. You can say a bit about your past work. Feel free to add in any interesting facts about yourself, too. We're a friendly company, not a bunch of stuffy suits."

I nodded, feeling a flutter of misgiving. Speaking in front of people wasn't a problem but being matey was a lot harder. I knew I didn't always come across as the most likeable person ever until people got to know me. This kind of sharing always felt forced.

"All right! So, the gang should be arriving any second now..." Zara said, picking up her phone and looking at the screen. It buzzed in her hand and played a shrill ringtone. She jumped and nearly dropped it before managing to accept the call and press it to her ear.

I politely looked away and studied the interior of the clearly hastily set up office. The most interesting feature was the big cork board behind the desk where Zara sat. Pendalay Zoo had been written on a piece of paper and pinned to the top. Beneath it were flyers from the zoo and then a whole bunch of random pictures - at least, that's what they looked like to me. There were giant pumpkins and screaming clowns. I tilted my head at the Halloween themed explosion and then gave up trying to decipher it all.

"Leave me alone! You can't do this. Go away!" Zara practically shrieked the words out before pressing hangup so hard that her phone fell to the floor and skittered away.

She looked at it for a moment before picking it up.

I opened my mouth to ask if everything was okay but she got there first.

"Scam callers... when will they stop?" she said with a cheery smile that I didn't buy for a second.

I thought about pushing her for the truth but decided against it. We'd only just met. Whatever the problem was, she didn't need my help.

"I think I hear the guys now. Let's go into the main room," Zara said and we left the office behind.

The PR team were seated on oversized school chairs in a circle. I was reminded of an alcoholics anonymous meeting, or at least, the film version of one. Five faces turned to look at me when I walked in behind Zara.

"Good morning, guys. This is Madigan. She's working on the Pendalay project with us overseeing... Well, I'm sure she'd tell you better herself," Zara finished with a smile.

She'd very obviously realised halfway through she actually had no idea what I did. Likewise, I wasn't crystal clear on what her job actually entailed.

I cleared my throat, self-consciously. "Please call me Madi. I'm an animal breeding and welfare specialist but I'm also here to observe the animals' behaviour and figure out what might be causing the zoo animals to be... less than happy," I finished. It was the warm and fuzzy version of the truth.

"Anything interesting you want to tell us about yourself?"

Zara asked, making me feel like I was back at school again. I was halfway through a head shake when I thought about my comic.

"I write and illustrate a webcomic called *Monday's Menagerie*," I said, immediately feeling foolish.

The comic had started out as a hobby. I'd only confided its existence with a few close friends but now things were different. The comic had more than doubled its funding target on a recent crowd funding campaign for a print version, and I had a publishing agent who was still trying to pin me down. It was probably about time I started to blow my own trumpet a little.

By the number of raised eyebrows around the room, I'd succeeded in sharing something interesting.

A tall, red-headed man with a slew of ginger freckles stood up and smiled. I took a moment to admire his neatly spaced teeth before trying to focus on what he was saying.

"Nice to meet you, Madi. I'm Alex, chief copywriter here at ZaZa PR. My 'something interesting' is that I was on TV as a contestant on Britain's biggest baking show."

"Out in the first round, unfortunately," the dark-haired woman next to him chimed in, not unkindly.

Alex grimaced. "I had a cake catastrophe," he confided.

The woman next to him got to her feet. "I'm Laura. I'm responsible for making sure this company doesn't collapse under a mountain of paperwork." This was met with sounds of approval and a couple of claps. "However, I don't give out interesting facts before being bought a drink," she said, completely straight-faced.

I didn't know whether to laugh or not. I was glad when the next woman stood up.

She had a blonde pixie cut and some prettily slanting green eyes. Unfortunately, there was also something about those eyes that immediately put me on edge.

"I'm Teagan. I help Zara come up with concepts. An interesting fact about me is that I'm married to the founder of Illiyrism."

I looked around the gathered group of people, but everyone was avoiding making eye contact.

"What's Illiyrism?" I asked and sensed a silent, but collective, group moan.

Teagan's eyes lit up. "It's a revolutionary new religion that pairs modern ideas with old faith. If you're interested, I'll be happy to introduce you to it," she said. I thought her bright smile looked just a little maniacal.

"Thanks," I said, in what I hoped was a suitably noncommittal way.

Fortunately, the next woman had already pushed herself to her feet. She was tall, but chunky, with hair a beautiful shade of grey blonde that I'd forever admired on the internet.

"I'm Lyra. My job is to deal with any fallout. Think of me as the company cleaner because that's what I do. If there's any mess surrounding a business we're working with, it's my job to clear it up."

"How do you do it?" I asked, curious about this rather interesting occupation.

"Blackmail, bribes, bullying... If it begins with a 'b', I've probably done it," she said with a smirk that I felt was intended as a 'just between us' joke that made fun of her colleagues. I thought I might have finally found someone that wasn't as fake as burger cheese.

"Tell us something interesting," Zara prompted when Lyra sat down.

She stood up again, but not without reluctance. "Let's see... the last time I took a couple of days off work for being sick, it was actually so I could binge watch *Game of Thrones*." She nodded as if that settled it and sat down again.

To my surprise, Zara just cleared her throat and inclined

her head towards the final man in the room. I'd been expecting at least a reprimand. I could tell from the vein which pulsed in Zara's forehead she wasn't happy but Lyra just looked amused.

She must be damn good at her job.

Lyra grinned at me across the circle and I suspected I might have made my first real friend at Pendalay Zoo.

"I'm Adrian. I do all of the graphic design and I'm also the only creative on the team." He gave me a stern look but I'd already caught his not-so-subtle meaning. I wondered why he saw me as a threat. For all he knew, my comics were a bunch of stick men. I'd never said they were successful, had I? *He'll probably have a nervous breakdown when he finds out the truth,* I thought, allowing myself a brief moment of smugness.

"My interesting fact is that I'm allergic to nuts. Please do not bring any in to work."

Lyra snorted with laughter and then had to disguise it with a coughing fit.

"Great! I think we're good to go," Zara said. I noticed the overly cheery facade was back in place. After hearing that phone call, I found it even harder to believe.

"If you just sit in on this meeting, you'll get an idea of where we're at. I'm sure you can work around us?" Zara continued. I noticed she hadn't said I could contribute anything - just that I would have to fit in around them.

Instead of arguing, I took a deep breath and sat down to listen.

It wasn't so bad in the end. Most of what the PR team did was done out of their rented offices. The reason they were on site in the first place was because one of their selling points was 'working closely and personally with business owners and the business itself'. Another reason was so they could put up posters and rebrand locally without having to pay someone else to do it for them. I could see there was something in that but I still thought it must be a lot of effort, having to hire new premises every time.

I was relieved when the meeting ended an hour later. One thing was for sure, I'd picked the right career. To me, PR sounded deadly boring. There was so much jargon flying around and discussions on how to best present 'the idea' of Pendalay Zoo. I'd also concluded that Jules had been right to hire me. While the PR team did focus on how the zoo looked and customer satisfaction levels, it was all too clear they had no animal experience whatsoever. I only hoped the other zoos they'd worked for hadn't been in the same dire straits as Pendalay.

The autumn air was fresh against my skin when I escaped from the confines of the group meeting. I sighed with relief and someone chuckled.

"Chill out, it's only me," Lyra said when I flinched.

She pulled out a cigarette and lit it. I watched as she held it and made no effort to bring it up to her mouth.

She saw me looking and smirked again. "I don't actually smoke but it's the smokers who get all of the breaks. Believe me, I deserve to have more breaks."

"So, you deal with complaints and things like that?" I was hoping for a more open explanation now that we were away from the others. *Not that Lyra was anything but forthcoming*, I thought to myself, remembering her open admission to skipping work in front of the boss herself. I still wasn't sure whether that had been a joke or not.

"Kind of," she replied. "Basically, if anyone says anything bad about a place it's my job to hunt them down and ask them nicely if they won't change their opinion, pretty please." She shot me a toothy grin. "There's an art to it and you definitely have to be a little bit of a masochist. If I didn't have a sense of humour, I don't know where I'd be." She hesitated. "Probably doing Alex's job."

"What's it like working for Zara?" I asked, wondering if my prying into her history was subtle enough.

"It's okay. My job is more interesting than most, despite having to deal with a big bunch of moaners. Zara's a decent boss most of the time but none of us have worked for her for long," she revealed.

"Really?" I raised my eyebrows enquiringly.

"Yeah. The company has been around for a bit, I think, but Zara and her husband only decided to move to Cornwall six months ago. They started fresh with a new team and decided to limit the moving around a bit more," Lyra explained. "She's nice for a boss, anyway. I know she comes across as fake, but when you get to know her a bit, the mask slips and she's actually fun to be around. We all work really hard here and she's the one who brings it all together and cracks the whip when needed." Lyra half-shrugged. "Someone's got to, right?"

I nodded keeping the light smile on my face. Whatever I'd overheard on the phone, it wasn't a regular part of Zara's personality from what Lyra was saying.

Perhaps she'd been telling the truth and it had been a particularly annoying scam caller. Even I'd been guilty of snapping at cold callers.

I was back at my rented cottage with a hot chocolate in one hand and most of Lucky in the other when my laptop started yelling that Lowell was calling me on Skype. I managed to unhitch Lucky's burgeoning claws from my jumper and popped him up onto my shoulder, where I hoped he'd settle down.

"You have a cat on your head," Lowell gravely informed me when I answered his call.

"Really? I had no idea," I returned, equally dryly. "How's work?" I asked, both of us casually ignoring the black kitten with the white socks, who was trying to build a nest in my hair.

"Work is bland. The only new case since you've been gone was catching a benefit fraud. You know I hate those cases."

I nodded. I was willing to bet the majority of private detectives hadn't imagined that catching fraudsters would be their bread and butter. Hanging around in the car all day, not even able to pop out to the loo, lest you be spotted, was not the glamorous lifestyle I was sure many hoped for.

"I've got some big news, but first I want to hear all about how your new case is going," Lowell said, smiling fondly.

I hesitated for a moment while I took in his dark, swept back hair and the creeping growth of stubble that was verging on a beard these days. My boyfriend was a handsome man and I often found myself guessing what particularly attracted him to me. I'd concluded it was just because I was me, which I supposed was a comforting thought.

"Things are okay here. I've had a look around the zoo and it's as bad as they said it would be. The outsides of the enclosures and some of the interiors have clearly been reworked. There's decent food here, too, so diet research has been done. All of that's good, but it's too little, too late. These animals have had a bad time and it's clear enough for anyone to see. I'm thinking about talking to the PR team..." I began and then trailed off. It had been my intention to discuss the spin that would be needed to explain the animals' state of being but it had slipped my mind. *It's not as if you were encouraged to share your views either*, I thought, reminding myself of how this morning's meeting had gone down.

"PR team?" Lowell looked puzzled.

I realised I hadn't filled him in on the situation that I'd only been appraised of yesterday.

"...They seem like an okay bunch and I think Lyra could definitely be an ally," I said, finishing my assessment of the group.

"That phone call does sound strange," Lowell commented. Even after I'd gone through, describing the ridiculously awkward introductions, he'd focused in on the phone call I'd overheard. It didn't surprise me in the slightest.

"I know, but perhaps she was just stressed out," I allowed. "Anyway, I'm hoping this job will work out well," I said, doing my best to sound chipper.

In reality, I wasn't so sure. This was a challenge unlike any I'd ever faced before. All I could think to do right now was take some time and look at each and every animal in their environment and go from there. I hoped the worst cases would reveal themselves and I hoped even more that I'd be able to help them. That was what I wanted most of all.

"I should tell you my news," Lowell said, snapping me out of my inner reverie. "I've been offered a case in Cornwall. It's not far away from you, either."

"Really? That's pretty lucky," I said, answering before I had time to think.

Equally luckily, Lowell smiled. "If I'm being completely honest, there were a few jobs on the table and I accepted the one that was in Cornwall."

"So, what's the job?"

"The job itself is not great." He shrugged his shoulders. "I actually think the agency director was surprised when I picked it, but I figured it would be nice to be near to you."

My heart did a little flutter when he said that.

"It's basically a glorified stake out. There's a big designer clothes outlet on the road to Padstow. I think it's out of the way on an industrial estate. They sell direct to both businesses and the public. Recently, they've suffered a number of thefts. It's nothing too big, just a few jackets and handbags, but the items are consistently going missing, and as they're designer, they've all got ludicrous price tags. The company contacted the agency asking for someone to come and work as an employee but be on the lookout for the thief. They suspect it's one of their staff who's responsible," he confided.

I raised an eyebrow. "Does the company in question know who they're getting?"

Lowell cleared his throat. "They were a little confused. They'd expected the newest detective on the agency to be sent over. Someone who still has acne… but they're very pleased, of course."

For a second, I thought Lowell looked a little worried. I reckoned I knew why.

"It'll be fine. You've done this a thousand times, right? If there's something to find, you'll find it," I reassured him.

He nodded and looked a lot happier. "It'll be a good refresher to do a job like this. It reminds you of where you've come from."

"Plus it's like another holiday with me!" I piped up.

We talked a little longer, figuring out the living arrangements, before I wished him goodnight.

Later, I lay in bed with Lucky curled up on the pillow beside me, but sleep was a while coming. Lowell's conversation had given me pause for thought. This job was beneath his pay grade, he'd said as much himself. He'd claimed he'd taken it so he could spend time with me, and I really hoped that was the truth.

I didn't want to contemplate the other option. If Lowell was keeping something from me, there'd be trouble ahead.

As it turned out, the rains of England had come and gone while Lowell and I had been in the South of France. The projected weather for October was mostly dry and sunny - albeit a sight colder than the little village in France had been. When Lowell and I went out for a walk that Saturday, it was one of these promised, sunny autumnal days.

We'd planned a walk across the cliffs and beaches to Padstow. Lowell was determined to try as many Cornish pasties as possible and Padstow was certainly the place to go for an authentic pasty experience.

We'd only made it a little beyond Pendalay village when we heard the scream.

We both looked over to our left at a little hamlet of traditional stone cottages. After exchanging a warning look we hastened over. I had no idea what to expect. Were we about to land in the middle of another violent crime?

When we rounded the corner of the boundary wall that encircled the properties, I got a surprise. Zara was standing on the prettily paved path that led up to one of the little cottages. At the same moment we arrived, a man rushed through the gate at the side of the house and Zara screamed again.

"What's wrong? What happened?" he said, rushing over to Zara. Even as Lowell stiffened next to me, the newcomer was throwing him an equally suspicious look.

I'd just spotted the real reason why Zara had screamed, and it had nothing to do with either of the men.

"That's horrible," I said, walking up the path towards the front of the house.

The man with his arm around Zara looked at me in confusion but made no move to stop me. I was able to get a good look at the scene of a foul crime.

There was blood splattered across the front step. Its garish red colour seemed to mock the subdued claret shade that the front door was painted. It hadn't taken me long to spot the source of the blood. A rat had been strung up by its tail in the ornamental lavender tree by the front door. Its throat had been cut and there was a sickening drip drip that continued to fall and stain the ground.

I turned back to the couple on the path and saw that Zara was crying.

"He's followed me here! I thought I was safe," she sobbed.

"Is there anything we can do to help?" Lowell asked, walking up the path to join our little group.

"Thank you, but no. It's kind of you to stop but I'm afraid there's nothing you can do," the man said, sounding remarkably defeated.

"Well, we can at least call the police for you," I tried, managing to shoot Zara what I hoped was a comforting smile. The business woman I'd met yesterday had completely gone to pieces.

"We've tried that before. Nothing ever happens. The police just ignore us," the man said.

"Oh, Madi! I don't know what I'm going to do. I thought this was all behind us. We've even been constantly moving around just in case. I thought it had done the trick," Zara said.

"Do you two know each other?" Lowell asked.

I nodded. "This is Zara, head of the PR firm I told you I was working with."

His eyes went a little wide when I mentioned her name but he covered it. I knew he'd remembered the odd phone call I'd described. Given today's display, I was definitely revising my opinion that it had been a scam caller.

"I'm Lowell, Madi's boyfriend," he said, offering a hand to Zara, who took it in a daze and gave the limpest shake I'd ever seen.

"I'm Darren, Zara's husband. It's nice to meet one of Zara's colleagues. I'm just sorry about the situation," the other man told us.

I thought there was something quaintly British about his apology for something that was completely beyond his control.

At that moment, a man poked his head over next door's wall and asked if everything was all right. Lowell left the group and went to talk to him.

"So, this has happened before?" I pressed.

Darren pulled a face, his arms still around Zara, who was clearly trying to get a grip on herself. "Yes, in a manner of speaking. The rat is new, but we've had dead things before. Mostly dead mice, pushed through the letterbox with threatening letters for Zara."

"You've been to the police with all of this?" I asked.

Darren nodded. "Yes, we've told them everything. They couldn't do a thing about it. They never found the person who was doing it and as neither of us have been physically harmed…" He shrugged.

"Even so, you should call them about what's just happened. You never know… a different local police force might be able to do more about it," I said, trying to be positive about a very scary situation. I couldn't imagine what it must feel like to be the victim of an apparent hate campaign.

"I'll call them when we're inside and have had a cup of tea. I think we need that much before we face them," Darren said with a thin-lipped smile.

"Okay," I said, as neutrally as possible. "Let me know if there's anything at all I can do to help. You've got my number," I said to Zara.

Part of the excruciating introductions yesterday had involved a number swap. Everyone on the team now had my contact number. It was antisocial, but I was already looking forward to deleting most of them from my phone book the minute this job was over.

I turned and discovered Lowell had returned with the neighbour in tow.

"This is Tom Riley, he's an off-duty police officer," he said.

The newcomer nodded his head, giving me a fantastic view of the tiny corkscrew curls that clung to his dark-skinned scalp.

"I heard someone in distress and thought I'd come and see if I could help. I hear you've been the victim of an attack?" The couple nodded grimly. "I'm your neighbour, by the way. Sorry to meet like this."

Zara and Darren mumbled about it being perfectly all right and that they were glad to have him there.

I noticed Lowell staring hungrily at the horizon in the direction we had been walking.

"I hope the police can help you both this time," I said, smiling kindly at the couple, before we excused ourselves.

"I'm glad that off-duty police officer was there. I'm not convinced they'd have called the police otherwise," Lowell said, breaking the silence when we were two hills away from the little hamlet.

"I got that impression, too," I admitted. "I don't know why they wouldn't. Someone with a history of being attacked like that... my first instinct would be to go to the police." I thought about it a bit more. "I guess they're just tired of it all. I can't imagine what it's like to constantly move around and think you've finally shaken your attacker, only for it to all start up again. I'm sure Zara's not done anything to deserve a stalker. Still, it's a little odd..."

"...That they're not doing more about it?" Lowell finished. "I'd set up cameras, surveillance - the works - if it were me, but not everyone would feel the same. I've worked on stalking cases before. At a guess, I'd say Zara and Darren are doing everything they can to live normal lives. They don't want to admit, even to themselves, that anything is seriously wrong."

"They said the police never did anything to help. Do you think maybe we could..." I trailed off when Lowell threw me a dark look.

"Believe me, you do not want to get involved. Someone has got it in for Zara. That's bad, but it's their business. If they wanted help, they'd be asking for it. Until they ask, we'd probably just end up making ourselves look guilty. Think about it... we'd have to spy on them to catch the culprit. All Zara and Darren would be doing is gaining another couple of stalkers."

"Well, I suppose at least there hasn't been anything actually violent against Zara. Darren just said it was small, dead animals and threatening notes. I guess the phone calls, too." I bit my lip, but Lowell didn't so much as budge. "At least the police know," I said, resigning myself to play by his rules for now.

He didn't think it was our problem. I could see his point, but that didn't stop me from having a very strong feeling that it wasn't going to stay that way...

11

A LOT AT STAKE

The first week passed by in what felt like a matter of seconds. I'd immersed myself in my observations of both the animals and their habitats. One week in and I knew I'd barely scraped the surface with a lot of them. My head was practically floating with ideas for the many damaged animals at the zoo, but I knew there was going to be a fair amount of trial and error. Solving a mental ailment was often far more difficult than treating a physical problem. There was no fixed timeline for healing and no guarantee that there would be complete recovery, or even any recovery at all. I'd known at the start of the job that it was going to be my most challenging case to date, and I wasn't about to change that assessment.

I'd been so busy, I hadn't engaged much with the PR team. I'd bumped into a couple of them during my observations, and these brief encounters had produced a surprising slew of information about the team I was supposed to be working with. I guessed because I was working with them but not a part of the team it made me the perfect person to vent their problems at.

From Adrian, I'd heard that Lyra was exceedingly arrogant and self-centred. From that I'd gauged that she'd turned him down at one time or another.

Alex had described Adrian's past as a student, fresh from uni, who'd attempted to set up his own business and had fallen flat on his face. Alex had implied that he was the PR company's charity case and had only been offered the job because he was Zara's second cousin.

Laura had told me that Alex was secretly trying to gather as much information as possible about the PR company before launching his own competitor business.

Laura herself wanted to save up enough money to quit her job and then go on a trip around the world, while she was still young enough to enjoy it.

To my surprise, no one mentioned anything particularly negative about their boss at all. It would seem that Zara was liked, but not interesting enough to warrant much discussion. From the lack of chatter, I also assumed that none of her employees knew about her history with a stalker. With things starting up again, I didn't think it would be long before they found out that their boss wasn't as bland as they'd believed.

Of all the members of the PR team, Teagan was the one who'd taken a real battering. Whilst most of the team members had dismissed her as being 'pretty nuts', I thought there was more to it than just a quirk of personality.

When I'd come across Teagan outside the bat aviary, she'd been achingly polite whilst simultaneously doing her very best to delve into my past. I'd answered her questions, but had felt my skin start to crawl at the back of my neck. There was nothing visible that I could put my finger on, but some extra sense of mine warned me that Teagan was not what she appeared on the surface. She had something wrong in her head and every inch of my goose-fleshed skin warned me not to push her to reveal what it was. Of one thing I was sure - Teagan was a ticking time bomb.

I hoped I wouldn't be anywhere near her when she finally exploded.

This morning I was glad to see no sign of the PR team. I assumed that their first week (much like mine) had involved a lot of reconnaissance and getting to grips with what Pendalay Zoo had to offer. Now they'd retreated to their office to come up with ideas, and I'd been left to work my own magic.

I'd decided to start with the big cats. My most recent case in France had involved a lot of close work with these magnificent animals, and I was hopeful that the knowledge I'd gained would come in handy at Pendalay.

If I were being honest, I was hoping to see a quick result, both for mine and the zoo owners' sake. If we could both point to the big cats and say 'look what a difference we've made' it would mean breathing space was more likely to be granted for the rest of the zoo. The threat of the animals being seized by an animal welfare group was imminent. I knew something had to be done - and quickly - if they wanted to retain the zoo.

It wasn't the first time I'd silently cursed the previous owners of Pendalay. While I watched the half-starved lions lying despondently on the sparse grass, I hoped that one day karma would catch up with the people who'd allowed it to happen.

The Johnsons had obviously worked on the exterior of the lions' enclosure. It was coated with freshly-cut wooden boards, and the information plaques were every bit as engaging as those at the award winning Avery Zoo, where I'd once worked. It was also obvious that the lions were being fed a vastly superior diet to what they'd been used to.

The problem was, they no longer wanted it.

I could see a carcass lying off to the side in the enclosure. It looked like the lions had barely picked at it. They were supposed to eat around eight pounds of meat a day in captivity.

The first thing to change was their immediate surroundings. The lions were beyond bored. In fact, they were probably out of their minds with boredom. Putting a human into a box with nothing but flat ground and four walls would be torture, and it was no different with animals.

I took a deep breath and got out my sketch pad. It was usually reserved for drawing comics, but today I would be turning my hand to interior design. I was hoping that the Johnsons would see my ideas as an opportunity. I'd studied many big cat enclosures and had learned what worked well. I also had an idea or two about things that could possibly be improved upon. This was a chance for the zoo to try something new - and potentially get ahead of other zoos.

Of course, it'll only be a success if you can get the lions to be lions again, I thought, feeling a little dismal.

I'd also found time to draw up plans for various interactive toys, like treat balls, and meat that hung on a string and had to be leapt at to catch.

I knew it was good stuff. The problem was, the lions would have to want to participate, and I wasn't sure what I could do to encourage them to take those first few steps. I couldn't force them to make the choice to get better and enjoy life. I just had to hope that they decided to change.

I'd picked the lions of all the big cats as the place to start. They were in a wide, open enclosure, big enough to house a medium-sized pride. While there (unsurprisingly) hadn't been any offspring for years, I was hoping that if even one member of the pride tried out a treat ball, or climbed up on a wooden podium, the rest might follow suit. Then I'd be able to *really* start work, making a difference here.

The major problem I'd uncovered at Pendalay, beyond malnourishment, was a complete lack of stimulus. The animals were almost completely sedentary, and I knew that had to change.

I raised my eyes to look at the dozing pride, with their breakfast still lying, forgotten.

I prayed I wouldn't fail them.

In spite of not seeing any of the PR team for the entire day, I was still summoned to their meeting.

Zara had texted to let me know that they were doing a 'team meet' quite late in the evening. I'd read the text a couple of times and had been forced to assume that she was asking me to come along. Otherwise, why tell me? I'd grumbled to myself about both the text and the time of the meeting. In the interests of diplomacy, I'd decided to suck it up. Now here I was again, walking across the car park towards the community hall.

I pulled my scarf a little tighter against the bitter wind that had started up and comforted myself a little with the thought that I hadn't missed any quality time with Lowell. His new work colleagues had gone out together for drinks to celebrate one of the staff's birthday. He'd confided with me that he strongly suspected they'd all got together and arranged their 'birthdays', so it was almost as if they had a birthday to celebrate every week.

Birthday fiddling was not the crime Lowell had been employed to investigate, so he had to join in the fun.

I walked up the steps, kicking dry leaves out of the way as I climbed. *A bit of rain and they'll turn into slippery mush!* I thought, contemplating how treacherous that would be. I shook my head, wondering when I'd turned into such an old worrywart.

"Hi Madi, I'm not sure if anyone else is here yet."

I was greeted by Teagan, who hovered anxiously by the door.

"Is it open?" I asked.

"No, I tried it already. It's weird. Zara stayed behind instead of going out for dinner. I don't know why she'd have locked the door."

I tried not to roll my eyes at the amount of time that had already been wasted. Perhaps the PR team were paid overtime for working this late, but it was definitely above and beyond the hours I'd arranged to work for the zoo. I wasn't usually a complainer. My zoo reviews tended to be written as much after hours as during the day, but I did try to limit myself to working regular hours, despite my passion for the job.

I was feeling more stressed about it than usual, due to the comic work I had to do. A lot of my readers were waiting for the stuff they'd paid for, and instead of working on it, I was stuck waiting outside a community hall, waiting for a door to be unlocked.

We both turned at the sound of car doors slamming. Alex and Adrian joined us on the steps.

"Are we having the meeting out here? I know we're trying to cut down on the heating bill, but this is surely a bit much," Adrian said.

I was sorry to note he was deadly serious.

"Zara's locked the door," Teagan said.

"That's odd. Her car's here. We passed it on the way in. The lights are on in her office, too," Adrian commented when he'd peered round the side of the building.

"So, she stayed behind?" I asked, a little confused as to why the team had separated.

Adrian nodded. "We worked late but still have to get this meeting in today. It's vital for planning things in time. Zara said she'd text you and say to come over. In the meantime, we could all go out and get some food."

"Where are the others?" I asked.

"We all wanted different things. I fancied pizza and Adrian wanted a kebab. We went separately, but I picked Adrian up on the way back because his car broke down."

Adrian grunted. "Piece of junk. I should have known that car salesman was spinning me a line."

Alex looked a little embarrassed for Adrian and pressed on to cover it up. "The girls all wanted boring healthy stuff, like sushi. I don't know where they all went," Alex said, generating a glare from Teagan.

"Lyra's car's here," Adrian said, turning back from the examination of the car park he'd been making.

"Hey, why are we outside?" Laura said, joining our group huddle on the top step.

"Where's Lyra?" Teagan said, voicing our thoughts aloud.

I knocked on the door and shouted Zara's name and the others joined me. It soon became clear that no one was coming to let us in.

For some reason, I felt the hairs on the back of my neck start to rise up.

"I'll call her." Alex turned away to dial.

In our silent state, we all heard the thin sound of Zara's ringtone from somewhere inside the building. She didn't answer and Alex cut the call off when it went to voicemail. "She's probably just put her phone down," he muttered.

I bent down, having spotted something sticking out beneath the door. It seemed to be a thin sliver of wood. I tried to pull it out, but it didn't budge. Acting on a hunch, I pushed the door.

"Already tried that," Teagan said, when the door didn't

open. But I'd noticed something important. The door had bowed inwards at the top when I'd pushed it, suggesting that it wasn't locked in the usual manner. I pressed my face flat against the thin window and tried to look down at the floor of the corridor.

"I think something's wedging the door shut from the inside," I said.

"Maybe the door kept coming open in the wind and one of the other groups using the building put something there to keep it closed?" Laura suggested.

"Maybe," I allowed and then banged on the door again. Nothing happened.

"We need to get inside. Laura, you've got the longest nails. Could you try and push the wedge out?" I asked.

The secretary obligingly knelt down and scraped against the piece of wood. It wasn't long before she made a noise of triumph and pushed the door open.

No one made a move to go inside. I wasn't the only one who'd got goosebumps.

"We should go in," I said.

"But don't you think it's weird that no one answered?" Teagan said, her misgivings plain for all to hear.

"Sure, but perhaps Lyra and Zara are already doing something and didn't hear us," I said, hoping it was that simple.

Alex looked across at Adrian.

"Doing something, eh?" he said, waggling his eyebrows.

Adrian looked blank.

Seeing as no one was making any progress towards getting the already delayed meeting started, I bit the bullet and walked inside the building.

I could hear the others shuffling along behind me, as I slowly walked down the main corridor. The lights hadn't been turned on in the corridor itself, but light spilled out from Zara's open office door, halfway down the corridor. It was just enough to see by, but didn't exactly help the creepy atmosphere.

"Hello?" Teagan called, but just as quickly fell silent again. No one said anything, but I knew we all sensed the same thing.

No one was going to answer us.

I understood the source of the growing feeling of dread when I reached the office and poked my head around the corner.

Someone had added to the Halloween decorations on the cork board.

A woman I'd never seen before hung amongst the paraphernalia, held in place by the large wooden stake that had been hammered through her chest. *Did someone think she was a vampire?* My shocked brain threw out, even as I heard the exclamations of horror behind me, as everyone else arrived in the room.

I stepped around the side of the desk to take a closer look at the victim and tripped on something. My hands landed on the board, either side of the victim's pinned body. I had time to note that the stake wasn't the only thing holding her up, before I looked down and saw what had made me trip.

"It's Lyra!" I shouted, immediately dropping to her side. There was blood coagulating in her hair and I feared the worst. "She's got a pulse! Someone call an ambulance right now. Call the police too," I added, raising my gaze to the hanging corpse.

"I'm the office first-aider," Laura announced, rushing forwards and kneeling down next to me. She gently tilted Lyra's limp head and inspected the wound.

"Does anyone know who she is?" I asked, inclining my head towards the unfortunate woman on the board.

She had short brown hair and was dressed in jeans and what had once been a cream, cable-knitted sweater. My eyes naturally skated over the gaping wound in her chest and instead focused on the cable ties around her wrists. They were hooked onto nylon thread. There was a single coat hook on either side of the cork board that had been used to anchor the nylon and aid in her gravity-defying position.

I couldn't remember if the coat hooks had been there before tonight, but I was willing to bet they hadn't been.

"I know her. She's Jayne Fairfax," Adrian said, breaking the silence in the room. "When I was running my own business, I employed her company to help with promotion. She and her husband call themselves 'business psychologists'. What they are is a couple of scam artists. They're the reason why..." He trailed off, blinking. "It's terrible what's happened to her," he tagged on, far too late.

"Who would do something like this?" Alex said, his already pale face now looking the colour of curdled cheese.

I didn't have a clue about who was responsible for the woman pinned to the board, but I thought I already had a clue or two about the motive. The memory of the dead rat swinging in the tree resurfaced in my mind.

I stood up and walked back to the entrance of the office.

"Where are you going?" Alex asked.

Four white faces looked back at me.

"Zara's car was in the car park, so it stands to reason that she's still here. Unless she did it," I added as a careless afterthought. I bit my tongue. "Sorry, I don't mean that. There's no way she could have lifted this woman up."

I noticed that Laura was the only one who gave me a remotely withering look. *Interesting, they're not sure about their boss' character*, I thought, saving that knowledge to mull over later.

"We should go and look for her in case she's..." I made myself look over at the woman with the short brown hair, who'd been staked to the cork board. "...in trouble," I finished, a little weakly.

I wasn't immediately overwhelmed with offers of assistance.

"I'll just go," I muttered and walked out the door. After a second, I heard someone follow me out.

"Do you think the killer's still inside?" Alex whispered, loudly enough to make me jump. I wondered if he'd gone to stage school and had been taught a different kind of whisper from the conventional quiet option.

"I don't know," I said, feeling horribly defenceless. "We weren't exactly silent on our way in, so they're probably long gone." I hoped so, anyway.

Alex gulped. "I knew I should never have quit karate."

We reached the door of the main hall. I tried the handle.

"It's locked," I said, the sense of foreboding growing again.

"Police! Everyone stay right where you are!" someone yelled, nearly making me jump out of my skin.

I lifted a hand to my face, shielding my eyes from the bright beam of light.

"The body's in the office with the light on. A woman in there needs medical attention. I think she was knocked out by the person who did it. Zara's missing," I told them and briefly explained about the PR boss' car being in the car park.

Someone flicked a light switch and the fluorescent strips flashed and stuttered into life, leaving me with white spots in front of my eyes. Some of the feeling of dread melted away, but not much, not much at all.

The next several minutes passed in a flurry of coordinated activity. Backup arrived and it wasn't long before forensics were in situ. The police were currently searching the building for any sign of Zara or the killer.

Most of the PR team were huddled near the entrance in

the icy wind. I'd stayed further down the corridor, keen to try and keep at least some of the feeling in my fingers.

"Hello, I'm Detective Maynard and this is Detective Toyne. What's your name?" someone asked, pleasantly.

I turned and found myself facing the woman I'd seen directing all of the personnel currently present. She had blonde hair, streaked with grey, and a face that was still attractive despite the lines which crossed her forehead and creased her eyes. A younger man stood next to her. He had dark hair swept into a deep side-parting and a mouth fixed in a permanent pout.

"I'm Madigan Amos. I'm working as a consultant for Pendalay Zoo. I was invited here tonight for a meeting with ZaZa PR, who I'm supposed to be coordinating with. But when I got here…" I briefly explained everything that had happened after I'd met Teagan on the steps outside the building.

"Is there anything else you think we ought to know?" Detective Maynard asked.

"Yes. When I first met Zara, she received a phone call that upset her quite a lot. She told the person to leave her alone. I also happened to be passing by her house when she discovered that a rat had been killed and tied up in the tree by her front step. Apparently things like that have happened to her before…"

"I knew it," Detective Toyne cut in.

Both the detective and I looked at him in surprise.

"I'm sorry?" The detective managed to fill her voice with a warning that somehow implied her many years of experience and the consequences of crossing her.

"It's obvious, isn't it? Of course she's involved. This is all about her," he said. Something about his tone of voice seemed to imply that Zara was the one responsible, as opposed to being the victim.

Apparently I wasn't the only one who thought that.

"It sounds to me as though this woman, Zara Banks, is the focus of a stalker," Detective Maynard corrected.

"Don't be so sure. I was on another case just like this one before I came down to Cornwall. There was a woman who sent herself death threats. She even pretended to break into her own house and graffitied on the wall. It was all for attention. These women... they do it to themselves," he said.

"Jack, please consider our company," the detective said, now openly angry. She turned away from me a little, but that didn't make it any harder to overhear her next words. "You may have come highly recommended, but remember you're new here. I'll be discussing this in greater depth with you later."

The other detective just shrugged. He opened his mouth to say something else, but a shout went up that the main hall door had been unlocked.

"I found her!" someone yelled a second later.

I looked up in time to see Zara being led out of the hall by another police officer. He seemed to be supporting her.

"Are you okay?" I asked when no one else did.

She nodded and then shook her head.

"Ms Banks, are you aware that a homicide has taken place?" Maynard asked.

"Oh no, not again!" Zara said and then bit her lip.

To anyone who wasn't aware of Zara's history, that would have been a pretty strange statement to make. Fortunately, I'd already given the detectives a brief history of my own experiences.

I noticed Detective Toyne shake his head from side to side. He received the full wattage of Maynard's glare. I was willing to bet there'd be fireworks later on tonight during his disciplinary meeting.

"It's Jayne who's dead, isn't it?" Zara asked, earning herself a sceptical look from the detective. I too, was curious about how much Zara had known about what was going on.

"Ms Banks, we need to talk to you about tonight's events. Shall we find a quiet place?" Detective Maynard said, adopting a soothing tone.

Zara bit her lip again and shook her head. "I'd rather stay with Madi, if that's okay. I might need help getting things straight. My head's in a spin."

I could tell the two detectives were reluctant for me to stay, but they needed the information, and after what I'd told them, they knew how much this must be affecting her.

She's holding up remarkably well! I privately thought. When Lowell and I had witnessed the rat incident, she'd been in tears. Now there was a body pinned to her cork board and she merely looked a little pale. *It could just be the shock,* I mentally allowed.

"Would you mind taking us through what happened tonight?" Detective Maynard prompted.

Zara took a deep, trembling breath and began. "We all worked late today, finalising ideas for Halloween. Unfortunately, we haven't got much time at all to put an event together and promote it. I'd been piling on the pressure all day when I remembered I'd arranged to meet with Jayne. Because of the deadline, I realised it would be sensible to get everyone together for a group meeting to make sure we were all on the same page about what's coming up. I sent the rest of the team out to get some dinner for themselves. I didn't go because I'd asked Jayne to come early, so we could discuss exactly what I needed her and her husband to do."

"Had you met Jayne before?" Maynard asked.

Zara shook her head. "She approached me with a business pitch and I was interested. I invited her down here tonight to talk through her ideas with the rest of the team. I wanted to see what everyone thought before I made a final decision on what she was offering."

I mentally raised an eyebrow, knowing exactly what Adrian would have had to say about a collaboration.

"Did you know the victim?" Detective Toyne suddenly addressed me.

"I did not, but Adrian knew her."

"Oh? What were the circumstances of their relationship?"

I shook my head apologetically. "You'll have to ask him that. I only know what he told me."

Detective Toyne looked annoyed but refrained from making another comment.

"Ms Banks, you were telling us what happened after you'd dismissed the rest of your team," Maynard reminded her.

Zara nodded, her face looking pinched. "Jayne arrived and I took her into the office. We chatted about what was going to happen in the meeting. Our talk turned to the Halloween event we've got to plan, and I got a little carried away. We'd been working on it all day as a group and I wanted to show Jayne the branding we've come up with. I'd left the posters in the hall, so I left Jayne in the office and went to go and get them."

She took another shuddering breath. "I'd got the posters and was about to walk back across the corridor when I dropped them everywhere. A second later, I heard Jayne say something to someone. She sounded surprised, but then I heard... I heard..."

"You heard her being killed?" Toyne finished, and this time he sounded serious.

Zara nodded. "It was horrible! I had my keys in my jacket pocket, so I quickly locked the hall door and turned the lights out. I was terrified. I thought that he'd break down the door and do something horrible to me, too."

"Did you hear the assailant enter the building through the

doors down the corridor?" Maynard enquired.

Zara tilted her head from side to side before letting out a big sigh. "I'm sorry. I don't know. The doors open and close all day long, so I can't say I notice it anymore. We're not the only people who use the building, you see. I think there's another entrance around the back, but it's meant to be a fire escape."

"Ms Banks, what happened after you heard what happened to the woman you'd been meeting with?" Maynard asked.

"I stayed where I was and prayed that whoever it was didn't know I was in the building. I heard footsteps right outside the door and I thought I was done for. But then I did hear the double doors open, and it sounded like someone ran back into the office. I heard someone calling…" She broke off again to bite her lip. "I wasn't sure who it was. I just hoped that the person who'd done something to Jayne would stay hidden, or run away."

She paused to rub her fingers together in a nervous tic I hadn't noticed her do before.

"There were some more footsteps after that, going up and down, but I didn't know who it was. A little while later, I heard voices again, but I was too afraid to move. I wasn't sure what was happening, so I stayed hidden. I was there until you opened the door and I realised it was okay to come out. I heard someone shout that the police were here, but I just thought it could all be some horrible trick," she finished, limply.

I did my best to keep my face blank, but I was having a hard time of it. I knew that Zara was at the centre of a storm of nasty behaviour, but I still found it difficult to swallow that she'd locked herself in a room and hidden - both when the murder took place and when Lyra had unwittingly walked in on the killer.

I noticed Detective Toyne giving her a look that plainly showed he didn't believe there'd been anyone else in the building at all - just Zara.

I tried not to roll my eyes. I was willing to believe the story he'd told about his last case, but I was pretty certain that this was a different matter. From a physical perspective alone, I didn't think Zara was able to have hoisted the dead woman up onto the cork board, even with the help of the cable ties.

I also didn't think she had it in her.

Cowering in a room (unfortunately) rang true as more her style. I'd already witnessed her reaction to things that upset her, and I didn't think this was an exception.

Unless she's an Oscar-worthy actress, I added, playing devil's advocate with myself.

"Zara? Are you okay?" The double doors burst open and a man with thinning brown hair ran in, despite the efforts of two police officers, who were trying to restrain him.

"Sir, this is a crime scene!" One tried to tell him.

"It's okay. It's my husband, Darren," Zara explained to the baffled detectives.

"How did you know?" she asked him.

"Alex called me to say you were missing. I'm glad you're all right. What happened?" he asked, brushing a hand across her hair to push a few strands back into place.

"It's him. This time he killed someone," Zara said. Her bottom lip wobbled a little, but with a remarkable effort, she stilled it. Something that looked like determination crossed her face.

"Is it true?" he said, addressing the detectives - as though Zara was prone to having flights of fancy about murder.

"Yes, it is. A woman has been killed and displayed in a very disturbing manner," Detective Maynard said, shortly.

I could tell she was considering Darren.

"You're okay though? You're sure?" He rested his hands on Zara's shoulders.

His jaw moved back and forth and I realised he was grinding his teeth to hide just how furious he was. I imagined how powerless he must feel, knowing that someone was affecting his wife's life in such damaging ways and not being able to stop it.

"I'm fine... really!" she said, even managing a little smile.

"Mr Banks, where were you before you received the call about your wife being missing?" Detective Maynard asked.

"I was back at our house, working. There wasn't anyone there with me, I'm afraid," he said with an apologetic shrug. "I work freelance from home as a financial advisor to businesses. Often, I help ZaZa PR's clients, who could use a hand with their financials. I also do the business' books. When Alex called me, I jumped straight in the car. I just knew this had something to do with *him*."

"Do either of you have any idea who might be targeting you?" Maynard asked.

The couple looked at one another and shook their heads.

"I think it's about time the police earned their money and did something to figure that out, don't you? We're the victims here!" Darren protested.

I suddenly wondered if Zara had noticed anyone leave the building after she'd heard the rest of us come in. I was about to open my mouth to ask her when Darren spoke again.

"We're going home. You can come and see us, but this sort of treatment just isn't fair!" He gently took Zara's arm and led her back down the corridor towards the doors at the end.

The detectives and I watched in silence, as the double doors slammed closed behind them.

"You'd have to be deaf to not hear that," Detective Toyne commented.

BOOKS IN THE SERIES

Penguins and Mortal Peril

The Silence of the Snakes

Murder is a Monkey's Game

Lions and the Living Dead

The Peacock's Poison

A Memory for Murder

Whales and a Watery Grave

Chameleons and a Corpse

Foxes and Fatal Attraction

Monday's Murderer

Prequel: Parrots and Payback

A REVIEW IS WORTH ITS WEIGHT IN GOLD!

I really hope you enjoyed reading this story. I was wondering if you could spare a couple of moments to rate and review this book? As an indie author, one of the best ways you can help support my dream of being an author is to leave me a review on your favourite online book store, or even tell your friends.

Reviews help other readers, just like you, to take a chance on a new writer!

Thank you!
Ruby Loren

ALSO BY RUBY LOREN

HOLLY WINTER MYSTERIES
Snowed in with Death
A Fatal Frost
Murder Beneath the Mistletoe
Winter's Last Victim

EMILY HAVERSSON OLD HOUSE MYSTERIES
The Lavender of Larch Hall
The Leaves of Llewellyn Keep
The Snow of Severly Castle
The Frost of Friston Manor
The Heart of Heathley House

HAYLEY ARGENT HORSE MYSTERIES
The Swallow's Storm
The Starling's Summer
The Falcon's Frost
The Waxwing's Winter

JANUARY CHEVALIER SUPERNATURAL MYSTERIES
Death's Dark Horse
Death's Hexed Hobnobs
Death's Endless Enchanter
Death's Ethereal Enemy
Death's Last Laugh

Prequel: Death's Reckless Reaper

BLOOMING SERIES

Blooming

Abscission

Frost-Bitten

Blossoming

Flowering

Fruition

Made in the USA
Columbia, SC
31 January 2021